BOOK TWO,
THE BROOM CLOSET STORIES

The Boy Who Couldn't
Fly Home

Sawyer,
look! charlie's
adventure continues!

♡ jeff

BOOK TWO,
THE BROOM CLOSET STORIES

The Boy Who Couldn't
Fly Home

Jeff Jacobson

NewFreedomPress.com

The Boy Who Couldn't Fly Home:
A Gay Teen Coming of Age Paranormal Adventure about Witches, Murder,
and Gay Teen Love

Book Two, The Broom Closet Stories

Jeff Jacobson

NewFreedomPress.com
© 2013, 2017 by Jeff Jacobson

This is a work of fiction. Names, characters, places, and incidents are either products of the author's imagination, or if real, are used fictiously.

Trademarked names appear throughout this book. Rather than use a trademark symbol with every occurrence of a trademarked name, names are used in an editorial fashion, with no intention of infringement of the respective owner's trademark.

ISBN 978-0-9989145-1-0

Overview from Book 1

High school sophomore Charlie Creevey flees his hometown in the California mountains with his mother one night, after discovering that she, and therefore he, hails from a long line of witches, and that he is being hunted.

Charlie begins a new life in Seattle, living with his Aunt Beverly, a witch, and her husband Randall.

The hunt continues, for Charlie as well as for other teens in the Seattle community. Beverly and her fellow witches try to find ways to stop Grace and her cronies from kidnapping Charlie and other teens.

At the same time, Charlie develops what seems to be more than a friendship with high school junior Diego Ramirez, but does not want to accept the possibility that he might be gay.

Malcolm, a witch mentor and trainer, tells Charlie that he has to be honest about the feelings in his heart if he wants to gain his full power as a witch, leaving him with an either/or ultimatum.

Charlie has several frank conversations with himself, with Diego, and with Malcolm, before agreeing.

He and other same-age teens go through a "popping" ceremony and become full-fledged witches. Charlie's abilities go berserk for a few days after the event, and then eventually calm down as he regains his footing and prepares to settle into his new life as a full-fledged witch with a lot to learn.

Contents

BOOK TWO,
THE BROOM CLOSET STORIES

The Boy Who Couldn't Fly Home

Prologue

TODD LARAMIE SAT AT A BUS STOP in downtown Seattle waiting for the Number Forty-Nine to take him home. Industrial music in his headphones drowned out all sound around him. He didn't hear the man in the tailored jacket and pants sit down next to him.

"Hey, Catman," the man said to the high school junior, who, oblivious, kept looking for his bus.

The man tapped him on the shoulder. Todd jumped, seeing the stranger for the first time. He pulled off his earphones.

"I said, 'Hey, Catman.'" The man stared at him. His dark hair swept back from his forehead, and black stubble peppered his jawline and cheeks. The man's shirt was unbuttoned at the chest.

"Wha- … what did you say? Why did you call me that?"

"Because, my man," the stranger said, his striking face moving closer to him, "I know that you know that I know what I'm talking about. The cats, brother. Dig it? You, the cats, your vision, all of it." The man stood up and began to moonwalk in front of the bus stop bench. He ended it with a spin.

"H-how did you kn-kn-know?" Todd asked, not caring that he stuttered.

"Want some help with it? I know about you and your cat vision. It's freakazoidinally radical, and I can tell you about it. If you want," he said, spreading his arms in front of him the way a vendor does when displaying his wares.

"What? Yes, please. What do you know? Please, can you help me? I feel like I'm going crazy!" The boy removed the headset from around his neck and turned off his music with a shaking hand.

"Crazy is as crazy does, my main man."

"I, uh, it started a couple months ago. My buddies and I were watching the Mariners game, and suddenly I could see myself, see us, sitting there, like I was across the room looking at us through the eyes of my family's cat. We'd had some beers, and they said I was just drunk."

"Anything traumatic," asked the man, stretching out the word and wiggling his eyebrows, "happen to you recently?"

"Like what?"

"Death of a parent? Violent crime? Major body injury?" The man ticked off the points with his hands.

"No, no, nothing like that. I just ... oh wait! I fell and hit my head pretty hard on the bench at basketball camp. Had to go home."

"Yep. That'll do it," winked the man, cocking his pointer finger at Todd and squeezing his thumb like the trigger of a pistol. "You started seeing things in black and white? No color?"

"Yes! And I started smelling things, and everything felt, I don't know, different."

"That's the network, my man."

"What network?" Todd whispered.

"The network. Wanna know some more?"

"Yes. Please. Please help me. I don't know what to do. I keep listening to this loud music to drown everything out. I don't even like industrial rock!"

"Lay me some skin and follow me," said the man.

Todd didn't care that this white man, who looked like he came straight out of an Italian menswear ad, was trying to sound like a funky homeboy. He was desperate for answers. So he gave the man a high five and followed him down the street.

They walked next to a chain-link fence, then turned into a municipal parking lot. The man approached a bright red Ferrari. The alarm system beeped as both the driver and passenger doors opened with a soft whoosh.

"Climb in, brother," the man said to him.

The scent of new leather, mingled with something wet-smelling, like moldy wood, rose from the interior as Todd slid into the passenger seat.

"But how did you know?" he asked the man, who turned to face him.

"What you've been hearing is the cat network, my friend."

"The what?"

"The cat network. All over town. The cats stay sharp. Report in. Keep an eye on things and share the news, if you know what I mean."

"Not really. I mean, I just see things through their eyes. And my hearing … it's so sharp. Lately, I sort of, I sort of feel what they're feeling. Why is this happening? Do you know?" He put his right hand on the dash and leaned toward the man, who smelled like aftershave.

"Sure do. You're leaking. And pretty soon you'll just be one of those echoes."

"I don't understand."

"I know. And buddy, I could give a flying frick," the man said. He reached over, closed both of his hands around Todd's throat, and began choking him. Todd recoiled and tried to pull the man's hands off him. But they were too strong. His legs beat and jerked, trapped beneath the low dashboard.

"Hey, baby, yeah, feel the love, just feel it," the man whispered, moving his face close to Todd's as the boy's eyes bulged.

The boy hit and slapped at the man, who, barely blinking an eye, leaned in even closer and bit down on Todd's lower lip, drawing blood. Todd gagged and shook, trying to scream, trying to pull away. Eventually he stopped moving, his head dropping forward on his neck, arms slack at his sides, unconscious.

"You, my friend, are a lousy kisser," Tony said as he licked the blood from his mouth and turned the key in the ignition. Rap music blared inside the Ferrari as the engine roared to life. Tony stepped on the gas pedal. The car lurched out of the parking lot and skidded onto the street.

"You cat, me cat, everybody we cat," he shouted along with the song.

CHAPTER 1

Chrome and Glass

CHARLIE CREEVEY DIDN'T GO TO SCHOOL that Friday. He still didn't feel back on his feet, and his Aunt Beverly suggested he take the extra day to see if things calmed down.

"Besides, you'll have the weekend to get back to normal again. Well, your new normal, that is."

Charlie helped around the house for a while, carrying things to the basement with Randall.

"You ever see her workroom?" his uncle asked as they passed by a closed door near the garage.

"No." The house was so big that there were still parts of it he didn't know.

"Have her take you in there sometime. It's a bit of a surprise."

"How so?"

"You'll have to find out for yourself. My lips are sealed."

Diego called Charlie that Saturday morning. "You back in town, or what?" he asked.

"Yeah, got home, uh, late last night."

"I'm so glad you're back. It's been wild at school with Principal Wang's heart attack. Monday was so awful. Teachers were crying, everyone walking around all spaced out. Then when we heard he would be okay, it was crazy. Like a huge school party. You missed the whole thing!"

Not really, Charlie thought to himself. He felt the mixture of guilt and relief that came up whenever he thought about Principal Wang. What if the man had died?

When he talked about it earlier with Beverly and asked why he had also had the dream of the young Chinese girl saying "dangerous" in Chinese, she shrugged her shoulders.

"I don't know, Charlie. It's hard to say. It could mean that one of your gifts will be dreams of premonition."

"What's that?"

"Some witches gets clues about the future in dreams."

"That would be weird."

"It's too early to tell, Charlie. Nothing is very clear after someone gets popped. We'll just have to wait and see."

"Do you?" he heard on the other end of the phone. He hadn't been paying attention to what Diego had been saying.

"Do I what?"

"Wanna hang out? Today?"

"Uh, yeah, sure," said Charlie. He hadn't broken anything in the house for several days. Nothing had flown into the air and wrapped itself around anyone. It would feel great to get out of the house. Besides, he wanted to see Diego.

"Why don't you come over? You can meet my mom, and maybe I could take you to Lincoln Park."

Beverly agreed to drive Charlie over to Diego's house.

"He seems like he's becoming a good friend to you," she said as she stopped at an intersection and waited for an elderly woman and her dog to cross the street.

Did she know? He wondered if she suspected. But it didn't seem like she was hinting at anything. He had begun to learn that she was pretty direct about things. He liked that, even if he wasn't used to it.

"Yeah, he's pretty cool."

"That's good. I really liked him when he came over the other day."

They pulled up in front of a very odd-looking house. More geometric than any of the traditional homes in the area, it was painted beige, red, and black.

"Oh, it's this place! I've always wanted to see the interior," exclaimed his aunt.

Charlie wondered about this. Wouldn't it be an easy thing for his aunt, someone who single-handedly drove two witches from her home, to figure out a way to see inside a person's house?

"Now, Charlie, call me for any reason, okay? If you start to feel funny or if it seems like you aren't able to hold up the charade of having been in California anymore, just call."

"Okay."

"Remember, Diego thinks you've been sick. It won't be strange if you're not completely yourself. But just call me for any reason." And then, "What a house!"

The front door opened and a smiling Diego walked out, dressed in jeans, tennis shoes, and a red sweater. Charlie opened his passenger-side window, smiling in spite of himself, hoping he didn't look too eager. He was really happy to see the boy.

"Hi, Charlie. Hi, Beverly," Diego said, bending down and looking in the car.

"Beverly, would you like to come in too? My mom's here, and she would love to meet you."

"That would be great. Yes, I'd like that."

Lydia Ramirez waited on the front porch. She stood barely over five feet tall, nearly a foot shorter than her son, dressed in yoga pants and a loose top, her black hair pulled back in a clip. Her son's bright eyes and wide smile were echoed on her face.

"Welcome, welcome, Beverly," she said, her slight Mexican accent warming her words. "So nice to meet you finally. And Charlie, you too. I've heard so much about you!" she said. Diego blushed a bit but smiled even more.

They exchanged pleasantries then walked inside the house.

"I've always wanted to see this place," his aunt said. They removed their shoes and left them near the front door.

Lydia took Beverly's arm in a friendly gesture and the two women fell into a tour of the house, discussing remodeling nightmares, views of Puget Sound, and the differences between modern and classic architecture.

"They'll be at this forever," Diego said. "Come on. I'll give you my own tour."

The house was unlike anything Charlie had ever seen. His aunt and uncle's home was very big, grand on a scale he was not used to, but it still felt like a house to him. Basically, it was what he was used to, only bigger and nicer. This house was completely different. He remembered Diego's description of chrome and glass but only now realized what he had meant.

Stainless steel appliances sparkled in the pristine kitchen. The countertops were concrete, cut in sharp angles. A glass-like surface covered the cabinets, and a soft green light warmed the plates and glasses within. Diego explained that the surface, which was the colored part, not the soft white light bulb hidden inside the cabinets, could be exchanged for a blue effect.

"Mom changes it about every two weeks. According to her mood, I guess," he shrugged as if to say, "Mothers and their moods. Go figure."

Charlie had never seen such a stark living room before. There were only two pieces of furniture, both upholstered in leather, on the wide light wood floor: a black recliner chair and a red curved couch, both of which sat near a black metallic freestanding fireplace. Floor-to-ceiling windows gave an unobstructed view of Puget Sound. Since the house was situated farther south than Beverly and Randall's place, Charlie could see more of Vashon Island than from Washington Street.

A wood and glass staircase rose up to the second floor. Diego hopped up the steps in his stockinged feet. Charlie followed.

Evenly spaced skylights lit the second floor. Soft pale carpet ran the length of the hallway. Lydia's bedroom was also very spare, with a large bed and a simple set of dressers, nearly everything painted white.

Charlie was therefore completely unprepared for the train wreck he saw when Diego opened the door to his bedroom and invited him in.

"This is what my mom calls 'The Land that Time Forgot.'"

Utter chaos and disaster reigned over Diego's room. A king-sized bed was shoved against one wall, with most of its bedding lying crumpled on the floor. Books and papers were scattered on every available flat surface, including the desk, a folding table in the middle of the room, and the floor. Posters of male models, male and female Hollywood stars, and South American soccer players covered most of the dark blue walls.

A two-tiered set of stacking tables rested against a wall in one corner. Several large decks of cards, bigger than those used for poker, covered the surface of the top table, which was draped in a gauzy yellow material. Leaning against the wall sat several framed photographs of dark-skinned people, some of whom looked quite old. However, there was one of a beautiful young woman with a bright smile and a red dot painted on her forehead. The woody scent of incense filled the room, and Charlie spotted a thin stream of smoke rising from a silver disk on the smaller of the two tables.

Clothes hung out of drawers, sat where they had been tossed on the floor, or draped, half in and half out, of the full closet on the far wall.

"This place is a mess!" Charlie said, so surprised by its contrast with the rest of the house that he forgot to be polite. It didn't seem to match the bright, well-put-together young man he had been getting to know.

"It sure is," said Diego, laughing. "Isn't it great?"

He walked into the room and threw himself on the bed, stretching out and folding his arms behind his head.

"A man needs his own kingdom," he said, smiling. "My mom hates it. But we made a deal when she bought this house three years ago. She could have it any way she wanted as long as I got to have my room any way I wanted. Her rule is that there can't be any rotting food or really stinky smells. My rule is that I get to have as much clutter as I want. I didn't think she'd agree, but she did.

"But," he added, "I have to keep the rest of the house as neat as she wants. It's a good deal for her. She's picky about it and figures that as long as I know how to clean the kitchen and the bathrooms and help her cook and do chores around the house, it doesn't matter what I do in my own space. Oh, and she has to knock before coming into my kingdom. It works out pretty well. She's a lawyer and taught me everything I need to know about negotiating."

Charlie couldn't imagine negotiating with his mother. How it worked in their house was that she would say something like "We're going to put up a new shelf in the bathroom" or "I'm pulling that old rug up in your room and refinishing the floor," and Charlie would say "okay" and then help her. She was the captain. He was definitely just a crew member.

He wasn't surprised that Diego was clear about what he wanted. The boy was so sure of himself that it made sense he and his mom would negotiate things. *How do you learn to do that?* he wondered. Maybe he could become more forthright with his opinions. Sometimes he wasn't even sure he had any. Did people just make them up and then demand that others agree to them?

"It's pretty cool," Charlie said. The room was definitely cluttered. But it wasn't dirty. The only smell seemed to be a combination of laundry detergent and incense.

"Another thing my mom said is that I couldn't do drugs. No way. And that if she found out I was burning incense to hide smoking pot or something, she'd sell me to a glue-making factory. Did you ever see that movie *Young Frankenstein?*" he asked, then continued without waiting for an answer from Charlie.

"Remember that part with Frau Blücher? Every time they said her name the horses would whinny really loudly? My mom always laughed at that part. She said that 'blücher' means 'glue factory' in German. I have no idea if that's true. But she thinks it's funny so I just go along with her.

"Anyway, that's a long way to say I don't do drugs. So my mom has nothing to worry about. God, I'm talking a lot. I'm kind of nervous with you being here."

Charlie relaxed, realizing that he was nervous too, standing just inside the doorway while Diego chatted away on his bed.

"Why are you nervous?" he asked, not ready to admit that he felt the same way.

"I dunno. I was excited for you to come over and see our house. But I was worried you'd think it was really weird, or that my room was awful, or that I'd say something stupid."

"You? You never say anything stupid. You always know what to say."

"Are you crazy? I do not. I blab away all the time."

"Diego, I'm the one who doesn't know what to say. I always feel shy around people, even around you, even around my aunt and uncle. Everyone seems so smart all the time."

"Maybe this is the case of the grass always being greener. You seem so wise and contemplative—great use of the word, if I do say so myself. Me, I have to say nine thousand words before I even know what I think sometimes."

"You're crazy. I just sound like a stupid shy kid," said Charlie.

"You're such a bonehead!" Diego yelled, hopping off his bed and running at him. Before Charlie could react, Diego tackled him and brought him to the floor, pinning his chest with one arm while he tickled him with another.

"Hey, no fair, get off!" Charlie shouted, laughing.

"Make me!" Diego said, his eyes twinkling while he wiggled his eyebrows.

Charlie tried to push him off, but the other boy was too strong. At first he couldn't move. Then a slight pulse of electricity rose up from the floor into his back and legs. He closed his eyes, and before he understood how it happened, he felt a spinning sensation and found himself atop Diego, straddling the boy's body and leaning over him, his hands pressing down on his chest to hold him in place.

"Whoa! That was cool! How did you …?" asked Diego, smiling up at him with a look of wonder.

"Oh, uh, just some, uh, wrestling move that my friend taught me," Charlie lied, hoping what he said not only sounded believable but also hid his shock from Diego. How the hell had he done that?

"Remind me not to meet your friend in a dark alley," Diego said, laughing.

"Nah, it's pretty easy, it doesn't take any …"

"As easy as this?" Diego interrupted, slapping Charlie's arms off of him. Charlie fell forward, and Diego grabbed him by his shoulders and sat up, then kissed him very quickly on the lips before throwing Charlie off and to the side.

"I got you, I got you!" Diego yelled. He jumped up and started prancing around the room, laughing.

"Boys, don't hurt each other up there," came Lydia's voice from downstairs. "Charlie, your aunt is about to leave. Come say goodbye to her."

Charlie lay back on the floor and saw Wolverine from the X-Men staring back at him from a poster on Diego's ceiling.

Charlie's lips hurt from where Diego's mouth had hit him. But they also tingled in a not entirely unpleasant way. Different parts of his body—his inner thighs, his arms, his chest, all the places where Diego had touched him—felt warm and quivery. Fear of what he had just done mixed with anger at Diego for having forced a kiss on him. All of this was covered over with worry: worry that his newly released ability had slipped out, worry that Diego would ask him more about it, worry that something else would happen, something that he wouldn't be able to explain away so easily.

He hopped up off the floor and shouted "okay" in response to Diego's mother.

"You mad?" Diego asked, looking much less confident than he had only seconds ago.

"Nah," said Charlie, wiping his mouth with the back of his hand. He turned, hurried past his friend, and headed downstairs.

CHAPTER 2

Foliage

THEY SAT ON A CEMENT LEDGE at Lincoln Park overlooking Puget Sound. Leafy ferns brushed the outsides of their legs, and all sorts of vines and climbers coiled together in the mass of foliage below. Sometimes the sheer volume of all the greenery in Seattle overwhelmed Charlie. You couldn't look anywhere without seeing something green and growing, twisting up out of the ground.

He wondered what would happen if he were to fall off the ledge and land in the soft underbrush beneath his feet. Maybe he wouldn't get up. Maybe the vines would grow up over him, covering him, while everything else continued to run at its breakneck speed up top. He would rest, and he would stay the same. Nothing would change down in the green world. Maybe he would like that. Being swallowed up.

A shudder ran along his chest.

"You cold?" Diego asked him, his words close to Charlie's ear.

"Nah, I'm fine. You?" He kept his voice neutral. He liked it better that way, near the other boy but distant. Distant enough to keep things normal, to breathe. After what happened back in Diego's bedroom, he wanted to stay on the alert.

"Charlie," Diego said. His voice sounded strange, as if a door were about to open up somewhere, and something scary would walk out.

No, don't, don't say it. Whatever it is, don't ..., Charlie thought. He didn't even know what he was worried about. But he imagined himself peeking up through the greenery below, his eyes barely visible through the foliage. He could stay hidden down there, just watching, because no one would know to look through the leaves.

But instead of feeling the green mass hiding his face and the soft soil beneath him, soft like a bed, like sleep, he felt the cold of the cement wall seeping through the seat of his pants. He shifted, trying to get comfortable.

"What?" he heard himself ask Diego. "What is it?"

He hated how his voice sounded, like the bleating of a scared little lamb.

"Charlie, can I ask you something?" Tall Diego, the politician and the charmer, the confident apple hawker, seemed worried. No, timid. Charlie felt angry at him then. He wanted to shout, "Man up, will you?"

"Uh, yeah, sure. What?"

"This is kind of silly, but ..."

Charlie looked at Diego as the boy stared straight ahead. He looked at the length of the side of his face, the line from brow to chin, his lashes like half-drawn shades over his eyes, the freckle at his temple a pinpoint, like the start to a conversation.

The freckle disappeared as Diego turned his head and looked at Charlie.

"Do you like me?"

The boy's eyes didn't change color—they stayed brown. But they could have. They should have, his question seemed to ask so much. Charlie could imagine them swirling, could nearly see gray clouds of color roll across them like the sky above their heads.

"Yeah. Yeah. Of course I like you. Why? You know I ..."

And he paused, because he didn't want to say it out loud. He wasn't ready. He thought of what Malcolm had said. But it was confusing. On the one hand, he couldn't lie about this stuff and be the witch he wanted to be. On the other hand, it wasn't anyone else's business. When Malcolm had said it all, it had made sense. But now, it didn't tell Charlie what to do. What was he supposed to say?

Diego looked back at the water, and maybe his eyes did change a little then, maybe the gray-green depths of the Sound rose with the tide and crept into his eyes right then, for they shimmered.

A drop of the Sound spilled out of his left eye and made it halfway to his mouth before Diego ran the back of his hand against it.

"Shit."

Don't, Diego. Don't let's have this talk now. The vines are green, the air is nice, and I'd like to sit here with you, Charlie thought, *maybe for a long time. What you're asking, what I think you're asking, will rush things. I don't trust myself to say the right words, to keep things safe and quiet, and I'd like to spend a lot of time just hanging out with you. Those other thoughts I have about you are low thoughts, deeper than the vines down below, and I want to leave them there, let them sleep in the wet soil down there, covered by ferns, while you and I sit on this wall above them. Safe. Just friends.*

These thoughts ran through Charlie's head faster than he could understand, but he knew them as a warning, knew them to be true even if he couldn't grasp their meaning. He wished he could stop the cold from sinking into his butt and his legs. He wanted to lie down on the warm soil below, mostly hidden beneath the soft ivy, watching Diego and Charlie above him.

Then his mind began to race. What do people do when someone is crying? They pat them on the shoulder, don't they? They just reach up and pat them and say "There, there." That's what good people do, right?

He reached up to pat Diego with his right hand, just as the boy turned to face him, his lips and left cheek quivering. Without quite knowing why or how, Charlie's left arm reached out and up, and now there was a circle wide enough for Diego. Charlie's betraying limbs extended out and around the boy, pulling him close.

Diego's face was so large then, so close to Charlie's that it doubled, just before his nose tilted to the side and he was pressing his mouth against Charlie's lips, a sound like a cry and a grunt pouring out of him.

No, no, that's not what I meant to do! I was just trying to reassure you, for God's sake, he wanted to cry out. He wanted to slow everything so that he could watch it pass by, the way he watched leaves floating in the stream at Carson Park.

But it wasn't happening that way, and there was no space in which to back up and gain any distance.

And besides, the vines from below had crawled up through Charlie's heels, had spread their leafy climb up his legs and were sprouting shoots along his spine as his own mouth, his traitor mouth, took Diego's in itself.

The boy tasted warm, and the warmth spread from Charlie's mouth and his tongue down his throat, pushing back at the vines in his spine, spreading out along his scalp, numbing his mind. He didn't know this was what it was like to touch his mouth to another boy's. Didn't know there would be so much teeth and tongue and heat. Didn't know Diego would taste like this, like the end of summer and pine needles and the sheer volume of things Charlie hadn't even known he had wanted.

The boys lay back on the cold hard cement, not so much kissing as feeding on each other, while the worried mind of at least one of them burrowed down into the soil below, trying to fill itself with loud noise, hoping to drown out what was happening, wishing none of it were true.

CHAPTER 3

Takeoff

"JUST FOCUS, ROBERTO, JUST FOCUS. Try a little harder, buddy!" Phil Sanchez shouted from the side of the large grassy field adjacent to Malcolm's cabin. Malcolm looked over his shoulder at the man and then waved his hands for all the kids to set down their broomsticks. They did so without complaint. Their training wasn't going very well.

Charlie watched as Malcolm walked to where the adult helpers stood. To him, they looked like parents watching from the sidelines of a soccer field, cheering their kids on. The hood of Malcolm's rain parka resembled a large orange light bulb surrounding his head. Mr. Sanchez looked chagrined. He held out his hands to placate Malcolm.

"Uh oh, you're in trouble," one of the other adults said to Mr. Sanchez.

"I'm sorry. I know I shouldn't be yelling. It's just that I know Roberto can do better. He ..."

Charlie couldn't see Malcolm's face, but his voice was very clear.

"Phil," said Malcolm, "you shouting things from the sidelines isn't helping. The kids need time to fail and recover. Fail and recover. It makes them stronger."

"I know, I know. I just ..."

"Yes, you do know, Phil. I seem to remember you failing quite a lot when you were a WIT, without anyone yelling at you to try harder when you were learning!" Malcolm's voice was getting louder.

Charlie watched as the man's posture sank in on itself. It was too gray and drizzly for him to be certain whether the color really did drain from Mr. Sanchez's face, but Charlie imagined it did.

"Now, I don't need a herd of soccer moms and little-league dads interfering with my training. From any of you," he shouted. Mouths hung agape from the ten adults standing in a line. All teasing and lightness had stopped.

"You have one job and one job only: to keep these kids safe. That's it! Does anyone need a reminder of his or her responsibilities?"

A lack of response indicated that no, none of the adult witches needed to be reminded.

"Good. Then stay ready to help if one of those rug rats over there gets off the ground. Other than that, keep your mouths closed!"

"I think I'll go see how dinner is coming along," said Phil, turning away and heading up to the house.

"Great idea!" yelled Malcolm, then stormed back to the twelve kids waiting in the middle of the field.

It was the following Saturday afternoon, a full week since Beverly and Charlie had gone to Diego's house. They had been up here since school got out the day before. It had been raining the entire time, and Charlie was glad that Randall had outfitted him with waterproof everything. At first he had thought that his uncle was being excessive as they shopped at REI's downtown store.

"Believe me, you'll thank me later," said Randall as he threw several pairs of waterproof socks into the basket Charlie was carrying.

This was their first official training weekend, nearly two full weeks since he and his fellow new witches had been popped. Malcolm's cabin was actually a massive wooden building. It looked more like a ski lodge than the little wooden cottage Charlie had imagined. It sat secluded on one hundred acres of privately owned forest land on Snoqualmie Pass, and it slept fifteen people comfortably, or nearly thirty if lodgers, in this case the kids, slept on the floor in sleeping bags in the carpeted basement.

To Charlie, the training was flying by. Malcolm covered so much theory, and they moved from one activity and spell to the next with little or no break. His head was spinning with it all.

He could tell that the other kids were getting frustrated.

No matter how much Malcolm seemed to teach them or how much they practiced, none of the kids had been able to actually do the spells. Any of them. Except one time, a quiet thoughtful girl named Lucinda caused one of the windows to open, and two black crows flew into the large living room area, squawking loudly. Unfortunately, the purpose of that specific activity had been to learn how to look into a scrying bowl in order to see things that were happening far away. The kids didn't know whether to applaud her results or worry that Malcolm would get angry. It took three adult witches and several different spells to transport the birds safely back outside.

Malcolm had simply said, "That's okay, Lucy. You failed, so recover. That's how you'll all learn this stuff. You'll fall down, you'll get back up, you'll try again, you'll fall down, et cetera. Fail and recover."

It had become a mantra of his, and Charlie thought that some of the other kids were going to scream if Malcolm said it one more time.

He could understand their frustration. These kids had grown up seeing their parents, family members, and other adults in the community do amazing things with witchcraft. Their own expectations for how easy and how fast it should be were getting in the way of just trying.

Charlie didn't care about getting it right. He was just excited to be learning it all. Other than having seen the violent display of witchcraft back in the kitchen in Clarkston or watching Beverly handle both a candle and late-night intruders, he hadn't known what to expect. It was a new world for him. He would have been happy just to watch Malcolm perform tricks all weekend.

He had been surprised, however, when Malcolm announced after lunch that they would be going out into the field to learn to ride broomsticks. All the other kids had yelled in delight and enthusiasm.

Charlie grew worried. They had failed at every single thing Malcolm had tried to teach them. None of them had been able to change the color of their hair or otherwise affect their appearance, nor had they been able to make small objects float, have their voices carry from one floor to the next, or even ignite a simple candle flame. (Charlie remembered Jeremy's comment about his own candle-lighting frustration when first learning the craft.) Other than Lucinda's one strange window/crow trick, they had produced absolutely no results whatsoever. They were tired. Many of them had headaches from concentrating so hard, and they all complained about being out in the wet weather.

How then, were they supposed to mount a wooden stick, and get it to fly them around in the air? He figured it would be either hopeless or dangerous, or both.

"Now you may be wondering why we're progressing to broomsticks," Malcolm said as they stood in the field as if reading Charlie's mind (he had to remind himself that witches couldn't do that). Twelve clunky-looking training brooms lay in the wet grass, one next to each kid. The ten adult helpers stood on the side, each of them carrying their own sleeker, smaller riding sticks.

The young witches in training, or WITs as Malcolm liked to call them, all wore helmets, elbow-pads, and knee-pads. They looked like they were trying out for hockey or about to go rollerblading.

"… especially since it seems to you that none of you have made any progress. That's okay, that's okay. Frustration is part of the process. What's our motto?"

"Fail and recover," they responded in dreary unison.

"That's right, good," Malcolm said. Charlie had to give him credit. He seemed utterly undaunted by his pupils' inability to work any of the spells that he had been trying to teach them.

"The reason we're switching to flying next," he explained, "is that activating a broomstick is a relatively easy thing to do, much easier than the things we've been attempting so far. Riding it is a bit tricky, but that's less about witchcraft and more about balance.

"These broomsticks, like many of the objects we witches use, have been charged with spells to make them work. In this case, the broom makers invoked the power of the wood to stay solid and true and to fly straight. They invoked the power of the wind to allow the wood to rise in the air and to carry a body or two on them. They've already been imbued. You don't have to do it.

"All you have to do is learn to activate the brooms, then hope like hell you can hang on," he laughed. None of the adult helpers seemed to think this was funny.

Malcolm gathered them in the center of the clearing, which was about the size of a football field, and explained that the other adults would be there to help out once the WITs learned how to get the brooms off the ground.

He taught them the few Words that were needed to activate the broomsticks. He had been teaching them many Words since they had arrived the day before.

"Words are very powerful. Don't go around saying them willy-nilly. Not until you're ready for something to happen," he said.

Charlie was still getting used to the idea of the Words. He couldn't really understand them, even when Malcolm or one of the other adults helped him form each sound individually. It was as if they were in a language so foreign, mumbled so quietly, that they would slip right out of his mind before he could hold them in.

When the adults said the Words, Charlie felt them. He remembered going to a birthday party as a boy. Somebody's dad had rubbed an inflated balloon along the kids' arms, then lifted it a few inches away so the kids could feel the static electricity pull at the hairs on their arms. The Words pulled at him much the same way. And when he heard the Words, it sounded like several people were whispering them at once.

When he and the other WITs tried to say them, nothing happened. No hair-raising electricity, no multiple whispers, nothing.

"It's okay, kid," Malcolm said when Charlie hadn't been able to reproduce the right sounds. "Try again. Fail and recover."

Now the kids stood in a wide circle. They had each laid a broomstick on the ground beside them. One by one, a WIT would place his or her hand over the broom, whisper the quiet Words, and see if the broom would do anything.

They went around the circle several times. Nothing happened.

"Like this," Malcolm said, standing in the middle of them and placing one of the training brooms down in the grass. He pretended to concentrate very hard. His lips began to move.

Just as he finished mumbling the last Word, the piece of wood popped up from the ground and snapped into his hand, and he affected a surprised look on his face. The WITs laughed at his antics.

"You have to clear your mind and let the Words work the way they're supposed to."

"Yeah, whatever that means," said Jenna Tompkins. She looked bored half the time, angry the rest, and was continually rolling her eyes or huffing when Malcolm offered her corrections.

Now it was Roberto Sanchez's turn. He was the pudgy kid who'd worn the navy blue sweater at the warehouse when they had all been popped. Charlie was pretty sure they had talked together at some point during that fuzzy night, but he couldn't remember any of their conversation.

The boy moved his lips, squeezed his eyes shut and held his hand open.

"Easy, easy, not quite so hard," Malcolm said.

Nothing happened. The boy opened his eyes, then shook his head.

"Nope, sorry," he said.

"Don't be sorry, kid. Just wait your turn and try again."

Several more WITs gave it a try. Not a single broomstick rose up in the air. They didn't even wiggle on the ground.

Charlie's turn came around again. This was his fourth time. He was cold and hungry, but it dawned on him that he was having a strange sort of fun. He just couldn't believe he was standing out in a field with a group of witches, trying to learn how to activate a broomstick. He didn't even care if he succeeded this round or not. He believed what Malcolm said about failing and recovering. At some point, one or more of the kids would make it work. The adults had all started where the WITs were now, standing in a field somewhere, cold, hungry, and failing. Even his Aunt Beverly had started out not being able to do anything.

Charlie took in a deep breath, cold air with the scent of pine and damp earth filling his lungs. He closed his eyes, held his hand over the long chunky piece of wood in the wet grass, and moved his lips. As usual, nothing happened. He tried again. Nothing.

"Good try, Charlie. Next," said Malcolm.

But something felt different this time. Almost … almost as if what he really should have done was open his mouth a little and let the Words say themselves. That was strange. How could that be right? But it did feel right, somehow.

"Charlie, time to stop and give someone else a chance," Malcolm said.

But he didn't stop. He felt a stirring in his chest, a sensation of rushing forward, as if a wide expanse had opened up in front of him. He could feel the thrilling vastness of something just beyond his reach.

"Charlie," said Malcolm, his voice sterner.

Charlie opened his mouth, and this time the Words themselves moved his lips as if tiny invisible fingers were lifting and pulling at them. He heard the Words near him, not as if he were saying them, but as if a crowd of people a short distance away were mumbling them, and the sounds carried to both of his ears simultaneously.

A sensation of vertigo descended on him. He felt sure that if he opened his eyes he would find himself standing on the edge of a cliff with endless miles of drop-off just beneath the tips of his rain boots.

He could feel the Words inside his ears, as if they were small live insects tickling the nerve endings along the rows of cartilage inside his ear drums.

With a soft whooshing sound and a hard smack against his palm, the broomstick landed right in the middle of Charlie's hand. He closed his fingers around it before he could drop it, then opened his eyes.

At first, there was no sound. Only the sight of the other kids, Malcolm, and the adults that he could see standing off to the sides, eyes and mouths wide open.

Then one of the kids shouted, "Hurray!" Soon everyone was clapping and cheering. Malcolm's smile beamed, and some of the younger kids even jumped up and down.

"I did it," Charlie muttered to himself, shaking his head in disbelief.

The broomstick quivered with tiny vibrations in his hand, confirming that he had, in fact, been successful.

After the cheering died down, Malcolm spoke.

"Now, my boy, do you remember the Words to return it to just a piece of wood?"

He nodded. He knew how to do it now. All he had to do was stop trying to make it work and instead let the Words say themselves through his mouth. He closed his eyes, the Words came through, the feeling of vertigo left him, and the broom dropped to the ground. It seemed so obvious, so easy. How could he not have seen it before?

More clapping, more smiling from Malcolm, even more of a sense of understanding on his part about how it all worked.

"Okay, do it again, Charlie. Call up that baby, and you can take it for a spin."

The Words came through with even more assurance. The sense of vertigo and slipping forward wasn't as strong the second time. The broom snapped up into his hands in a way that felt right, like catching a stick someone had tossed to him. Its weight felt good in his hand. Familiar.

"Okay, kiddo, hold on a second," Malcolm said. He called two adults over from the side. Charlie wished Beverly had been there to help. He would have appreciated her calm caring attitude.

"I'll be here when you get back on Sunday night. I'll help you practice all the things you'll learn with Malcolm," she had said as she handed him a sleeping bag and helped him load his things into the minivan that was taking a group of kids and adults to Malcolm's place.

"I've got to stay here and make sure this community keeps itself going while you're all off having fun," she had said, giving him a wink.

One of the adults called over by Malcolm was the tall black man who helped subdue Charlie when he had started breaking things after learning of Principal Wang's heart attack. His name was Sean Crenshaw.

He smiled at the boy and said, "Good job, Charlie. Looks like you're getting the hang of it." He lifted his right leg up and over his own broomstick and stood ready.

The other adult was an older white woman he didn't recognize. She had arrived earlier in the day and had been observing the training for most of the time. She gave him a nod and mounted her broomstick too.

"Rose and I," Sean continued, nodding to the woman, "will go with you as you take your first solo flight. Now remember, you steer by moving the tip of the broom up or down, side to side, with your hands. You only need to move it a little bit to change direction."

"How do you speed up or slow down?" Charlie asked, coughing slightly. Now that they were about to take off, his mouth had dried up and his hands were shaking.

"Mostly from leaning forward or back. But it's hard to explain. You'll figure it out as you do it. Don't forget to wrap your feet up on the bristles behind you to protect the family jewels," he added, motioning below his waist with his hands. The girls in the group laughed. The boys' faces turned green.

Malcolm told the WITs to open up the circle and stand out of the way. Charlie pointed the broom toward the far side of the field.

"Nice and slow, Charlie," said Rose to his left. Strands of gray hair were loose beneath the hood of her jacket. She had on purple gloves and smelled like flowers. She gave him another nod.

Charlie lifted his leg up over the broom and grasped the shaft with both hands. It seemed lighter than it had before. Was it hovering? He couldn't tell. He brought it right up between his legs, bending his knees a little.

"Have you ever surfed before, Charlie?" asked Sean.

Charlie shook his head.

"Oh well," Sean said, shrugging his shoulders. "Forget that metaphor then."

Charlie looked out across the field.

Is this really going to work? he wondered. The idea of flying on a broomstick had seemed fun. But now he wasn't so sure. He wished another WIT had activated a broom first so Charlie could have watched.

"Just push off gently with your feet and ..." Rose said.

Charlie shuffled his feet a few steps, then pushed.

The broom slid forward, causing his boots to drag along the wet grass. He felt the handle dig into his crotch.

Charlie winced. "Ow!"

"Feet up and beneath you," Sean said from his right side. The man had mounted his own broom and was gliding along next to him. Charlie turned his head to try to see where the man put his feet, causing the front of the broom to jerk to the right.

Before he knew what happened, he slipped over the side and flipped upside-down. He held tightly to the handle and managed to wrap his legs around the back near the bristle end, hanging bat-like from the shaft.

Cheers and laughter came from the group of WITs behind him.

He continued to float forward at a snail's pace, his head only a few inches above the grass.

"I can't ..." he grunted. "I don't ..."

Rose giggled as she flew on his other side. "That's certainly one way to mount a broom. See if you can climb back on top."

"We can give you a hand if you can't," said Sean. He and Rose were flying at the same slow pace to match his.

Charlie tried not to look at the trees coming slowly toward him, upside-down. Instead he focused on righting himself. He attempted to swing his body upright, but that only forced the broom to shake from end to end, nearly prying it from his fingers. For just a moment he tried to recreate the move he had done back in Diego's bedroom when he had flipped the boy onto his back, but since he had no idea how he had done it, he dropped the idea. Eventually he pressed his chest to the broom handle and squeezed his legs to the side until he slid back on top, huffing and puffing the entire time. He stayed stretched out along the length of the broom, not quite ready to sit up. He was glad he was wearing kneepads. Somehow it had been his knees and his ankles that had helped to right himself.

"It's working!" he shouted, voice shaking with laughter and relief. The slight breeze on his face cooled him off.

"Way to go, Charlie," said Sean. "Now, scoot back with your feet underneath you. You'll have more stability."

He slid back until he sat almost completely on the bristled end and felt much more anchored. He extended his forearms until he sat straight up. His arms shook from effort, but a thrill ran through him.

Oh my god! I'm flying! he said in his head. It wasn't what he expected. He thought it would be like riding a bike. But a bike was heavy. When he rode one, he could feel all the bumps in the road as he pedaled along. This was softer. The broom floated up and down on the air currents, and the sensation of having nothing beneath him, of being three or four feet above ground, was pure heaven.

"Kind of fun, isn't it?" Rose said from his left side.

"Yeah!" he yelled, the word carrying out across the field. They were inching along, so a quieter tone of voice would have been appropriate, but he was too excited to be able to manage talking normally. He lifted his face and enjoyed the soft droplets of rain sprinkling down on his cheeks and nose.

Rose reached over and put her hand on the tip of his broom.

"Hold on, okay? We're going to steer clear of those trees." She guided him to the left.

They were approaching the outer ring of the forest at the far end of the clearing. Together, they turned in a slow arc, eventually flying parallel to the trees.

He was reminded of riding a small pony at the county fair when he was little. The handler had kept her hand on the saddle's horn as they had walked about the corral.

"There you go," said Rose, letting go of his broom.

Charlie heard Sean's voice above and behind him.

"Charlie, pull up a little on the tip. Give it a try, but don't lean back too ..."

He pulled the broomstick end up toward his chest, which caused him to slide backwards, the shaft burning his palms. The broom shot skyward, going from a snail's pace to what felt like lightning speed in seconds, nearly yanking his arms from their sockets. His entire body slid off the end of the broom, his hands barely managing to maintain their grip. He was about to crash into the treetops, which were approaching at breakneck speed.

"No!" he screamed.

Sean appeared in front of him, then slid off his own broomstick so that he was hanging from it by one arm.

"Let me!" he yelled to the boy. He grabbed the end of Charlie's broom with his free hand and pulled up toward the sky.

The two of them climbed at an even steeper angle. Charlie clung tightly to the broomstick, sure that at any moment his fingers would lose their grip and he would plunge to his death. Both he and Sean had to tuck their knees to avoid hitting the treetops with their feet.

Once clear of the trees, Sean let go of Charlie's broom, letting it level out, and in one swift movement pulled his own broom down and swung up and over it, once again in a mounted position.

"Right as rain," Rose said as she and Sean lifted Charlie up into a sitting position on his own broom. Somehow she sounded calm even as she shouted to be heard above the wind.

Charlie's chest heaved as he tried to catch his breath. His palms stung where the broomstick had slid between his hands, and his thighs felt weak and wobbly from their vice-like grip on the shaft. He shook his head, then looked at the witches on either side of him. He was in awe of the grace and casual confidence they possessed as they rode their brooms.

"I have a lot to learn," he yelled to them.

"Fail and recover," Rose reminded him, giving Charlie a warm smile.

"Welcome to the friendly skies," Sean shouted. "The only way to fly."

Together, the three of them soared higher above the treetops and circled the perimeter of the clearing a few times. Charlie had just relaxed enough to enjoy the complete rush of flying so high in the air before Rose pointed back to the field.

They descended slowly. Charlie only had a moment to panic, having no idea how to actually land on the ground. Malcolm had barely covered Takeoff 101 in their lessons, let alone landing. Was he supposed to slip off the side of the broomstick, or touch down with it still between his legs?

Before he knew it, the ground slammed into his feet while he was still straddling the stick. Because the broom was activated, it continued flying straight ahead. Not knowing what else to do, he gripped tightly to the handle while it yanked him forward for a good twenty yards, his legs stumbling along in an awkward run on either side of the broom. He could hear shouts coming from the crowd of adults and kids watching him.

"Help!" he cried, unable to comprehend what anyone was yelling at him, let alone how to stop his crazy lurching across the grassy field. Finally he made out one adult shouting, "The Words, Charlie! The Words!"

The Words! He had completely forgotten.

He opened his mouth, letting the Words find, then move, his lips. The broom stopped pulling him along. He barely caught himself from sliding forward off the end of the handle and landing on his face. He stumbled to a standstill, then collapsed down into the grass and lay on his back, the dead weight of the broom in his hand. As everyone crowded around him, laughing and clapping, he began to giggle, thinking how he must have looked, running the length of the field and unable to stop.

Several of the younger WITs, filled with excitement, dove on top of him in a pig pile. He laughed harder, until someone accidentally kneed him in the stomach.

"Ouch! You're killing me!" he grunted. The adults pulled the kids back up on their feet.

He looked up and saw Sean's face smiling down at him.

"A really good job, Charlie," the man said. "A fine first solo flight."

*   *   *

Hidden behind an illusion of mist and cloud banks, two witches circled above on their brooms, watching the people in the field below and exchanging glances with each other.

"One little, two little, three little witches, fly on broomsticks, soar over ditches ..." Tony began singing.

"Shut it. I hate that song!" barked Claudia. "Let's get back and report in."

"Someone put on her cranky pants today, didn't she?"

"Yeah, I guess I did. It's just that ..."

"I know, I know. She isn't going to be happy about this. All right then, let's get back," Tony said, then looked again at the commotion below. "So mama's little baby has learned to fly. The plot sickens."

The two broomsticks became dark streaks as they sped off through the afternoon dusk.

CHAPTER 4

Stories 'Round the Fire

THAT NIGHT MALCOLM MADE a fire in the big fire pit on the front patio. The rain had let up enough to sit outside, though the adults placed tarps on the still-wet benches surrounding the pit.

After Charlie's unexpected breakthrough, many of the other kids were able to activate their brooms. With varying levels of success, six of them flew around at varying heights, shadowed by two or three adults each. The thrill of flight was thick among the new witches; even those who couldn't activate their own brooms were given rides from some of the adults, and the experience of the entire group racing and dipping in the air had broken the frustrated mood from earlier in the day, elevating it to excitement and focus.

As the flying lessons came to an end and everyone was gathering up the helmets and kneepads, Charlie watched as several of the adults threw their own brooms with great force to the ground. He heard a cracking sound and saw the sticks shrink to narrow pieces of wood less than twelve inches long.

"Makes it easier to lug it around. Though you gotta be careful not to accidentally sit on it if you forget it's in your pocket," said Roberto, who must have seen Charlie staring at the brooms.

The last session of their training, just before dinner, had also been much more successful.

"It usually happens this way," Malcolm told them after they had watched Malcolm Paulsboro, whom they called Little M in deference to their teacher, make words appear on paper like a fast-developing Polaroid image. Nine years old, he was the youngest in the group, and after the sentence "Malcolm is a rad name!" finished materializing on the page, he had hopped up from his kneeling position in front of the table and started jumping around on one foot in delight. His spontaneous expression of joy and triumph was so infectious that some of the other WITs joined him. Everyone laughed and clapped, and Charlie saw Little M's mother dab at her eyes with a handkerchief.

"Charlie's success with the broomstick earlier in the day unclogged you all," said the teacher, smiling at him. Charlie blushed, not wanting the attention. But he was still so enraptured by the sensation of flying on a broomstick that it was hard to stop smiling.

"It always seems to spur on a group of WITs. Helps them believe they can do it, and also starts to create some competition," he said, winking at them all.

"Have you ever had a group where no one could do anything?" asked Jenna, much more focused on the lessons now that she was one of the WITs who hadn't been able to make any of her spells work.

"Yes, it happens. Though what that usually means is kids get it when they go home. I've also had groups who make the spells work on the first night. It doesn't mean anything really. It's like babies learning to walk. Some take to it faster than others, but they all get it eventually."

The fire spat and sizzled in the large pit. Adults and kids alike made s'mores, though they were unlike any Charlie had never eaten. There was chocolate with lavender, chocolate with bacon, chocolate with sea salt, and chocolate with chili peppers. There was even a white-chocolate raspberry combination that was a group hit. The marshmallows were soft and gooey, unlike the dusty things he was used to pulling out of plastic bags at his friends' homes. In place of graham crackers, they grilled halved croissants over the fire. Charlie was sure he had never tasted anything so delicious.

The mood between the adults and Malcolm had changed. Where it had been tense before, with Malcolm in charge and the grown-ups doing what they were told to do, it was now collegial. At dinner many of the adults gathered around the kids and chatted with them, and some of them even teased Malcolm about his strict ways.

Rose, the witch who'd flown with Charlie earlier in the day, sat with him at dinner and told him about her first time riding a broom, about her son David who worked in Europe as a witchcraft researcher, and about the Words. Charlie liked her gentle manner and soft voice, so different from some of the louder, cockier adults at Malcolm's cabin.

"I watched you today out in the field, Charlie," Rose told him while they finished the last of their meal. "It was interesting. At first I could tell that you were trying out the Words, saying them and hoping that they would work. But then something changed. Even when Malcolm was telling you that your turn was over. The look on your face told me you understood how the Words worked."

"I don't think I understand them."

"No, you don't fully. You have a lot to learn about them. But you understood that it's less about saying the Words and more about letting them be said. Through you."

"Yes! That's what it felt like. I … I didn't know."

Rose nodded. "It can be a difficult transition to make. I appreciate that Malcolm didn't come flat out and tell you young people to 'let the Words speak through you.' I think that would be too confusing. It takes trial and error, as well as a certain amount of self-discovery, to understand it.

"Anyway," she continued, "I haven't been to a new witch training in a long time. It was a delight to see you catch on the way you did. It reminded me of when my son was little and even of my own discoveries of the craft so long ago. Congratulations on your breakthrough today. It will take you far."

"Thank you. And thanks for all your help with the broomstick today."

"You're welcome, Charlie," she said and then fell silent as she looked out the window. Charlie joined her gaze, and together they sat quietly together, surrounded by, but not joining in, the raucous chatter of the others. He wondered if this is what some friendships were like: enjoying silence together, rather than having to talk, like so many people tended to do. It was strange, but also pleasant, to imagine being friends with a much older grown-up like Rose.

After the s'mores were finished, Malcolm stood up.

"We have a treat for you tonight. Something even better than this delicious fireside dessert. Rose Patchke, community historian, famed storyteller, and one of the few people who can keep me in my place, is here tonight to share her gifts with us."

Rose stood up as the other adults clapped for her.

"Malcolm, please, you are too kind. As I was telling Charlie earlier," she said, nodding in his direction, "I haven't been to a training weekend in a long time. It has done these old bones some good to be among you new witches as you discover your talents and abilities.

"I've been asked to tell you a story tonight about a young witch and her exploration of the craft. Please keep in mind the spirit in which it's being told: as a reminder that with your new abilities comes great responsibility. You can no longer pretend that you are a single human being with merely personal consequences. You are part of a community of people who must make hard choices about how to interact with the greater world, sometimes on a daily basis.

"There was once a young woman named Catherine, or Cat, for short. She was from a rural town in the southern state of Kentucky, born in 1943. She had long red hair, a lovely face, and a good head on her shoulders."

"Is this really about Grace, that red-haired lady who …" asked Little M.

"Malcolm Rudolph Paulsboro!" scolded his mother. "What have I told you about interrupting?"

Little M's face fell, and he looked down at his lap. "Sorry," he said.

"That's all right, Malcolm," said Rose.

Charlie looked around and saw the expressions of unease on the adults' faces, as well as many of the WITs, at the mention of Grace's name. He had forgotten that everyone else knew who she was too.

"No," continued Rose. "This is not about Grace. She's not the only witch with red hair," she said, winking at Little M. "It's about someone else. Now I invite you all to sit back and listen.

"As I was saying, there was a young woman named Cat. From the South."

As Rose spoke, Charlie saw the fire grow brighter out of the corner of his eye. He looked into the flames and was surprised to see an image of red hair emerging, then the face of a fair-skinned girl. Soon the flames, as well as his surroundings, disappeared. He found himself transported to the edge of a garden patch, watching the young woman weed flowerbeds near a quaint-looking cottage.

"Like many of our kind, Cat lived alone on the outskirts of town. She worked mostly as a healer for the local community. Her parents died when she was very young. For a while she lived with a great aunt, who taught her things about healing, medicine, and plants, until the old woman passed away. Cat grew herbs, made unguents, helped with midwifery. The townspeople had a love-hate relationship with her, like they do the world over with people like us. Tall tales about her family had been passed down from generation to generation. Many publicly ridiculed Cat, all the while visiting her secretly in the middle of the night with their worries of money, health, and love.

"As you can imagine, Cat's existence was rather lonely. She did not have the support and camaraderie of a vibrant community like ours and had to learn most things on her own. Though she hadn't been popped, she carried strong echoes of the blood in her."

Charlie watched as the young woman trimmed herbs and gathered plants from her garden. He followed her inside her orderly pleasant home.

The scene changed. Cat sat in a wooden rocking chair by the fireplace in her living room talking to a young man in a white T-shirt and jeans who was sitting cross-legged on the floor with his head in his hands. His dark hair was combed back from his forehead and shiny with hair gel, like someone in a movie from the 1950s or '60s.

"It's okay, Tom. It's okay."

The man looked up at Cat. "But what if she is pregnant? What am I gonna do?"

They spoke with strong southern accents. Cat seemed to be trying to placate the man, all the while keeping her distance from him.

"You always have choices, Tom. You know that."

The man leaned forward and rested his head in Cat's lap. The young woman looked uncomfortable at first but then began to pat, and finally stroke, the man's hair. For a long time they sat in silence. Eventually, Tom raised his head and looked into Cat's eyes. He moved his face closer to hers until she leaned down and gave him a gentle kiss on the mouth. Tom pulled away, then threw his arms around her. The two stayed locked in a passionate embrace, kissing each other deeply, he upright on his knees, she sitting on the edge of her rocking chair.

Charlie felt extremely embarrassed, thinking that he shouldn't be watching this, and yet unable to pull his eyes away.

Tom broke the embrace first.

"Ah, Jesus, I shouldn't have. I'm sorry, I ..." he said as he stood up and backed away from the rocking chair.

"I shouldn't have," Cat said, looking horrified.

"Don't tell Miriam, for God's sake!" Tom begged, his hands up at his head, walking in quick small circles.

"Of course not! It was a mistake. Tom, I'm so sorry."

The scene faded, and Charlie found himself looking at Cat, asleep in her bed, with a storm raging outside. Two cats slept at the foot of the bed while lightning flickered outside her windows and raindrops pelted the roof.

Cat's eyes flew open as a large crash came from somewhere in the yard.

She sat straight up in bed and fumbled about in her nightstand until she found a flashlight. Gathering a raincoat around her and slipping on an old pair of shoes sitting near the back door, Cat stepped outside to investigate.

A large tree had fallen onto a storage shed in her backyard.

She walked around the building to investigate, shining the light here and there to assess the damage.

A strong gust of wind blew through her yard, and Charlie heard a loud crack from somewhere close by. Before she could react, a branch ripped free from the fallen tree and struck her in the back of the head. Cat fell forward into the mud, the light spinning as her flashlight flew from her hands. She lay in the mud, face down, not moving.

Charlie heard someone gasp, and remembered that a group of them were sitting around a campfire, as the story progressed. Somehow Rose was showing them the story, as if they were actually in the small Kentucky town, not at Malcolm's cabin in Washington state.

As the wind died down, the light changed, and Charlie found himself back inside Cat's house. It was daytime, but all the shades were drawn. The woman sat upright in bed, her red hair spilling down her shoulders, a bandage around her head.

Rose's soft voice carried through, as if coming from inside the living room.

"Cat was lucky she wasn't killed. She sustained no brain damage from the injury, but the violence of the accident served as her own private popping ceremony, surfacing all of the witchcraft in her blood. She had always known she had abilities that other people didn't. Her great aunt had taught her to keep this a secret and to serve others well. But she had no idea how much more potential ability she really possessed."

Several books floated near Cat's face, and scrying bowls filled with water showed scenes of people and places. Cat's brow furrowed in concentration, her mouth forming small soundless words. A knock at the door startled her. The books fell to the floor and the surface of water in each bowl once again turned clear. The knocking continued.

"Cat, you in there?" a man's voice shouted from outside. Charlie wondered if it was Tom.

"I just want to know if you're all right!"

The young woman sat still in bed, staring at the door and making no sound.

"Cat!"

Eventually the knocking stopped. Footsteps crunched on the graveled path leading away from the front door, and a shadow passed by one of the windows as the visitor left.

Rose continued narrating. "The young woman stayed away from

people until her wound healed. When she was back on her feet, she discovered that she was more capable than ever to help the townspeople with their ailments. Her lotions and salves were stronger, her ability to spot trouble for them was more accurate, and she was able to imbue certain objects with protective qualities. Even though she was untrained and had no one to guide her, she was determined to learn as much about her abilities as possible."

More scenes, this time of people coming to her home at night, sitting in her living room, giving her money in exchange for bottles of liquid and other items. In some scenes Cat placed her hands on people's heads. In others, she looked into scrying bowls and offered advice.

"But her loneliness and isolation began to catch up with her. Having no one with whom to share her discoveries, a part of Cat began to foment and fester. She had been attracted to the young man Tom since she was a girl, and on the day they kissed, a seed of hope was planted inside her. Had her abilities stayed the same, her feelings for him would have remained quiet. Under the surface.

"Cat found herself spying on Tom and his young fiancée Miriam, watching their time together, learning how Miriam loved the man, hoping to copy her acts to woo him away. Her attempts led nowhere.

"She spent more and more late evenings in town hoping to get closer to Tom. She discovered ways to stay hidden behind shadows and to ride the wind for short distances."

Charlie saw Cat darting through the woods, then standing unnoticed near a car parked on a secluded lane, watching as Tom and a young woman sat kissing inside the vehicle. He watched as Cat changed her appearance and followed the young couple through a grocery store. And he saw her alight atop a modest home, then slide down a wall and peer in through a window.

"Cat convinced herself that she could change Tom's heart, making him love her and have no more desire for Miriam. She didn't know that witches cannot directly affect a person's heart or mind. Failing at this, she attempted spells to dissuade Miriam from loving her fiancé.

"Faced with more failure, nearly crazy in her desperation, she experimented with a most dangerous idea: to inhabit the body of the young Miriam.

"Unfortunately, while this is a very difficult thing to do, not to mention profane and corrupt beyond words, Cat discovered that it was not, in fact, impossible."

Charlie watched as Cat walked to the edge of the woods near her house, spread her arms wide, and begin to sing a sad wordless melody.

Within minutes a large raccoon came crawling from the forest, low to the ground and quivering, as if trying to to resist the song's enchantment. Just as it reached Cat's feet, she pulled a hunting knife from her coat pocket and drove it through the beast's back, killing it instantly. Unable to look away, Charlie was forced to watch her carry its body into her home, throw it flat on her kitchen counter, and with the same knife, saw off its head, which she then skinned and cleaned until its skull emerged, small, white and hollow.

"Cat had created a vile witch's receptacle, a crucial tool for her plan.

"Without bothering to wash up after butchering the raccoon, Cat telephoned Miriam and invited her to her home under the pretense of giving the woman a warning about Tom."

The scene changed to the living room of the witch's small home. Cat stood facing Miriam, who looked uncomfortable and confused by the blood covering her hostess and the kitchen counter. Cat leaned in to her as if to tell her a secret but instead began to sing the same melody into the woman's ear.

Charlie watched as a small wisp of white vapor emerged from Miriam's body while the shocked look on Miriam's face changed to a vacant expression. Raising one hand in the air, Cat coaxed the vapory substance, the way a child plays with a soap bubble using a plastic wand, down and into the raccoon skull.

Acting quickly, she mumbled quiet Words, whispering her own life force free into the air between the two women, then guided it until it entered and inhabited the rigid shell of Miriam's body. Through new eyes, she watched as her own form slumped to the floor, red hair spilling everywhere. She quickly dragged the body into a sitting position in the rocking chair, then fled the house in anticipation.

"Using Miriam's body, Cat deceived Tom into believing that she was his young fiancée and spent several days and nights with him in borrowed bliss."

A montage of scenes flashed before Charlie's eyes: the young couple holding hands and laughing as they walked together in town, eating fried fish at a local restaurant, pressing their bodies against each other as they kissed on a couch in Tom's house.

"But for all of Cat's strength and ability, she lacked focus and control as well as the experience needed to maintain her trickery."

Charlie saw Tom extract himself from Cat's embrace and sit up on the couch, staring in confusion at the person he thought was Miriam. Soon the young man and woman began to yell and shout at each other. At one point Miriam/Cat screamed in frustration, then reached out and struck Tom across the face. With his hand holding onto his cheek, the man stood still and stared at the woman, who returned his gaze with a look of shock. Striking Tom seemed to snap Cat out of her obsessive mindset. She looked around her as if discovering for the first time where she was and what was truly going on. Without a word of explanation, she fled Tom's house.

"Horrified at what she had done, she forced Miriam's body to race home, hoping to repair any damage she might have caused. But once there she discovered her own body, rigid and lifeless in the rocking chair, next to the cold fireplace. Most human bodies cannot survive more than a few hours without an internal life force. Cat had vacated her own for days. There was no life left to which she could return.

"With only one able body remaining and no witch available to help her revive her own form or reverse her nefarious spell, she panicked. Picking up the raccoon skull, she released Miriam's life force and impelled it back into her body.

"Had the young witch stopped to consider her actions, she might have realized the impossibility of two people trying to inhabit one body. The human mind is a complex protective entity. Just as a physical body creates an immune response when it is invaded, the mind reacts similarly. Two human minds, two life forces thrust together in the same physical form, simply cannot coexist. Miriam's and Cat's essences attacked each other, forcing the structure holding the two of them together to crumble."

Charlie watched as Miriam's body ran helter-skelter inside the cottage, screaming, crashing into walls, throwing things. It slapped and shook Cat's lifeless form, trying to will it to live.

Cat's body slumped forward and fell off the chair, while Miriam's body, filled with two competing life forces, fell to the floor and writhed.

The scene changed again. In a small hospital room, Tom sat on a chair next to a bed where Miriam's body lay. Several tubes were attached to places on the woman's arms. Her mouth lay open and her eyes stared out the window, seeing nothing. Occasionally, her body shuddered. Several doctors and nurses came and went, making notes on clipboards and shaking their heads.

"After interviewing Tom, the police concluded that Miriam had run off to Cat's house in the middle of the night and murdered her, though motive, as well as cause of death, remained unknown. It was assumed that the murder had driven the young Miriam mad. After a week in the hospital, Miriam's body expired, unable to withstand the war being waged inside it."

Now Charlie watched as Tom, looking haggard and grief-ridden, walked around the grounds of Cat's home on a cold gray afternoon. Boards sealed the windows shut while weeds overran the garden. Then the scene changed. Sunlight shone on what appeared to be a spring day. A cleaning crew removed the last bit of debris from the newly repaired storage shed outside of Cat's home. A smartly dressed older gentleman pounded a for sale sign in Cat's yard, then got in his car and drove away.

The flames of the campfire grew brighter, and Charlie found himself once again back on Malcolm's patio. Several of the WITs were crying, including Jenna. A couple of the adults wiped at their eyes and blew their noses.

"I wish this story were fable. But it really did happen. I tell it to you today to remind you," Rose said, looking each of the young witches in the eye, "that with authority comes responsibility. Cat gained great authority, great power, an ability to do things that were previously unimaginable to her. But she lacked the personal responsibility and fortitude to do no harm, to maintain her concern for other people's welfare over her own desires.

"I tell you this story because Cat was a fine young woman, with a sense of decency. She cared for her fellow humans. She was not a bad person with evil motivations. But she had no guidance, no one with whom to share her concerns, her fears, even her ideas. Unchecked, she made a series of decisions that led to utter devastation for three people, not to mention Tom's and Miriam's families.

"In the coming days, weeks, months, even years," she continued, " you will find yourselves in situations where it might seem like a good idea to use your abilities for your own personal gain or maybe to help or hinder the gain of another. The consequences of such ideas, such choices, are far more widespread and potentially damaging than you can possibly imagine. I urge each and every one of you to listen to Malcolm and heed his lessons well, to practice what you have learned in safe supervised environments, with your family as well as other adults in the community, and to only use your legacy for the benefit of the whole world, not just for your own personal advancement. Remember, the ends never justify the means."

"But wait," said Little M, where he sat near his mother. He was close to tears but doing his best to choke them back. "Didn't she, couldn't Cat use the craft to, to … make everything back like it was?" he asked. His mother rubbed his back. Charlie looked away, unable to bear the expression of heartbreak on the young boy's face.

"No, Malcolm, she couldn't," his mother said. "Some things can't be undone." The boy buried his head in his mother's side and cried.

Rose looked at several of the young witches one more time, then sat down. The people gathered around the campfire stayed quiet, sobered by the story of Cat and the inadvertent devastation she had caused.

Eventually Malcolm stood up and announced that it was time for bed. There would be much more to learn the next day, he explained, and Rose's story deserved to be pondered.

As the adults cleaned up the s'mores supplies, Charlie followed the other kids, ready to go to bed. But a hand on his shoulder stopped him.

"Can I talk to you for a second?" It was Malcolm, eyes shining in the firelight as he looked down at Charlie.

They walked to the far end of the patio and sat down. A light rain had begun to fall. Malcolm looked up at the sky.

"Quite a story, huh?" Malcolm asked. Charlie nodded, still haunted by Rose's images. "This won't take long. I want you to stay dry."

He smiled at Charlie and looked into his eyes as if searching for something.

"Kid, you did it. You really found a way to make peace with your heart, or at least enough to kick us off today. Well done."

"Thank you."

"How'd you do it?"

Charlie looked at the flames for a while not sure how to explain what he had figured out. Then he remembered his conversation with Rose at dinner.

"I guess I realized that I had to stop saying the Words and instead let them say themselves, through my mouth, you know? It felt really weird, but right, too, when the Words started making my lips move."

Malcolm nodded. "Yep, that's part of the trick, isn't it? But that isn't what I was talking about. I meant that you figured out something about the conflict inside of you, didn't you? About that boy?"

Charlie looked away, feeling embarrassed. As usual, there wasn't anything clear inside his head to say. But he knew that Malcolm expected something from him.

"I thought a lot about what you said, about not being able to be one person while hiding another part of myself. I didn't know what to do about any of it. But that boy, he sort of, uh, he brought it up."

"What do you mean?"

"He asked me if I liked him. You know, in that way? I wasn't sure. I mean, I thought I did. Or I think I do. But it all felt so confusing."

"So what happened?"

Charlie didn't want to say more. He wanted to run away instead of having this conversation with a man who was still a relative stranger. But he felt sobered by Rose's story and was tired of playing at hide-and-seek. Additionally, he had begun to trust Malcolm, with his consistent encouragement and the no-nonsense way he talked. Charlie figured he could be no-nonsense too.

"He kissed me."

"Wow, kid. Are congratulations in order?"

"I don't think so. I didn't really want it to happen."

"He forced himself on you?"

"What? No, nothing like that. He didn't understand me, and I think he thought I wanted to. The thing is, I kissed him back. Later. In the park. A lot."

"Oh."

Charlie turned his head, unable to look Malcolm in the eye.

"It's okay, Charlie. It really is. You acted on your heart, and you have the guts to tell me about it now. Your honesty will help you go far, kid."

"Really? You don't think that I'm, like, gross? Or weird?"

"Of course not. Who knows why we like what we like? Look at us, a pack of witches, kings and queens of the air. And we can't figure it out either. I think we're all pretty clueless when it comes to this stuff. So if anyone tells you what you're doing is wrong, just remember this: What the hell do they know?"

Malcolm tousled the top of his hair. Charlie pulled away, but grinned in spite of himself.

"You do realize, don't you," the man said to him, "that because you were brave and honest with yourself, you cleared things so the Words could find you?"

"What? I don't understand."

"Kid, remember what we talked about? I told you that you couldn't be a witch while hiding something big from yourself. You stopped hiding, which let everything inside of you relax. That made it easier for the Words to find the witch in you."

"Oh. I guess I hadn't thought about it that way."

"Well, that's how it works," Malcolm said, folding his arms across his chest and nodding as if he were explaining the laws of gravity.

Charlie smiled in response to Malcolm's praise, even as his face turned red.

"Go get some sleep, kid. You deserve it."

"Okay," he said, standing up.

"Malcolm?"

"Yeah?"

"Thanks for today. It was really, really great," he said.

"You're welcome, little man."

CHAPTER 5

Philosophies

"SO DID HE HAVE THAT whole conversation with you about Maria Callas and Michael Jordan?" Beverly asked, the liquid in her wine glass swirling plum-red as she brought it to her mouth.

"You mean about whether witchcraft is a religion or just a skill?"

"Yeah, that one. Seems like he's been using it forever. No offense to Maria or Michael, but you'd think he'd come up with new examples after all these years."

"I didn't even know who Maria Callas was at first until he explained everything."

Aunt, uncle, and nephew sat together at the dining room table the Sunday night of Charlie's training weekend. Rain pelted the windows at the back of the house. The temperature had dropped from chilly to downright cold. A fire blazed in the fireplace, where Amos lay kerfuffling in his sleep. They ate a shellfish stew, red and savory, with thick slices of bread and a leafy spinach salad.

"Um, this is really good," said Charlie, his mouth full of bread.

"It is, isn't it? Thank you," Beverly nodded. "I'm happy to feed my two guys."

"Wait a minute. What's the story about Michael Jordan and Maria Callas?" Randall asked, a look of disbelief on his face. "Are they witches too?"

Charlie laughed just as he was taking a drink of water. He was barely able to keep from spraying it all over the vase of flowers at the center of the table.

"Honestly, Rand!" said his aunt, laughing too. "No, they are not witches."

"Well? How am I supposed to know? Are you two gonna have all of these mysterious conversations now? That I won't understand? All these secret witch handshakes?"

"Probably. What are you gonna do about it?" Beverly teased.

"I'll make up my own stuff. And only talk to Amos about it. Isn't that right, Amos? Abracadabra bark bark!" Charlie's uncle turned his head and broad shoulders to the fireplace. Amos thumped his tail on the ground but remained prone, the warmth of the fire too satisfying to warrant standing up.

"Some witches believe," said Beverly, ignoring her husband's antics, "that our craft is a religion, or at least lends itself to religious doctrine. Others completely disagree. No research has come up with anything definitive on the nature of God in relationship to witch-craft. They feel that it's more like a unique talent not limited to one philosophy."

"For example, I can take this here …"

The silver napkin holder next to her soup bowl rose a foot into the air and began to spin in place, throwing shadows from the candle-light against the wall.

"… and do this. But does it prove the existence of God? Does it show me what will happen in the afterlife? No, it doesn't. I can do this and call myself a Christian. Or a Muslim. Or an agnostic."

"Or a Jew," Randall added.

"Or a Jew. I can do this thing, then attribute it to whatever phil-osophical or religious beliefs I have. The opera star Maria Callas had a freakishly good singing voice. That didn't make her a devotee of the religion of opera. Michael Jordan's basketball skills are superhuman. He practically flies through the air. But it doesn't mean he has to see life a certain way. He could be a Buddhist or an atheist and still have made slam dunks and winning seasons for the Chicago Bulls. That's the debate."

Randall made a tut-tut noise, raised his eyebrows at Beverly and pointed to the napkin holder still spinning above their plates.

"Oh. Sorry," she said. The metallic ring floated back down to her place mat.

"What do you believe?" Charlie asked.

"I believe it's a little of both, actually. I mostly agree with Malcolm, who thinks our craft is just a unique ability. Especially when I look at the demographics in our community. We have some highly philosophical witches among us, while others are much more secular. Some of them have strong religious practices. Others have never stepped foot into a place of worship in their lives. What we can do isn't necessarily affected by what source we believe it comes from.

"But," she added, looking into Charlie's eyes, "I do believe that our craft affects how we view the world. Before I was popped I had never heard that music, that song that seems to come from all living things. Sometimes when I hear it today, I find myself weeping because it's so beautiful. I believe it allows me to sense a certain beauty in the world that I wouldn't have been able to if I didn't have this legacy in my blood or if I wasn't a full witch. I care deeply for this planet and its welfare. It definitely has affected my philosophy of life."

Randall interrupted. "Yeah, but Grace can do all the stuff you can. Doesn't sound like she has much concern for the planet other than what she can get out of it."

"True. To me it isn't as cut and dried as the people on either side of the debate try to make it. I mostly know that I stand with the secular side. But I can't help wondering how Maria Callas's talents affected her worldview. Or Michael Jordan. Look how strong, how elegant, he is. His ability to manipulate the ball like that, or his shooting precision—don't you think that if he were just an average guy, he would experience life differently?"

They ate in silence for a while, each lost in thought.

None of them noticed the slight change in the way the fire flickered in the fireplace as if a sudden draft made the flames flutter.

None of them noticed one flame licking at the air, higher than the others, stretching slightly, becoming more solid. As the three people continued to eat their dinner, they were unaware that several flames leaned in together, looking for a moment like bound stalks of fiery wheat, bending forward as if listening.

Charlie talked more about his training weekend, especially about his maiden voyage on the broomstick.

"I couldn't believe it when I slipped off. My head almost hit the ground while the broom was jerking forward. But then, when we rose up in the air …"

Amos awoke, walked over to the window, and stretched. He looked out into the night and began sniffing the air near the windowsill. Then he ambled back and peered at the fireplace, his head cocked to one side.

"… other kids seemed to get it too. More of them did today. So that by the time we left, everyone had been able to work at least one spell."

"That's amazing, Charlie," Beverly said. "It's not uncommon to have less than half the group able to do anything that Malcolm taught them."

The dog moved closer to the fire. He sniffed more of the air and then barked twice in quick succession.

Beverly, Randall, and Charlie jumped.

"Amos!" Randall began. "For God's sake boy, you scared the …"

His wife's hand, extended forward in a warning gesture, cut him off. She stood up from the table and walked into the living room.

"What is it, boy? Did you see something?"

The dog's tail wagged, and a slow, deliberate whine came from his muzzle.

"Is there something …?" she asked, bending down and peering into the fireplace, having just missed the flames shrink a half inch, returning to their normal size. The whiff of damp wood was too faint for her to notice.

"Huh," said Beverly. "Guess it was nothing." She returned to the table and announced that she had made an apple tart for dessert.

"My boy," Randall said to Charlie as he began to take the dinner dishes into the kitchen. "You are in for a treat. Try to take a bite of it and not weep for joy. As a matter of fact, just see if you don't convert to the religion of Apple Tartism."

Charlie laughed. "Sounds better than any religion I've ever heard of," he said.

Beverly and Randall smiled at each other while Charlie helped clear the table.

*   *   *

In a bedroom across the city, a vertical length of fire, the approximate size of a human body, burned just above the floor. Gradually, the center of the fire changed. A woman's face emerged, then hair, shoulders, a body wrapped in a silky peach-colored dress. The flames hovered above the woman, then shrank to a thin jet of fire that ran along her right arm as her bare feet floated down to the carpet. She pointed her hand toward a candlestick on her boudoir, and the fire leaped from her fingers. By the time it touched the wick, it had dwindled to a small bud of flame.

"So, the boy's home from witch camp, is he?" she said out loud, her dress fluttering as she turned and walked over to a small table. She flipped her ginger locks from her shoulders and sat down on a wooden chair, examining the objects lying there.

"The good news is that Beverly's wards are weak. Easier to penetrate than I thought they'd be. The bad news," she paused, holding two small glass vials in her hand, "is that they have a dog."

Setting the vials down, she reached over and picked up a small white apron.

Tying it around her waist, the woman gestured in the air behind her. Her bedroom window opened wide. A large crow hopped onto the window sill and gave a loud caw, then spread its wings and flew into the room, landing on the table in front of her.

"Hello," Grace said to the crow. "Thank you for coming."

The bird bobbed back and forth, its head bowing up and down, claws making a skittering sound on the shiny wood of the table's surface. It turned its head to the side and looked up at the woman with one of its black-marble eyes.

After she stared into the eye for several seconds, the crow stopped moving. It didn't make a single noise as she removed a hairpin from her tresses and drove it straight into its breast. Its body shuddered as blood seeped from its feathers, pouring into an unstopped vial the woman held in her hand.

After a time the crow fell to its side on the table. She placed the cork back into the small bottle, then wiggled her fingers. The bird carcass lifted off the table and floated out the window.

"Always good to stock up on supplies," Grace said, wiping her hands off on the apron. She walked over to the far side of her room and regarded the person who was gagged and bound to a chair in the corner. Eyes wide open, body straining against the rope that bound it, feet trying to push away from her.

"Now, what are we going to do with you?"

CHAPTER 6

The Crash

DIEGO AND CHARLIE WALKED down A-wing together after
Chinese class, headed toward biology. It was the Monday after the
first training weekend up at Malcolm's cabin. The nervousness Charlie felt now had nothing to do with whether or not he thought he
was good enough to be Diego's friend or even whether or not Diego
thought Charlie worthy of his attention.

After the Saturday at Diego's house, and the surprise kissing at
Lincoln Park, the two boys had avoided each other at school. They
had thought it best, lest people get the wrong idea. Actually, Charlie
had thought it best.

But they texted each other. They talked every single night on the
phone. And on Wednesday afternoon they snuck into Diego's car,
parked a few blocks from school near a small neighborhood park, and
kissed for quite some time.

"I can't stop thinking about you," Diego had said when Charlie
pulled back to catch his breath.

Charlie's mind had clouded with conflicting thoughts. Ever since
he lay back on the cement path at Lincoln Park and let himself kiss
and be kissed by Diego, sinking deeply into the confusing desire he
felt for the boy, he hadn't been able to think clearly about what he
wanted or what he should be doing. Diego's charm, his personality,
was so big, so enticing, it seemed easier to give in and ...

And yet, he was afraid. He was afraid of what it all meant. He was afraid people would find out. People like Julio and Dave Giraldi. What if they teased him in front of everyone? Or beat him up? He wanted to keep things quiet, to slow things down. And yet nothing else seemed to slow down. Not his escape from Clarkston to Seattle, not the whole witchcraft situation. Why should he expect this to be any different?

Charlie wasn't ready to tell his aunt and uncle anything yet, so Diego agreed, albeit reluctantly, not to see him after school all week. Wednesday in the car was an exception for both of them, a rule that in the end Charlie was glad they had decided to break.

On Friday, before heading up to Snoqualmie, he had told Diego that he was going camping with his uncle and some friends. Diego looked surprised, then sad.

"I can't see you this weekend? I thought we could hang out some more."

Charlie assured him that they would see each other at school the next week.

As they walked past the lockers and school posters ("Girls' Swim Team Bake Sale Thursday – BRING CASH!" and "Get Well, Principal Wang, We Love You") he knew he wasn't nervous because of what Diego thought about him. He was nervous because he was sure everyone in school was talking about them. Not because he could hear anything from his newly acquired listening abilities, which had decreased in intensity just like everyone had said they would. It was because it felt like he was walking around with a sign taped to his shirt that read "We're kissing now!" and was paranoid that he and Diego were the talk of the school.

Diego sauntered down the hallway with a smile as big as Texas, waving to people, holding himself tall. Charlie wanted to duck into the bathroom and hide in a toilet stall, or at least splash water on his face. Alone.

He also worried about the excitement he felt when he was with Diego. He couldn't stop thinking about him. Images of the boy flooded his brain when he tried to concentrate on all the makeup homework he had to do since the week of school he had missed after he had been popped. Memories of how it felt when he bit Charlie's lower lip, when he ran his hand along Charlie's lower back, his legs …

Diego had asked him if he could walk Charlie to biology on Monday.

"I miss you. It'll be fun. No one knows."

At this point Charlie was sure that everyone knew and that Diego was either clueless, didn't care, or wanted to flaunt it in front of the whole school.

"Yeah, sure," he had said.

"How about coming to the GSA meeting tomorrow after school?" Diego asked as they climbed the stairs to the second floor. "You'd like it."

"Um, well, I don't know. Maybe."

"Come on. It's really chill, and Ms. Barry is awesome."

"Ms. Barry? Everyone says she's the hardest teacher here."

"She is. As a history teacher. But as the GSA faculty advisor, she's totally chill."

Charlie didn't want to go. But he felt badly that he had to lie to Diego about camping over the weekend. He was trying to think of a way he could say no when he heard a girl's voice coming from somewhere behind them.

"Hey, boys, what are you up to?"

They both spun around. There stood Tawny with her long blonde hair and a look of surprise and delight on her face.

"You two look so guilty!" she said, laughing. "Did I catch you doing something?"

Diego had asked Charlie if he could tell Tawny about them. Charlie still wasn't sure what "them" meant, but he had relented. He felt his face burning as Tawny looked at him now.

"Relax, Chuck, really," she said as she walked in closer. Then she whispered, "Your secret's safe with me."

"What? Well …"

Tawny hid her smile behind her hand and then looked at Diego.

"I get it, Mr. Ramirez. He's cute anyway. But then, that shy look he gets? Yum, yum!"

"Totally," said Diego, grinning like a fool.

She turned to Charlie. "Oh, and I'm not just saying that to make you feel good about yourself. It's true. You just don't know it."

Charlie had no idea what to do. He mumbled thanks and ducked his head. The strap of his backpack slipped from his shoulder to the crook of his elbow and somehow managed to turn upside down. Because it was unzipped, the entire contents spilled out onto the floor. He watched in horror as his pencil case opened and pens skidded under a nearby drinking fountain. Books lay scattered on the tiles near his feet.

"Oh geez, I just …" he started.

Tawny and Diego were down on the floor in a flash, gathering the dropped items and trying, unsuccessfully, not to laugh.

Charlie stood in painful silence, unable to do anything but hold his backpack open while the two friends filled it with the spilled contents.

"Well, okay then. Looks like I've completely flustered you," Tawny said. "I'll take that as my cue to leave." She leaned in and kissed Charlie on the cheek, then gave Diego a hug before walking back down A-wing.

"Charlie, don't worry about that, it's no big deal," Diego started to say.

But Charlie wasn't listening. He realized how tired he was of hearing himself say that he wanted things to slow down. If he really did want things to slow down so much, then he was going to have to do something about it. No one could or would do it for him. Waiting for someone else to make it better for him was a stupid idea.

Yeah, 'cause look how good that plan has been going.

"I'm not going to the GSA meeting with you tomorrow."

"Oh. Okay. Why not?"

"Because," Charlie said, worried that Diego was going to get mad but determined to speak his mind. "I'd like to take things one at a time. I really like hanging out with you. Can we just keep it to that for a while?"

The frown lines on Diego's forehead deepened, then vanished.

"Of course. I'm kind of like a puppy, all excited and everything. Sorry."

"No, no, it's okay, I ..."

"Charlie, I get it. I've had a lot of time to figure a bunch of stuff out. And to take lots of small steps. This is new for you."

Funny. Diego's words sounded just like what Beverly had said to him about the legacy of witchcraft. How could two things which seemed so opposite end up running around him in the same way?

In spite of trying to maintain his cool, Charlie's shoulders actually shuddered as he relaxed. He was relieved that Diego understood. "But I'd like to hang after school, if that's okay with you."

"Are you just saying that because you're trying to be nice?" Diego asked, crossing his arms over his chest and furrowing his brow.

"No. I want to. I just don't want to go to some big public meeting, is all. Not yet."

Diego smiled so widely that Charlie wanted to shield his eyes with his hands. But he found himself smiling back. And then his mind flooded with sensory images, of tasting the boy's mouth, of feeling Diego putting his hands on the back of his head as they kissed.

Charlie shook his head. "Okay then. Time to get to class."

At lunch he called his aunt to ask if he could go to Diego's house after school.

"Will you be home for dinner?" she asked him. "Randall's making his famous stuffed pasta shells. They're too amazing to be missed. Maybe Diego would like to come over?"

It was decided that they would go to Diego's house for homework, since he needed to feed their cats as his mom was working late. But Diego had a Wicca meeting to go to later that night and couldn't make it to Washington Street for dinner.

"But tell your aunt I'd love a rain check," the boy said.

And so this was how Charlie found himself in Diego's house, with no adult around. He drummed his fingers on the kitchen counter while Diego pulled out cereal boxes from the cupboard and two large white bowls.

They ate their cereal and watched part of an Adam Sandler movie on TV.

"I should really get to some homework," Diego said. "Wanna join me?"

The idea of going to Diego's bedroom excited Charlie but also made him nervous. He remembered his realization earlier in the day that he needed to speak up about things. But he wanted to be with Diego in his room. Alone. He tried not to think about how much he wanted to kiss this boy. Unable to figure out what he wanted, he kept his mouth shut.

They walked up the wood and glass staircase, down the hall, and into the bedroom. Charlie did a double take. The mess was gone. Everything was picked up off the floor. The closet doors were closed, and the bed was trim as a soldier's uniform.

"Wow!"

"I know. Some difference, huh? Every so often I go on a cleaning binge. Plus, I was reading in one of my Wicca books the other day that if I wanted to have a clear mind, I should make sure my environment is free of obstacles. It made sense to me. I'm not promising to keep it like this forever, but ..." He smiled, hands on his hips, like a proud captain presenting his sailing vessel.

He walked over to his desk and turned on his speakers. Soft world-beat music began to play. He lit a candle and some incense.

"Can we just hang a bit before doing homework? Whaddya say?" His eyes softened. At any moment Charlie expected him to walk over to him and embrace him. Instead, he stood still near his desk waiting for Charlie's response.

Charlie now knew what "hanging out" meant. He was worried. Worried he would get behind in his schoolwork, worried that hanging out was swiftly becoming a habit for them. But the sheer fact that Diego was making an invitation, that he seemed to be willing to go slowly the way Charlie wanted, made him relax even more. And it made Diego look that much sweeter as he waited for his answer across the room.

"Okay, but we need to do ..."

"I know, I know. Our homework. We will, I promise. But let's just ..."

He walked over to where Charlie stood, took him by the arm, and brought him over to the edge of the bed. He sat down, and his eyes darkened as he pulled Charlie close to him.

The first time they had kissed at the park, Charlie hadn't paid much attention to the mechanics of it all. He had wondered before, while watching a movie or reading a book, how people ever figured out how to kiss. Where did you put your nose so it wouldn't bump into the other person's? How did you know when to turn your head?

It was a lot easier than he had realized.

Now he knew what to do, how to lean in, how to open his mouth slightly ...

Charlie could feel waves of warmth coming from the boy's chest. Diego's lips were thick against his, and he tasted like sweet granola and milk from the cereal they and eaten. He put his arms around Charlie's back, pulling him closer. The gentle smacking sound of their lips coming together and drawing apart excited Charlie.

Diego responded by lying back on the bed and pulling Charlie on top of him. Diego's chest rose and fell beneath him as their kissing grew deeper.

Charlie let his tongue press into the boy's mouth farther than he had before. A low grunt escaped Diego's mouth.

Charlie pulled back. "Oh, sorry, I didn't mean to ..."

Diego, whose eyes had been shut, looked up at him. "Didn't mean to what?" he asked, his voice deeper than normal.

"I, uh, I thought I hurt you. I thought ..."

Diego interrupted him. "You goofball. That felt really good. What you were doing with your tongue. Do it again."

Charlie smiled in spite of himself and leaned back down over the boy. Their tongues began to push against each other, and Diego groaned. Loudly.

Charlie slid onto the side of the bed so that they were facing each other. Diego rubbed his hands along Charlie's chest. Then he slipped his fingers up under Charlie's shirt and ran them along his belly.

The muscles in his stomach contracted each place the boy's hand touched. He surprised himself by groaning even louder than Diego had and pulling at the boy's ears, tugging him closer, as if trying to fit him into his own mouth.

Diego's hand slid below the waistband of Charlie's pants, fingertips brushing the skin just above his hipbone.

Λ loud crash sounded across the room. Diego jumped up off the bed.

"What the …?" he exclaimed. He walked over to the far side of the room. Charlie sat up and saw three of the framed photographs from Diego's altar lying on the ground near several large shards of glass.

"That was weird. I must have bumped them when I lit the incense," he said. "Oh well, I'll take care of them later."

Charlie knew they hadn't fallen accidentally. He thought that all of the post-popping, out-of-control-stuff was over. Maybe it wasn't.

All the excitement he had been feeling drained out of him as fast as it had come on.

Diego walked back to the bed.

"Now where were we?" he said.

But Charlie was sitting up, his legs hanging over the side of the bed. "Diego, have you ever, uh, have you ever, you know, done it?"

"What? You mean, had sex? Nope, not unless you count me and *la mano mio,*" he said, holding up his hand.

Charlie felt his cheeks grow hot.

"I was hoping we might, you know, if you wanted to …" Diego started, then stopped when he saw the look on Charlie's face.

"I don't think I'm ready," said Charlie. A part of him really wanted to. It just felt so good with Diego. But another part knew that if going to the GSA meeting seemed fast, then having sex with Diego would be like a rocketship ride to the moon. And he also worried about what would happen. If pictures broke when Diego touched him with their clothes on, what if they went further? Images of the Ramirez's home engulfed in flames flashed through Charlie's head.

"Hey, of course not. If you're not ready, then fine. I wouldn't want you to do anything you wouldn't want to do."

"Are you mad?"

"What? Mad? Charlie, come on. Of course I'm not mad. I'm not going to pressure you into doing anything you don't want to do. I mean, yeah, I want to. You're totally hot and it feels really, really good. But only if you do too. If not, then well, I liked what we were doing. Or we could even just hang out," he said, smiling. "I mean, really hang out … and talk and stuff."

Diego lay back on the bed and pulled Charlie up beside him, so that his head lay on the boy's chest. He could hear Diego's heartbeat in his ear. He breathed in the boy's familiar scent, a combination of butter, raspberries, and warm skin. Charlie had begun to equate the smell with both excitement and contentment. He thought a lot about that scent this last week.

Diego began to talk about his mother, his uncle's apple farm, and the trouble he and his cousins used to get into, all the while stroking Charlie's messy hair and the back of his neck. Soon his eyelids grew heavy, and it wasn't until his phone rang in his pocket and he woke with a start that he realized they had both fallen asleep, cuddled together on Diego's bed.

"Dinner's just about ready, Charlie," he heard Beverly say into the phone. "Come home soon, okay? You don't want to miss these shells. And tell Diego he doesn't know what he's missing," she said, her voice teasing with laughter.

CHAPTER 7

A-Plus

"VON'T YOU COME VITH ME down to my spooky lair?" Beverly said in a fake Transylvanian accent as they walked downstairs to the basement. Their slippered footsteps echoed on the cement floor as they passed by the garage and stopped in front of a door that Charlie had never opened.

"You may think it odd that I lock this door with a key. I have so many wards on this room that Esmerelda of the East couldn't get in here. But my mother, your Grandmother Margaret, used to do the same thing. Like mother, like daughter, I guess."

She selected a small key from her key ring.

"How do wards work? How do they keep people away?"

Beverly's hand stopped midway to the lock as she considered the question.

"There are many different kinds. Some of them are what I think of as a soft deterrent. If someone were to pass by, say, they might not see the door. Or the door might look so unimportant and uninviting that they'd just ignore it and move on.

"Others are more aggressive. They work to keep the door shut. If anybody pulled on the door, it wouldn't budge. If a witch were able to break through the first layer of wards, then things could get a little more serious. My dad forgot to remove one of them when he had some friends over one night, some folks from the community. One of his buddies had asked if he could get something out of Dad's den. They all heard a yelp, and the next thing they knew, Jerry was flattened against the wall, trussed up like a rodeo calf. I think they'd all been drinking a bit too much. They used to crack each other up, telling that story again and again."

She inserted the key into the lock, passed her hand over the knob, and moved her lips. Charlie felt a small wave of heat flush over his arms and chest. He wondered how many times in his life his mother had done something like that in their own home. Had she set up wards? He wouldn't have been able to feel them. Now he could, after being popped. He felt a confusing mix of emotions—antipathy, frustration, sadness—when he thought about her. In a way that was becoming habit, he pushed them away.

Beverly opened the door and stepped inside, motioning for Charlie to follow.

While he certainly hadn't expected a dark and creepy dungeon, what he saw still surprised him. The room was larger than he had imagined, at least forty feet long by thirty feet wide. At the top of the wall opposite the door, warm light spilled through a set of windows. Soft beige carpet covered the entire floor. A table ran down the middle of the room. It reminded Charlie of Mrs. McMeniman's craft table back at home, though Beverly's sat much lower to the ground.

A white shelving system covered the entire length of the left-hand wall. Large mason jars filled most of the shelves, though there were also several white boxes, the kind his mother used to store tax documents. These were labeled in clear handwriting with things like "Aunt Lula's Papers," "Photos of Dad," and "Ideas." Charlie wondered what was in the small yellow box sitting off to the side marked "Lithuania." The mason jars contained brightly colored powders, round objects, dried flowers, red and brown liquids.

Black-and-white photographs hung on the right-hand wall. He recognized a younger version of his mother in a few of them, and a younger Beverly too. To the right of the photos was a closed door. Probably some sort of closet.

A low cement shelf jutted from the far wall near the floor. On it sat a small speaker system, a vase with dried flowers, and a stone sculpture of a heron.

"Randall calls it 'Bed, Brooms, and Beyond,'" Beverly said.

She walked over and turned on the speakers. "Stevie Nicks and I like to hang out here together, though sometimes we invite Joni Mitchell too."

Soft vocal music began to play. Charlie didn't know who his aunt was talking about but figured they must be singers she liked.

"Want some tea?" Beverly asked.

She opened a cupboard on the far left side beneath the shelves and pulled out an electric kettle, two mugs, a teapot, a small mesh ball, and a brown paper bag. She slid a cushion out from beneath the table and sat down, crossing her legs, then motioned for him to join her. He sank down onto his own cushion's softness.

"I've made my own tea before, but I can never get it to be quite like this stuff," she said, handing him the brown bag to sniff.

He inhaled. He smelled the strong scent of orange, along with mint. There was another smell he couldn't identify.

"It's called 'Spring Spice,' and we get it at—oh my god, Charlie, we haven't taken you to Pike Place Market yet! This whole time and …"

"What's that?"

"Only the oldest-running farmers market in the nation, thank you very much. Parts of it can be really touristy, but people forget that it's an actual farmers market. It's right downtown. Great produce, amazing flowers, and a shop that sells this tea. Rand and I love to spend hours at the market. We get all kinds of different foods and sometimes sneak up onto the roof of the Inn at the Market as if we were guests and watch the ferries cross Elliot Bay."

She slapped at his arm and laughed. "How can you let us be such bad hosts? Charlie, I know a lot has been happening. It's not as if you've had a normal 'Welcome to Seattle' kind of introduction to this place. But really! There are so many beautiful things to see here. There are great hikes. Waterfalls to explore. Do you ski? Oh, and we haven't even talked about the Olympic Peninsula yet. I want to show you so many things!"

Her enthusiasm was infectious, and he found himself carried

away by images of mountains, the water, a large market. Just as he was wondering why she had never mentioned any of these places and activities before, she said, "I think I was worried I'd be one of those fussy people who try to shuttle you all over the place as if life is one big bus tour. But it looks like I've just been neglectful!"

The kettle boiled, and she busied herself filling the tea ball with the spiced leaves.

"What do you do down here?" Charlie asked.

"This is my workroom," she said. "Most witches like to have a place where they can work. I make many things down here. Teas, for instance. Not any that taste this good. And you'd think I'd be able to recreate it. How could it be that hard? But I swear there's a secret ingredient that the shop owner won't tell me."

"Couldn't you just, you know, use the scrying bowl on them and get the answer?" he asked, remembering their lessons at Malcolm's cabin.

She laughed. "Of course I could. But you know, I enjoy mystery. It's more fun not knowing, and trying to figure it out. Plus I like teasing the people at the shop. Every time I go in, one of the clerks says, 'Hide the recipe. The spy's here!'"

She placed the ball into the teapot and poured in hot water.

"Let's let that steep for a bit. Do you like yours strong?" she asked.

He had no idea if he did or not. He hadn't drunk much tea in his life.

"Yeah," he said.

"Anyway, this is where I work. I dry flowers and herbs down here. I make teas and lotions. I also wrap birthday and holiday gifts, which may sound funny to you because it's not very witchy. But it's quiet. I like being down here," she said, spreading her arms wide and indicating the walls around her.

"I also make other things. I'm sure Malcolm talked to you about the objects we can make."

"Like broomsticks?" Charlie asked, intrigued.

"Yep. Like broomsticks. And your bracelet. If you can imbue an object with a certain task, it will remember that task. That frees you up to cast other spells. A witch can only keep track of so many things at once."

She poured a stream of gold-colored liquid into a mug and handed it to Charlie.

He sipped at it carefully. He first tasted the bitterness of the black tea itself, but then the flavors of mint and citrus spread throughout his mouth.

"I know it might not be as good as a sugary soda, but ..."

"I like it. I haven't had anything like it before."

"I swear those people who make it are witches in their own right. I'm just kidding. I know for a fact that they aren't. They just make really good tea. I'm pretty sure they use basil too, but how do they keep it tasting so fresh?"

He liked how the warmth of the tea spread down his throat. For the moment, he wasn't worried about Diego, or catching up on his schoolwork, or even learning more about witchcraft. He simply enjoyed the tea and the company of his aunt.

Beverly took a long sip from her mug, then set it down on the table. "The responsibility now falls mostly on me to help you develop your skills. Other adults will also teach you. But I'll be overseeing everything. I thought we could do some practice now. Try some things out. See how it goes. What do you think?"

"Yeah, that would be cool," Charlie said, eager to learn the things that Beverly could do.

"Okay, but we have to promise each other that if either of us doesn't like it or gets mad at the other, we get to raise our hand and say, 'I don't like this.' Deal?"

"Deal."

"Good. My own father could be a bit of a tyrant—he'd breathe down our necks, complaining that we never practiced enough. Plus, he corrected everything, no matter how good we did. 'How do you expect to be top-notch if all I do is give you praise?'" she said, imitating her father's deep voice. "I don't want to do that to you."

"Okay. Thanks."

"Remember the very first thing I showed you?"

"You mean with the candle?"

"Yes. Would you like to try that?"

He nodded. She stood up from the table, opened up a cupboard behind her and took out three white round objects.

"Are those Ping-Pong balls?"

"Yep. They're better to practice with. They won't break, and it doesn't hurt if they hit you in the face. Also, there's no fire to worry about. We'll work up to candles," she said, smiling.

She set the three balls on the table.

"Okay, here's how I like to think about it. First, you have to relax. Clear your mind of other thoughts. Did you practice that with Malcolm?"

"Yeah."

"Good. Then, you have to open your senses and focus on the object. See if you can hear its music, its sound."

"Um, am I supposed to do this now, or …?"

"Let me just walk you through it first, okay? Then you can try."

He nodded.

She held up her fingers. "So, number one, clear your mind. Number two, listen to the object's sound. Then … ," she paused, brow furrowing, searching for the right words.

"Then, I like to imagine that I'm offering it an invitation. As in, 'Hey Mr. Ping-Pong Ball, how about hanging out with me for a little bit, maybe float around some?'"

"You have to think that every time you do a spell?" It sounded like a lot of work to Charlie.

"Well, no, not now. It becomes second nature after a while. But I did when I first started. It helped me learn how to reach out to things."

"Okay."

"Then I picture in my mind what I want it to do, like an offer. And if it wants to, then I say the Words, and that's that."

"What if the thing doesn't want to?"

"Then it would be difficult. Think about it this way: if I ask it to float in the air, like this …," she said. One of the white balls lifted up off the table and floated between them.

"Hey, you didn't even say any Words!"

"No, I didn't. Or I did it so fast in my mind that it wasn't necessary. But Charlie, I've been doing this for decades. It takes practice. This is to help you start off doing something that will seem strange at first. Understand?"

"Yeah," he said, not sure if he did understand. But he was eager to try.

"So," she continued, looking at the ball, "it's easy for the ball to do this. It's made of light material. It's designed to be hit by a Ping-Pong paddle. What I'm asking it to do is 'imaginable,' if you will.

"But," she said. "If I wanted to turn the ball into tea leaves, that would be much harder."

"Why? I mean, that guy turned himself into a dog, didn't he?"

"Yes, but first of all, I bet that's one of his unique abilities. Not all of us can do that. Second and most importantly, the ball can't quite 'imagine' itself—and I use that term loosely—as tea leaves. I'm not suggesting the ball has a brain. I mean that its material is far from being a singularly organic substance. It's made of a polymer. Those things are very different. It's doable but takes a much longer spell and a lot of concentration. It's not the kind of thing you want to try in the beginning."

"Okay. I think I get it."

"Good. So why don't you give it a go?"

He watched as Beverly's white ball floated back down to the table. He decided to concentrate on one of the others, so he picked the one closest to him.

"Just clear your mind first," his aunt said, her voice soft. "I'll turn the music off so it won't distract you." She looked over her shoulder, and the music faded away.

Clear my mind, clear my mind, he repeated to himself.

Instead of clearing it, his mind flooded with thoughts: *Did I pick the right ball? Will I be able to make the ball lift off the table? What if I never figure this out? How long does it take most witches to do this? Will I be slower than everybody else? Does Beverly think I'm slow?*

"Maybe picture the inside of your mind as completely black as you take a deep breath," she suggested.

He saw a cave, a dark cave, and imagined it expanding until the walls were the borders of his brain.

But was the cave somewhere in the Northwest? If so, it was probably wet inside. So he made moss appear.

But that might not be the right kind of cave. How about a dry cave? That would be better.

But were there bats?

"Or just emptiness," his aunt offered. "Just let there be emptiness."

This was a lot harder than he had thought it would be. Ever since he had activated the broomstick on Saturday and performed correctly some of the other tasks Malcolm had given him, he had thought he was home free. Why wasn't it working today?

He concentrated on listening to the ball. He heard nothing except for some kids shouting to each other outside. Could he feel the ball inside of himself? That had been a suggestion from one of the adult witches up at Malcolm's.

The suggestion hadn't worked then, and it wasn't working now.

"Deep breath in and out. In and out," Beverly said.

He didn't know he had been holding his breath. He exhaled through his mouth. The air hit the three balls on the table and pushed them toward Beverly.

"Well, that's certainly one way to do it," she said, stopping the balls from rolling off the table with her hand.

He laughed. "You sounded like Randall when you said that."

"Well, after you get married, you become your spouse. You knew that, right?"

"Wait, so he's now a beautiful woman with long hair who makes lotions in the basement?" Charlie said, surprising himself with his bold comment.

"Charles Creevey! That's the first compliment you've paid me about my looks. You are so sweet I could kiss you!"

"Ew, gross, no way. Wouldn't that go against the teacher-student relationship thing?"

Beverly's held tilted back as she issued a deep-throated laugh.

"Right, right. I forgot about that. Okay, no more buttering up the teacher to get out of your studies."

Charlie smiled, enjoying the teasing and the easy banter.

Then he took a deep breath, focusing again. The laughter had relaxed him. His mind felt emptier than before. He listened to see if he could sense anything. At first, nothing. But slowly he began to notice what seemed like a sound coming from the white ball closest to his wrist. It was like a humming sound, perched almost beyond his range of hearing.

Then he began to feel the material of the Ping-Pong ball, the lightness of it. While he wouldn't have known what a polymer was, he could sense the smooth plasticity of the ball as well as the empty space inside it. It was made to be light. He sensed a part of himself, from somewhere in his chest, or maybe his forehead, extending out almost like it was leaning forward. This part of himself carried an idea of flight, of floating, of lifting into the air.

And unlike anything he had experienced at Malcolm's cabin, he felt the thing respond to him. My god! It wasn't like it was talking to him, but there was a form of interaction going on between him and the ball. Charlie grew excited. He had conveyed the idea of flying to it, had extended an invitation, like his aunt suggested, letting it know he wanted it to fly. And it had done something to the ball. Now the ball was responding.

He remembered learning about Venn diagrams in school. The template his teacher drew on the board showed two circles next to each other, slightly overlapping. She shaded in the part where Circle A and Circle B converged.

"The space shared between the two circles is part of a set, or internal to the set, while the space not shared by the two circles is external to the set," she had explained. He had had trouble grasping the concept at school, but now it made sense to him.

He and the ball seemed to be creating something internal to the set of them both, as if he were Circle A, the ball were Circle B, and now there was something shared between them.

As he maintained connection to the Ping-Pong ball, he waited until he could feel the lightness of the material, what it was made for, its essential purpose, meeting with his invitation, and even possibly what he was made of.

He sensed the two sides melding together. It felt exciting, normal, and satisfying all at once. The space between two overlapping circles. That part of the ball's purpose melding with the part of him that wanted it to fly, blending together, becoming a fixed set.

Now. Now's the time.

He opened up his mouth, letting the Words come to him, feeling the odd way they moved his lips and mouth.

Charlie watched as the ball quivered, leaning toward him and the invitation he held out to it. It lifted up off the table an inch or two, then hovered, quivering again.

It wasn't like Charlie was lifting something heavy. But he was straining anyway. He could feel something inside him resisting as if it didn't want to connect with the ball. He could also tell that the ball needed more imagination from him. He needed to provide more possibility. He wasn't sure how he knew all this, but he knew it nonetheless.

His head began to throb; he heard himself gasp out loud. He felt himself pushing hard. But the ball only rose an extra half inch before bouncing back down on the table, then rolling off and landing in Beverly's hand.

"Oh my god, Charlie! Look at that! You made it move!" she declared.

He blew out his breath.

"But yours stayed up forever. It floated there. Mine just ..."

"Hey, that was amazing. That was your first try since the weekend, right? It worked!"

He sat back, rubbing at his forehead.

"Head hurt?"

"No, not really hurt. It just felt like I was trying to, I don't know, hold a heavy door open or something. But I ... I could feel it, the ball, like it was listening to me or something."

"That's right. You hear each other. I mean, not really, since the ball can't really hear anything. But you get the idea."

"Yeah, and when it came forward a bit, it seemed like it was touching me inside my brain. Is that weird? Or is that how it is for you?"

"Something like that, yes," Beverly nodded.

"But the door was really hard to pull open. Like something was holding it from the other side."

"Ah, yes. Resistance. Your mind doesn't like it when it thinks that something else is trying to control it. That Ping-Pong ball wasn't controlling you, but your mind doesn't know that. It's such a strange feeling at first, isn't it? You have to learn how to calm your mind, to let it know that nothing bad is going to happen. That it's not being invaded by enemies. It's just strange and new, but not dangerous. That's where practice comes in."

Charlie nodded, remembering what Randall had told him in the parking lot at Costco, about how hard it was to have your mind be blown open and about how much it fought to hold on to reality.

"Charlie, you did it. You did it, you did it, you did it."

"Yeah, I guess so."

"No, not, 'I guess so.' It was an experiment. Most all other spells operate similarly. Clearing your head, sensing that thing, picturing it in your mind, and then offering the invitation. Or at least, that's how I like to think of it. If you asked a hundred witches, you'd probably get a hundred different answers as to how it works for them."

In spite of himself, Charlie smiled. He looked at the mason jars above Beverly's head filled with their bright contents. He smelled the fruity aroma from the tea in front of them. He heard a crow squawking just outside the room's high windows. He felt pleased with himself.

"Whew, that was a lot of work! Moving that little ball and all," he said.

"Class is over for the day, young man. You get an A-plus!"

CHAPTER 8

Aunt and Nephew

THAT NIGHT, AS CHARLIE WAS finishing up his homework, he heard a knock on his bedroom door.

"Come in!"

Beverly walked in, dressed in layers of polar fleece. She wore a knit cap on her head and gloves on her hands.

"Charlie, in celebration of your fantastic progress with the Ping-Pong ball earlier today, I thought we might take a spin together," she said, jutting her chin toward his bedroom window.

"A spin?" he asked, at first not understanding what she meant. "You mean ... you mean on broomsticks?"

"That's exactly what I mean. What do you think?"

He set his pencil and protractor down on his geometry book. "Yes!"

"After you finish your homework. How much more do you have to do?"

"About thirty minutes or so."

"Great. Come downstairs when you're ready. I'm going to take Amos for a walk right now. Dress warmly. The air gets really cold."

He could barely concentrate on his work. He had been thinking about his maiden voyage and hoping he could ride a broom again soon.

"Concentrate," he said out loud, trying to get his brain to focus again.

He finished his last math problem, then reviewed a few Chinese sentence patterns and copied the five new characters he had learned yesterday. Chen Laoshi was probably going to give them another one of her impromptu quizzes tomorrow. He would cram some more in the morning before class.

Charlie slammed his books shut and put them in his backpack. He threw on a sweater and a hat, then ran downstairs to the hall closet and grabbed the fleece-lined leather jacket that Randall had bought him. He hadn't had the chance to wear it because the weather hadn't turned cold enough yet. He caught a glimpse of himself in the foyer's mirror. His mother's voice, unbidden, ran through his head. "Two leather jackets, Charlie? One from Beverly and one from Randall? Isn't that just a tad bit excessive?" Her words were icy with sarcasm and contempt.

"No, it's not. And you aren't going to ruin my evening, either," he said to the image of her face that he pictured in the mirror next to him. "You left me here. It's out of your hands now." He felt a thrill as he talked back to her even though he knew she wasn't really there.

Randall was reading the newspaper in the dining room when Charlie walked in.

"You sure you're ready for Air Beverly? It's a suspect airline."

"Yeah, I think I'm ready. I, uh, I heard the pilots are better than Alaska Airlines."

"Those are fightin' words, buddy," Randall said, grabbing for Charlie's arm.

Charlie yelped and jumped back, laughing.

"Ready?" asked Beverly as she walked into the dining room.

She slipped a small backpack over her shoulders.

"Yep."

"Good. Rand, you and Amos hold down the fort. We're going to go for a real flight, not like what you do in that huge metal, gas-guzzling jetliner you call an 'aeroplane.'"

"Ooh, witchy witchy. Just because you float around on a little twig you think you're greener than the rest of us."

"That's right. We are model green citizens. See you, love bug," she said, giving her husband a kiss.

Beverly motioned for Charlie to follow her, then walked down the stairs to the basement, her voice echoing off the walls as she descended. "I brought you a pair of gloves. Your hands can get really cold flying at night."

She unlocked the door into her workroom and released the wards. Then she opened the closet door on the right-hand wall. Charlie saw several tall broomsticks inside, next to long raincoats, hats, and some more white boxes with labels on them.

"This one's mine," Beverly said, pulling out a broom made of a light-colored wood. "Birch. Fast and supple. But a bit tricky to maneuver when starting out."

She removed another broom from the closet and held it out to Charlie, sizing up how they looked together.

"This ought to do. It's mahogany. A very hard, solid wood. It should give you a feeling of stability."

The broomstick was a dark reddish-brown and a lot bulkier-looking than Beverly's. But it wasn't as thick as the training brooms they had used in the field near Malcolm's cabin.

"If you like it, we can call it yours. But I want you to be able to test it out first, okay?"

He nodded. The idea of having his own broomstick was so exciting that he was suddenly afraid if he talked out loud it would be taken away from him. He knew he was being silly, but he kept his mouth closed anyway.

Beverly locked up her workroom. Together they walked into the garage and out the door that led to the backyard.

"You'll have to get used to flying in the rain if you ever want to ride around in Seattle. But for tonight, you're lucky. Mostly a clear sky."

They walked past the hedges framing the sides of the yard and stopped where the grass ended. There was about a foot of soil beyond with small rose bushes and hydrangeas acting as a natural barrier. Then, a steep decline that led down to blackberry bushes about twenty feet beneath his feet. He peeked over the edge and could see the rooftops, far below, of the homes that extended from the end of their property straight out to the Sound.

Moonlight softened the edges of everything in the yard that was sharp and bright during the day, turning the grass a metallic gray, silvering the leaves of the trees. The twin lights of a large ferry, crossing over to Vashon Island, shone over the dark water. A slight wind was the only sound he could hear.

"How are we going to …?" Charlie whispered, for the night was quiet and it seemed like the right thing to do. "What if someone sees us?"

"Don't worry about that. I'll whip up a little concealment for us. It won't turn us invisible. It'll just help us blend into things."

Charlie's heart started to pound. The drop-off in front of him wasn't a sheer cliff face, but it might has well have been. If he fell from this height, he would definitely hurt himself.

"You scared?" whispered Beverly.

"Yeah, a little."

"Good. You should be. I want you to gain a healthy respect for broom flight. You'll grow to love it. I just know you will. But don't ever forget that it's just a small piece of wood holding you up, hundreds of feet in the air. There are no seatbelts. If you keep that in mind and stay smart, you'll do fine.

"And don't forget—I'll be right here with you. Now, go ahead and set your broom down. Do you remember the Words?"

"I think so."

He placed his broom down on the wet grass, held his hand over it, closed his eyes, and let the Words find him. The cold air helped to clear his mind. He parted his lips and could feel a tingling sensation gather around him as the Words began to flow from his mouth.

The broom didn't smack into his palm the way it did at Malcolm's. It rose gently up into his hand. He held it in his grip and looked at Beverly.

"Smarty! You're such a natural."

She lifted her leg over her own broom before nodding at him to do the same.

"Ready?"

"I think so."

"Good."

And with that, they pushed off the ground together and floated out over the black expanse of night awaiting just beyond the edge of the backyard.

CHAPTER 9

The Velveteen Night

CHARLIE LOOKED DOWN and saw the blackberry bushes far below the broom handle. He dropped several feet, causing his stomach to lurch.

"Whoa!" he shouted, his voice echoing off the hills.

"That's okay," he heard his aunt say from somewhere above him. "You just hit an air pocket. Come back up a bit."

He leaned back, stopping his descent.

The tip of his aunt's broom came up on his left side, and soon they flew side by side, soaring forward, the wind cold on his face.

"Keep breathing," his aunt yelled.

God, why do I always hold my breath? he wondered, exhaling.

He relaxed, convinced at the moment that he wasn't going to plummet to his death or at least to a painful encounter with the blackberry bushes beneath them.

He looked down and found that the distance to the ground didn't seem as frightening as it had been back at the edge of the yard. He watched as the pointed roofs of the homes passed beneath the length of his broomstick.

A minivan drove through the winding streets that ran through the neighborhood below. It was a strange vantage point to have: to watch the roof of the van from a good three or four stories above and the yellow light spilling out onto the street in front of it, illuminating garage doors, recycling bins, and juniper bushes as the van drove past house after house.

The taste of salt in the air grew stronger as they passed the last of the houses and flew low out over the water. He relaxed even more, knowing that he could survive a ten-foot drop into the water much better than a fall hundreds of feet above blackberry brambles, chimneyed rooftops, and TV antennas.

He wondered how fast they were going. It was difficult to tell. It felt faster than riding a bike downhill, but slower than being in a car on the freeway. And unlike a car or a bike, flying on a broom was smoother. The air pockets created dips and rises, but none of the bouncing or shaking you got when wheels spun over pavement.

He liked how his broom felt. It was solid, like Beverly said it would be, but glided through the air much better than the one he had used at Malcolm's, which compared to this felt like it had training wheels on it. He wondered if Malcolm's brooms had some sort of spell on them to make them go slowly.

He felt a tapping on his shoulder. He turned to see Beverly pointing down to the surface of the dark water and smiling, her teeth white against the night's background.

Charlie looked down and saw the silhouettes of two figures flying on broomsticks. Their shadows rippled and reformed as they passed wave after silver-crested wave, the moonlight pulling their dark shapes along the way a child pulls a toy on a string.

It was a breathtaking view, quiet and wonderful. The colors of moonlight, silver and gray blending in with the shadowy dark, created a soft textured sheen over the surface of the water. It was cold, but the lighting made everything seem gentle.

Charlie remembered a children's book that his mother used to read to him when he was young. In it, a family of bears drove their station wagon down a tree-lined country road at night. A large yellow moon rose in front of the car.

The sky in the storybook was covered with a black synthetic material made to resemble velvet, and Charlie used to rub it between his fingers while his mother read to him about the bears and their adventures.

The quality of the light around them, the weightless journey, the silver on the water, their shadows, all of it had the same velvety feel to him. Charlie wanted to extend his hand and rub the night between his fingers, convinced that it would feel as soft and as smooth. He resisted, deciding that it would be better to keep a firm grip on his broom handle.

A thought arose in his mind, surprising him. *Maybe I am home now.*

*　　*　　*

"We're going to land over there on Blake," Beverly yelled. Several strands of her hair had slipped out from beneath her knitted cap and were whipping past her head as she pulled up in front of him and looked back over her shoulder.

She was pointing to the small uninhabited island to the north of Vashon. All Charlie could see were trees and rocks as they flew closer. His vision was better than when they had first stepped out in the backyard, but it was still hard to distinguish shapes in the dark. How was he going to land on ground that was covered with rocks? What if he fell into the water? As they flew closer to the landmass, Charlie strained to see a clear landing spot.

Beverly shot ahead and slipped both legs over to one side of her broom. It reminded him of a documentary he had seen about the bicycle culture of the Netherlands. He remembered how people there tended to dismount, swinging both legs in front of them and to the side of the bike and then stepping down onto the ground. This was quite different from how he and his friends got off their bikes, by stopping first, straddling the bike with both feet on either side, and then lifting one leg up and over the seat.

As the island loomed closer, Charlie saw a long stretch of beach that was free of boulders. Beverly angled her broom so that it ran parallel to the open, sandy patch. She sank toward the ground, slowed down, and then simply slid off the broom, standing up gracefully.

He flew toward her, not exactly sure how to slow his broom down. He decided not to flip his legs over the side the way she had; he worried that such a movement would toss him headfirst into the water.

"Slow it down, slow it down," he heard Beverly cautioning him.

As he glided past the water and over the sand, he turned his broom parallel the way his aunt had. He also pulled back on the broom handle to slow his flight. It was too much at once. The broom nearly stopped in mid-air. He spun off the side like he had done in the field at Malcolm's. This time, however, he remembered to release his legs instead of clinging to the broom like a chimp hugging a tree branch. He hung from his hands about a foot above the sand, then let go of the broom and dropped to the ground.

"Oomph!" he grunted.

"An excellent, if unusual landing," Beverly said. "A high score for creativity."

"Thank you very much," he said, his legs wobbling as he stood up straight and took a bow.

"Aren't you forgetting something?" she asked, pointing to the air above him.

He looked up and saw his broom hovering over his head.

He reached up and touched it with his fingertips. He closed his eyes, letting the quiet Words escape his mouth, and then felt a dull thud as the broom dropped on his head.

He laughed. "I think that might disqualify me from the match."

*   *   *

Beverly unzipped the backpack she had been wearing and pulled out a small tarpaulin that she lay over a log. They sat down together. Then she removed some dried apricots, a package of almonds, a bar of dark chocolate, and a thermos of hot Spring Spice tea with two small porcelain cups.

"No need to starve to death out here. We can still be civilized," she added in a bad British accent.

The tea was spicy and delicious. So were the nuts, which his aunt had dusted with her own blend of wasabi-salt.

The beach wasn't as sandy as it had appeared when he had come in for his landing. It was actually made up of millions of small rocks, almost like gravel. When the surf broke over them, then rushed back away from the shore, the pebbles made clicking noises against each other. It sounded like dried beans being poured into a glass bowl. He found it mesmerizing.

"When I first learned to ride a broomstick," said Beverly, "I was just about your age. I wasn't very good at it. I told my parents it was stupid and made up excuses about wanting to be more modern. 'Clearly witches who ride broomsticks are too old-fashioned,' I used to say, forgetting that my parents both rode brooms themselves.

"But then one night a family friend came over, and suggested then and there that he take me out for a nighttime ride. Just the two of us. I think my mom put him up to it. At first I didn't want to, but he persisted, so I just went along with it.

"It was a night a bit like this. The stars were out, and it was cold. Autumn was definitely in the air. We rode out over Puget Sound. It was so quiet, and I liked how I could feel the sea spray on my face. The man gave me some pointers, but he also encouraged me a lot. What I remember most about that night was the sea spray and being with a nice older man who didn't drive me so hard, like Dad always did."

She stopped talking, then looked off into the distance. Charlie wondered about his grandfather. So far the stories he had heard about the man didn't paint a very nice picture.

"Whatever happened to him? And to my grandmother? How did they die?"

"Your grandfather died of brain cancer, and Mom of a heart attack. His was a long, drawn-out thing, and hers, well, she went peacefully in the night."

"Brain cancer? How can …? Can't you, you know, do …?"

"… something about it?" Beverly finished the question. "It's the darnedest thing. No matter how powerful and amazing we witches think we are, we succumb to illness just like everyone else. We do know ways to promote health. But there aren't any spells that cure cancer, unfortunately. You'd think we could do that, wouldn't you?

But we've never been able to. And I doubt we ever will. When it comes down to it, we're human just like the rest of the population on this planet. I think that's a good thing. It keeps us humble and levels the playing field."

Charlie remembered what Malcolm had said to him in the living room before he had been popped about how witches couldn't read minds and how that made it more fair to normal human beings. Witches couldn't read minds, they couldn't cure cancer, they died like regular people did. Maybe Charlie should be disappointed that witches weren't immortal superheroes. Instead, he was more than a little relieved. Being a mind-reading creature immune to disease might make him feel like a monster.

They sipped their tea in silence and listened to the gravel-rush of the waves washing over the shore. Beverly offered Charlie more of the dried apricots, which he chewed slowly, enjoying their tart-sweet flavor.

"In the meantime, there's life to live. Who knows when our number is up? I think death is a great reminder to live life the way we want to, to enjoy it and do what we can do to leave some good on this planet," she said. She reached down and picked up a rock, then threw it out over the water. He watched it skip several times before it sank, and at each place it skipped, tiny splashes of light exploded.

"Did you make it do that? Get so bright?" Charlie asked.

"No, that was phosphorous. Tiny particles that make light when something stirs the water. There is plenty of magic in nature that has nothing to do with witchcraft, Charlie."

*　　*　　*

They mounted their brooms and soared high above the water, flying side by side. Charlie looked over his shoulder and watched Blake Island as it gradually shrank in the distance. Beverly pointed out the skyline of downtown Seattle, Lake Washington, and its much smaller counterpart, Lake Union. The lights of the Fauntleroy Ferry dock shone in the clear night air.

As they approached the shoreline, Charlie spotted their house. Looking closely, he could make out Amos standing at the edge of the garden, wagging his tail. He had no idea how the dog knew they were returning but was glad to see him.

"Woof!" Amos barked one time as they came in for a landing. The lawn was much bigger than the small beach on Blake Island. Charlie came in low to the ground, slowed down, then landed with his feet solidly on the grass, his legs straddling either side of the broomstick. It was easy with no stumbling, flipping, or tripping this time.

Together they walked toward the house, Amos running back and forth between them. Beverly said, "Feel free to take your broom upstairs with you if you'd like. Play with it. See what it's like to float around in an enclosed space. That can be trickier than riding in a wide open area. Just no solo flights out your window, okay? Promise me?"

"I promise."

They stepped inside the basement and began removing their hats and gloves, their heavy coats.

"Thanks, Beverly. That was a really great ride."

"You are welcome, Charlie. My pleasure."

CHAPTER 10

Shame On You

DIEGO TOUCHED AND STROKED everything above the belt as the two boys lay next to each other on Charlie's bed. Their kissing deepened, and he could feel the boy's breath blow stronger on his neck and face. Charlie was more relaxed, knowing that they weren't going to do anything he wasn't ready to do. Therefore, he found himself exploring and touching his friend with a hunger he hadn't let himself express before.

Diego had such a beautiful face. Charlie marveled at the cinnamon brown skin, the long lashes that softened the intensity of his large eyes, the strong nose. And his mouth, his amazing mouth, with its white teeth and thick tongue, the full lips always pulling at him, receiving him.

He pressed his hips against Diego, who responded in kind. This quickened their kissing and their breathing. Charlie felt light-headed and decided that, while the hip part was amazing, it sped things up too fast. He pulled his mouth away and took a breath.

Sitting up straight, he leaned back against the headboard and exhaled.

"What's the matter?" Diego asked, his lips puffy and his eyes half-closed.

Charlie smiled and ran his hand over Diego's black hair.

"Nothing. Just out of breath is all," he said.

"Yeah, I know what you mean."

Diego lay his head down on Charlie's stomach.

"Do you think this is a good idea?"

"Do I think what is a good idea?" Charlie asked.

"This. Us. Kissing. Doing this together. Hanging out."

Fear stabbed at Charlie's chest. Was Diego regretting their friendship? Or whatever they were calling it?

"Uh, yeah. Why? Don't you?"

"Charlie, how can you ask me that? It's amazing. I really like you a lot. And I love spending time together. It's just that I don't want to pressure you. I can't tell what you're thinking half the time, and if you're not into it, well …"

"But I am. Can't you tell by how much I, you know, like doing this?"

"Yeah. I can tell that. But I don't know. I've been out for a long time. You aren't even sure if you're gay. Maybe you're bi. I don't want to force anything. Ms. Barry says that it's really someone's own choice when and how, even if, they come out. She says that those organizations that force people to come out are doing everyone a disservice. She says it's better to let people do it when they're ready."

He turned his head and looked up into Charlie's eyes. "Are you ready?"

"I don't know. I just know that I like you. Can't that be okay for now?"

"Of course it can. That's what I'm trying to say. I'm worried that every time I call you to hang out with me, I'm sort of pressuring you to come out more than you want to."

"It's okay. Don't worry."

Diego sighed, and then turned his head back to rest again on Charlie's stomach.

Charlie had been worrying. He was glad Malcolm had told him that lying would block him from being able to work his own witchcraft; that all made sense to him. But now what? Was he supposed to tell someone? Beverly and Randall? Maybe. He had thought about it. But he didn't know how they would react. Would they be embarrassed? Angry? Disappointed that he didn't seem to like girls? At least not right now?

If he continued feeling like this for Diego but kept it to himself, would that stop him from learning more as a witch?

"I should get going on my homework. I have a lot to do tonight."

Diego sat up on the bed and looked at him. "Did I say too much? I always say too much around you."

Charlie was still getting used to the fact that his outgoing friend needed reassurance. It surprised him. It also made him wonder if everyone else on the planet wasn't always as confident as they looked. That would be nice. If it were true.

Charlie smiled at him, hoping it looked reassuring. "I like what you say. I like talking to you. A lot. Even if," he added, "you are completely ridiculous sometimes."

"What's that supposed to mean?" Diego yelled, shoving him down on the bed. Charlie pushed back, which led to tickling and wrestling, which in turn led to more kissing. It was quite some time before they came up for air again.

*   *   *

Well past midnight, as Charlie headed down the hallway and back to his room with a bowl of half-eaten cereal in his hands, he saw light spilling from underneath his aunt and uncle's bedroom door.

What are they doing up so late? he wondered. Then he heard their voices rising up out of the heat vent on the floor.

"What are you talking about? I can't believe you're even suggesting that!" Beverly's angry voice bounced down the hallway toward him.

"I can't believe you're just sitting there with your head in the sand!"

"My head is not in the sand! Just because you have an opinion about this doesn't mean I'm being blind."

"Bev, I seriously doubt that this is just an opinion. Think about it!"

I shouldn't be listening to this, Charlie said to himself. He was just about to walk into his bedroom when he heard his name.

"I am thinking about it. Charlie's still getting used to being here. He finally has a friend, someone great, who likes him, and you have to suggest that?"

"What do you mean, 'that'? You make it sound like it's dirty!"

"He's not even sixteen yet."

"As if that's ever stopped a teenager before. Beverly, think about how much time they're spending together. Diego's openly gay. He's president of the Gay–Straight Alliance."

"So what! The last time I checked, gay kids could be friends with straight kids. Plus, all they're doing is homework, Randall! And going for hikes!"

"Every day after school? Homework at Diego's house when Lydia isn't there?"

"She works late on cases!"

Beverly's angry words thundered over the walls, pounded across them like carpenter's tools. A dull thud followed, as if something fell on the floor.

"Bev, calm down. Unless you want to remodel the bathroom."

"Okay. Okay. Sorry."

A long pause followed.

"Look, what makes you so sure you know what you're seeing?"

"Don't start that up again with me, Bev. We can figure things out too, you know. It's not like you people have cornered the market on seeing the invisible. You all think you know what's happening everywhere, yet you miss what's going on right beneath your noses!"

Silence. Thick, heavy, hair-prickling silence.

"Look, I'm sorry. I didn't mean to insult you like that. But why do I have the sneaking suspicion we'd be having a very different conversation if this were about Charlie and a girl?"

"What are you saying?"

"I'm saying that you don't like it that Charlie might be gay."

"Damn it, Randall, lower your voice. Of course I don't want Charlie to be gay!"

"Will you listen to yourself? I can't believe you don't ..."

*   *   *

Charlie had been standing still, barely breathing, one foot resting on the carpet inside his bedroom, the other one still in the hallway.

He shook his head, then stepped into his room and closed the door behind him, as quietly as he could.

He set the bowl of cereal on his desk and walked to the middle of his room. He stood silently, arms at his sides, hearing his aunt's words in his head: "Of course I don't want Charlie to be gay!"

He had wondered earlier today what they would think if they knew about him and Diego. He didn't have to wonder anymore. Or at least not about Beverly. A snort escaped his nostrils. Now he knew where she stood on the topic. Loud and clear.

"Of course I don't want Charlie to be gay."

He was surprised when he felt wetness on his cheeks. He didn't feel sad. Just empty, numb, and a little tired. Then why was he crying?

His mind began to race.

They knew. He thought he had been hiding it. But they knew. Everyone at school knew. His aunt and uncle knew. Maybe even his mother did too.

Embarrassment and shame filled his face, surged through his spine like grease, leaving a trail of slime behind. It seeped into his heart so that all the blood pumping through his body flowed with filth, with dirt, with scum.

His aunt and uncle didn't want him. His mother had said she couldn't raise him, that she couldn't protect him. Maybe she meant she didn't want to raise a gay son. That's probably what it really was. It hadn't made any sense to him that she would just leave him up here, drive all this way and dump him off on long-lost relative. Now it did. She had wanted to get as far away from him as possible.

But they didn't want him either. He was disgusting. What had he been thinking? That he could just sneak around, kissing a boy over and over again, and no one would find out? They always found out, didn't they? He thought of scenes in movies, on TV, where they teased boys about being girlie, about wearing women's clothes, about all those funny "single" uncles and their weird humor.

It was dirty, what he was. It was lower than low, the worst. And they always found out, didn't they? They came for you. The way they came for Ted Jones. They beat you into a pulp, leaving you by the side of the road.

They drove you from your school, like they did Diego. The kids beat you up while the teachers looked the other way. You couldn't count on anyone. You couldn't hide it, could you? It always leaked out, and they always found out.

They always hated you.

His body shook and his chest heaved. Snot ran down his nose.

"You little faggot, crying like a girl!" Charlie turned and looked at his red wet face in the mirror. He flung his hands out at the glass as if trying to strike his reflection. Even though he was several feet away, the mirror fractured, leaving webbed cracks down the middle of the surface like frozen streaks of lightning.

The sound of the breaking mirror startled him, yanking him from the dark swirl of hate and shame.

He felt his mind clear.

And he knew what he had to do.

Charlie walked over to his closet and pushed aside his hanging clothes. He saw the long length of wood leaning against the wall, the bristles at the bottom glowing a golden brown from the bedroom light.

He reached in and pulled his broomstick out of the closet.

Even though he had promised, he knew now that all bets were off. His aunt and uncle had finally figured out who he was, just what kind of monster, what kind of sick freak they had living under their roof. Promises didn't matter anymore.

"Fine," said Charlie as he dressed in warm clothing. He grabbed an extra sweater and some books and threw them in his backpack.

"If you guys don't want me ... " he said quietly, as he slipped his wallet into his pants pocket.

"Then I'm outta here!" he finished, hoping his voice sounded tough. It didn't. It shook and warbled.

He slid the straps of his backpack over his shoulders, then opened up his bedroom window.

Charlie, this is not a good idea. You're gonna get into trouble. You don't even know where you're going. What if you get caught? What if you fall somewhere and nobody finds you?

"Then everybody'll be happy," he said.

At the last minute he took off the bracelet from his wrist, the one that Beverly had told him to wear at all times, and threw it on his bed. He didn't know why he did it. It just seemed like the right thing to do.

He climbed out onto the sill with his broom in hand. As he turned to shut the window behind him, his foot slipped on one of the wet shingles. He grabbed the sill with one hand and slid into a crouching position an inch short of the rain gutter, stopping himself just before losing his balance and falling off the roof.

Trying to catch his breath, he felt his limbs begin to shake. He looked down at the cement sidewalk nearly two stories below his feet.

"Come on, Charlie, don't be a stupid baby. Get up!"

Carefully, still holding onto the rain gutter with one hand, he slipped the broom handle between his legs and let the quiet Words find his mouth. The stick shuddered to life.

"You're such a stupid baby," he said again, more quietly. He scooted the toes of his shoes out over the edge of the roof, looked to his right then his left as if checking for traffic, took a breath, then pushed off the rain gutter and floated out over the front yard, wiping the tears from his eyes so that he wouldn't hit the thick tree branches as he left the house behind him.

CHAPTER 11

Which World?

ALTHOUGH CHARLIE HAD MOSTLY stopped crying by the time he flew out over the street, his tears blurred his vision, making it hard to navigate. After nearly flying headlong into a telephone pole, he leaned back and rose above tree level. He wasn't thinking about where he was going or if anyone could spot him. He had the vague idea of heading west, out over the Sound, with its lack of telephone poles and tree branches.

But he looked down and found himself flying south over the top of Puget Academy with its solid brick structure and blocky HVAC unit mounted on the roof.

Charlie could feel defiance building in him. He had done his best to ignore the gay part of himself for so long, until he had been told that if he lied to himself about it he couldn't be a witch. He had decided to open up as best he could. But he couldn't even do that right. Diego wanted more, even though he said he would be patient. Beverly didn't want him to be the way he was. His mother dumped him off at her sister's house and drove away like he was radioactive material. It was time he decided for himself how he should do things. Too many other people had been making his choices for him for far too long. And none of it ever worked. He just kept getting yanked around or thrown away.

A pocket of air caused his broom to drop a foot. He gasped and tightened his hold on the handle.

For some reason an image of Mavis formed in his head. He remembered how she had grabbed his arm and the feeling of nausea and lightheadedness that came from it.

He thought about how she tried to get by, selling lotions at farmers markets, tricking people.

He thought of his mother, tucking herself away in some rural town, letting her gifts atrophy, unable to protect herself.

Their hidden lives. Being sly or scared all the time seemed awful. Could he do that? Could he be a hermit, or a scam artist? He didn't think so.

But then what world could he inhabit? What was left for him?

There was the normal world, where you clocked in at work, raised a family, worried about mortgages, grew vegetables. But that was the world where men and women liked each other. That wasn't going very well for him.

There was the witching world, where you learned your craft and you had a community surrounding you. But in that world, you had to be raised in a witch family your whole life, where you knew about your legacy and where you fit in, instead of being some freak castaway.

There was the world where boys liked boys. You could walk around, knowing who you were, reading pamphlets, and going to meetings. But you had to be popular, and confident. You had to be the president of things.

He couldn't find himself in these worlds. All the instructions seemed to be for other people. There wasn't anybody to tell him how to get it right. He really was on his own.

Why hadn't he seen this earlier? Why had it taken him so long to understand that all the rules, all the guidelines, weren't for him? He just didn't fit. He had tried to hide, but all those parts of him leaked out. The witch part that he didn't even know about leaked out in the kitchen during the Dog Man attack. The faggot part leaked out enough for Diego to spot it at the farmers market. What good was it to try to hide when everyone just found out anyway?

What good was it to try to live in any of the normal worlds when he was just a screwed-up freak who couldn't pull any of it off to save his life?

Charlie was surprised to see that the route he was flying had taken him along the coastline and had brought him to the northern tip of Lincoln Park. Maybe he had planned to head here the whole time. He didn't know. He just knew he wanted to keep flying.

He tried not to think that his mother had done the same thing he was doing, nearly sixteen years ago. He didn't want to be like her, someone who hid out, someone who was worried and shy all the time, someone who was weak. Someone who cared about dumb stuff like coupons and correct posture, while lying about all the things that really mattered.

No, he wasn't running away from things the way his mother had. He was running toward something, flying in a direction where he could figure out just what sort of world he could inhabit.

He heard the soft rustling of fabric beside him and turned his head.

"Hello, Charlie."

CHAPTER 12

The Promise

HE JERKED IN FRIGHT, nearly tumbling off his mount. Looking to his right, he saw a woman on a broomstick, flying parallel to him, her dress flapping in the wind. She had bright red hair pulled back from her face in a bun. She was smiling.

He barely managed to keep his hold on the shaft of the broom. His heart thudded cannon balls against the walls of his chest.

"Wh-wh-who are you?"

The woman laughed. She sat sidesaddle on her broom, perfectly balanced. As she laughed, her head tilted back exposing a creamy white neck.

"You know who I am," she giggled. "Don't be silly."

Charlie did know who she was. He knew it the moment he heard her say his name.

"Wh-wh-wh- ..."

His pulse was beating so hard in his throat that he feared his head would explode off his neck like a rocket.

"Are you stuttering? How adorable. Why, there's no reason to be nervous," the woman cooed. "It's just me. An outcast like yourself. Out for a nice evening ride."

She shot several feet in front of him, then turned her head and looked directly at his face.

"Isn't it thrilling to be out on your own, with no adults to boss you around, just you, that trusty piece of wood, and freedom?" she asked, her green eyes shining.

Charlie knew he should change course, but he wasn't sure where to go. He had no doubt she could outride him. He looked around, desperate to come up with a plan of escape.

He heard fabric rustling again and jerked his head to the side. She was on his left now, so close that he felt her breath in his ear as she talked.

"Charlie. Charlie. You don't have to be scared. I just wanted to meet you. Your reputation precedes you, you know."

The sound of flapping came from somewhere below. He looked to his right and saw two large crows flying next to him, side by side, their wings beating the air in steady movements, the glass-bead eyes on the sides of their heads trained on him. In them, he could see a reflection of his small shape and the gauzy, orange figure of Grace, the witch.

Two more crows joined them, flying just beneath his feet, and another pair soared into position above his head. They kept their spindly legs tucked straight behind them as they flew. Charlie could see the thickness of their black oily feathers, could see their beaks, curved like ebony knives.

His whole body began to shake. The sheer blackness of the birds, and Grace's warm soft scent overwhelmed him. He tried to make his broomstick descend, but it wouldn't budge.

More birds flew in front of him, behind him, all around him. The sky was filled with black feathers, the swoosh swooshing of flapping wings, a profusion of harsh bird calls.

They rose above the treetops and turned left, away from the water. He wondered what they must look like: an odd cloud of birds, a cluster of wood and feathers and hair.

He tried to turn his broom to the right, but again it wouldn't budge. It was as if a tractor beam had locked onto the tip of his handle and was pulling him. They were turning together in a long, wide arc.

"So many people seem to be talking about you these days, Charlie. Out of nowhere you show up, and then you're the talk of the town. Elizabeth …"

The sound of his mother's name on Grace's lips sobered him and stopped his shaking. He felt his veins heat up with courage.

"You leave her out of this, you witch!"

"Oh ho, a feisty little one. How very cute," she said, her voice as calm as if speaking to him from a park bench on a pleasant spring outing, not thirty stories in the air, flocked by black wings and razor-sharp beaks. "No, let me finish, Charlie. You deserve to know some things, things that nobody has told you.

"Your mother, Elizabeth, kept you hidden all those years, hidden away so you wouldn't know the truth of who you were and what you could do. But then we found out that you existed, even though no one else had been able to. You were hunted down. Do you know why, Charlie?"

"What are you talking about?" He had to yell now, for they were flying faster, and the wind was sucking the words out of his mouth. Somehow Grace managed to speak as if there was no wind to impede her.

"Didn't you wonder why that Dog Man, as you call him, came and tracked you down? Didn't you wonder why he went to all that fuss? I mean, really, who cares? You were just a young unpopped witch kid hiding out with his pathetic little mommy on a crap farm in the foothills? Didn't you ever stop and think, 'I wonder why these people are making such a big deal of me'?"

Charlie couldn't figure out what to do. He knew he was in danger. Grace had already taken control of his broom. He didn't know where they were going. But her words pulled at him. He hadn't thought much about what Grace was saying, at least not about why they had come for him. It had all gone so fast.

He felt stupid. Why hadn't he considered any of this? Could he really get away with the excuse that everything had gone too fast? Or was he just keeping his head in the sand?

The truth was, he didn't know why the man had come for him. Or why the two witches had broken in and tried to kidnap him. And now, in spite of the danger he knew he was in, a tiny spark of interest burned in him. Did Grace know? Could she tell him?

"Do you want to know, Charlie? Do you want to know the things that Beverly's precious ridiculous little coven is trying to keep from you? Because if you do, I'll tell you. I'll explain it, and a whole lot more, if you want to hear it. If not, fair is fair. You can fly on home to your cute little house and keep living your cute little life with your aunty and uncle. And that hunky Diego too. I must say, you do have good taste in boys."

His face flushed. How could she know about Diego? Had she seen them? Seen them kissing? How did she …?

Who was he trying to kid? She was the most dangerous witch around. Even normal people always found out. For her it was probably as easy as blinking.

Grace's voice dropped low. "Would you like to know, Charlie? Answer me now and we'll keep going. If not," she said, letting her voice grow louder, "I'll set you free." She waved her arm above her head. A rainbow of colored lights sparkled from her fingertips and floated around his face, mocking him.

No, Charlie, a voice said inside of him. *She's dangerous. You can't trust her. Say "no" and fly away. Go back to Beverly, where it's safe …*

Beverly doesn't want me, another, angrier voice said. *My mother doesn't want me. At least maybe I could find out the truth for once.*

Before he could ponder any further, he nodded. Grace laughed again, a tinkling sound that was clear even through the rushing wind and the myriad crow wings beating at the air.

"Wonderful!" she shouted, clapping her hands together in delight. "Then hang on to your broomstick, young man. I think you're going to enjoy yourself."

CHAPTER 13

A Murder of Crows

GRACE SPED AHEAD, AND CHARLIE'S neck snapped back as his broomstick shot forward to keep up with her. He clung tightly to the wood in his hands, not sure if the sound he was making was a prayer or a scream. The flock of crows surrounded them like a cloud of coal dust, their smell gamey and raw, their chorus of cawing awful in his ears.

"Do you know what a group of crows is called?" Grace yelled over her shoulder, her placid expression replaced by what looked like madness. She had tucked her feet underneath her legs and now sat with her shoulders hunched over the front of her broom, her neck twisted to look back at him, several strands of ginger hair whipping about her forehead and cheeks.

Charlie was too terrified by their breakneck speed to do anything other than shake his head.

"It's not a flock. It's a murder. We're surrounded by a murder of crows!" Even from the distance of two broomstick lengths in front of him, with the wind that passed through the crows' wings pounding at his face, he could see the crazed light flashing in the witch's eyes.

They flew north. Through the erratic gaps between black feathers, the lights of downtown Seattle twinkled several miles away.

A bright glow caught his attention far off below him, to his left. It appeared to be growing larger. Grace didn't seem to notice, and neither did the crows.

He blinked eyes to be sure that he wasn't imagining things. Sure enough, the bright light wasn't just growing. It was moving toward them, a blazing ball of yellow, rushing so fast that he had trouble tracking it.

A moment later Grace looked over her left shoulder. The air was filled with a terrible screeching sound, though Charlie didn't know if it came from the witch, the crows, or something else. Half of the birds broke formation and winged off toward the oncoming ball of light. Grace dropped back, closer to Charlie. The tendons in her neck strained as she reached beneath the bodice of her dress and pulled something out, something silver, hanging from a cord. It had a white handle, and moonlight reflected off its long curving blade.

With horror, Charlie watched as Grace gripped the strange-looking knife in one hand, and letting go of her broom handle with her other, leaned toward him. The distance between their two brooms disappeared. Before he could react, she grabbed Charlie around the neck and lifted him almost completely from his broom, choking him. Charlie batted at her iron-like grip, unable to breathe, as white dots began to swim in front of his eyes. Any trace of the previous softness in her face, which was now inches from his, had disappeared. Her teeth were gritted, her lips bared, her eyes narrowed to horrible slits. The hand holding the wicked-looking knife rose above his head.

And then the ball of light was upon them.

Shouting erupted in Charlie's ears. Broomsticks tangled with legs, hair whipped at his cheeks, arms and faces flashed in front of him. Grace's nails scratched hard at the skin of his neck before they were ripped away. He gulped for air. There were feathers, the cawing of crows, screams and grunts, swearing. Before he knew what was happening, his broom had spun out from under him.

He felt weightless for a split second as he was thrown in an upward arc. New shouts joined the cacophony. Hands grabbed for his back and legs. His body began to flip, head over heels, as he plummeted toward the earth, no more feathers to block his view as he fell away from the mess of birds and broomsticks colliding above him.

A sharp jab caught him on his back, knocking the wind from his lungs. Arms wrapped around his shoulders, his waist. He had stopped falling. He saw the strange yellow glow about twenty feet above him in the air. Two figures were mounted on Grace's broom. Arms rose and fell repeatedly, but he couldn't tell why, or what they were doing, or even who they belonged to. More screaming, more cawing. Charlie turned his head and saw the faces of a man and woman on either side of him, faces that should have been familiar, though he couldn't place them. It took him a moment to figure out that he was splayed across two broomsticks. Hands held onto him to keep him in place.

Crows dove and spun at them. The man … it was Daniel! Daniel Burman! The stern-looking detective. And the woman was Rita Lostich, her hair a mass of curls about her face. Daniel smacked at the crows with his hands. His face bled from several scratches. Charlie watched as a crow bit Daniel's ear, listened in terror as the man screamed.

More birds came, a seeming endless rush of beaks and claws, more fight than Daniel could ward off.

"Hang on!" Rita yelled. She gripped Charlie with one hand. The other reached up and grabbed a gold-colored ring hanging from a cord around her neck. He watched her mouth move. A colorless wave spread out from the ring, becoming black ripples in the air. The ripples struck the cloud of attacking crows, sending them spinning off like dry leaves in a gust of wind. The instant Charlie felt the wave wash over him, his stomach lurched with nausea. The next thing he knew, the cold cereal he had eaten earlier that night rushed up from his stomach. He barely had time to turn his head away from Rita before vomiting over the side of the broomstick.

She pulled Charlie over until he was mostly sitting up on her broom, in front of her.

"Go, Daniel! I've got him!" she yelled.

"No! There aren't enough of us!"

"Go!" she screamed.

Daniel veered off to the right and flew directly up at Grace and the witches surrounding her. Charlie wiped at his eyes, then felt his veins turn to ice as he figured out what he was looking at. His Aunt

Beverly was mounted on the back of Grace's broomstick. Her hair flew behind her in a dark stream. She had her hands around the witch's neck.

No! What was she doing? Didn't she know how dangerous Grace was? Didn't she …?

A sound cracked the air, something between a woman's scream and the boom of thunder. He watched as Beverly, Daniel, and the others were flung away from Grace, spinning faster than the crows from the terrible wave of Rita's ring. He saw his aunt tossed from her broom, her feet flailing in the air.

"No!" Charlie shouted. "No, they're falling!"

Rita looked over her shoulder. "They're all right! Don't worry about them!"

Freed from her attackers, Grace spun her neck around until she looked down at Charlie and Rita. Even from nearly twenty feet away he could see her face. For a moment, it was horrifying, crackling with murder and rage, spitting with war. Then she turned, bent low over her broom, and shot off into the distance, impossibly fast, faster than a fighter jet, faster than a witch should be able to fly. The pungent odor of moist wood filled his nostrils. The last he saw of her was the streak of long red hair freed from its bun, trailing behind her as if on fire.

Dark shapes surrounded them. He saw Daniel, Beverly, the older witch Joan, the one who'd argued with Randall that night in the kitchen, and another man he didn't recognize, all secure on their broomsticks.

"All accounted for?" Rita shouted.

"Yes!" Beverly yelled in reply, pointing west. "Back to my place!"

The broomsticks angled toward Puget Sound, with no crows, no red-haired witch, pursuing them.

CHAPTER 14

Someone Brave

THE DISHEVELED BAND OF WITCHES walked into the living room. Charlie jumped as he heard loud cracks behind him and turned to see the adults picking up their shrunken broomsticks from the floor.

Randall rushed at them, coffee mug in hand, the worry lines thick on his face looked as if drawn with ash.

"Bev! Is everyone all right?"

"We're okay," his aunt said. "We're okay." She took off her shoes, then walked over and threw her arms around her husband.

Charlie had only just begun to understand the magnitude of what happened, had only just realized that, because of his stupidity, Beverly and the others had risked their lives in order to rescue him.

"Mostly okay," Rita said behind him. She and Daniel were supporting Joan, who seemed barely able to walk.

"Joan!" Beverly gasped.

She pulled away from Randall and rushed over to where the rest of the group stood in the entryway to the living room.

"I'm okay, I'm okay, it's just my leg," Joan answered, trying to laugh it off. But her voice was weak, and her face grimaced in pain as she tried to take the next step.

Daniel and Rita brought her to the couch and had her lie down. Beverly and the man Charlie didn't know gathered around her.

Charlie stayed in the entryway, watching from across the room.

"I saw Grace strike at her with that dagger."

"How much does it hurt?"

"I'll be fine. It's just a flesh wound," Joan said, imitating an English accent.

"Did anyone else get hit?"

"No, no, we're fine."

They didn't look fine to Charlie. Their clothes were torn, Daniel and Rita's faces were covered with claw marks, and the detective's ear was bleeding.

"I'll get supplies," Beverly said, walking past Charlie without looking at him and heading downstairs. The man Charlie didn't recognize went with her.

"Well, what the hell happened?" Randall asked, looking at his nephew, then the remaining three adults.

Daniel took his attention away from Joan's leg and glanced at everyone in the room, stopping last at Charlie, who stood frozen with his arms folded over his chest, not sure if he should sit down or go to his room and hide his face in shame.

"Grace had your nephew and was taking him north somewhere. She had an army of crows surrounding them for cover."

"I tell you, Randall, your wife is one badass witch," Rita said from the end of the couch near Joan's feet. "She led the charge, flying right into Grace and her coterie. Grace had Charlie's broom locked up, but Bev broke the lock by taking her straight on. I couldn't believe it."

"What?! She flew right into Grace?! What the hell was she thinking?" asked Randall, freezing in place in front of the couch, a look of horror on his face.

"It's okay, Randall," Daniel said, putting his hand on the man's shoulder. "It was the only thing that would have worked. Grace has a tremendous amount power, more than all of us combined. But I don't think she's used to being confronted directly. Beverly's attack threw her off and allowed us to get Charlie away from her."

"It was so satisfying to land on that bitch's broom and smack her around," Joan said from her prone position on the couch. Her voice shook, but her eyes gleamed with fierceness. "She didn't know we had it in us."

"But ... but ... how did you get away?"

"Rand, it's okay, don't worry about it. We managed."

"Don't placate me, Daniel. Goddamn it. My nephew takes off in the middle of the night, and my wife and the rest of you go on a rescue mission against ... the most dangerous witch in the cosmos, and you tell me not to worry?!" He yelled, his voice bouncing off the walls of the living room. Charlie cringed.

Beverly and the other man entered the room carrying jars and bowls and candles.

"Hey, hey, the worst is over," said the man. He was short, stocky, and mostly bald, but what hair was left was brushed in a not-so-subtle combover. In spite of himself, Charlie wondered how his hair had managed to stay plastered to his scalp after the midair fight they had just had.

"Randall," Rita said, turning to him, her face solemn. "Beverly contacted us, as you know, after she heard Charlie's mirror break. It didn't take long to hone in on where Grace and Charlie were. As I said, we flew straight at them, surprising her. Daniel and I got Charlie back. Joan, Bev, and Morty attacked Grace. She had crows everywhere, so I blasted them with my trusty ring here ..."

She reached up and pointed to the cord around her neck.

"... and took care of them. Daniel joined in the fray until Grace was overpowered. She took off. We flew back here. End of story.

"Now," she said, looking from Randall to Beverly to Charlie. "Why don't you let me take care of Joan? You probably need to have a little chat."

Beverly, who stood next to her husband, finally turned to Charlie. He saw the fury in her eyes. He felt his knees weaken and had the sudden urge to open the front door and flee.

"Do you want to tell us just what the hell you were thinking, Charlie?" His aunt yelled, her voice ringing sharply in his ears.

"Easy, honey. Let's take this easy now, okay?"

"I will not take this easy. Charlie, do you realize how much danger you were in? I don't know why Grace hadn't already killed you. She was about to when we got there. I don't ..." She stopped, the fury draining from her face. A choking sound escaped her lips. Her head dropped to her hands, and she started to weep.

"Aw, honey," Randall said, draping an arm over her shoulder.

Charlie wished that the floor would open up and swallow him whole. He wanted to do too many things at once: run to his aunt, pound his fists on the couch, throw something, beg for forgiveness, and rush out the front door, never coming back.

Instead, he did what he always did. He stood still, unable to say anything.

The man whose name was Morty walked over to Charlie and looked up into his face while Beverly continued to weep.

"Why don't we all sit down and talk? There's gotta be some food in this joint somewhere. I'm starving!"

*　　*　　*

Tea, coffee, and juice had been poured. Apples, cheese, and banana bread were passed around. Rita made some sort of ointment from Beverly's supplies. She dabbed it on the cuts everyone had sustained in the fight, including the scrape on Charlie's neck from Grace's fingernails, which she assured him would not leave a scar, then massaged a large quantity onto Joan's leg. When it had been determined that no poison or spell had infested her wound, the older witch smiled and said, "I told you so" as she sipped her tea.

Charlie sat in a chair as far from the adults as possible. He knew they were waiting for an answer from him. And he knew that it was time to give one. They had put their lives on the line for him tonight. This made his fears and worries seem stupid, seem meaningless. He would no longer hide behind his shame and shyness in front of these brave people.

He had found the courage to speak with Diego, and with Malcolm. He could do it again. His aunt, Joan, and the others deserved it.

He wasn't sure where to start. He looked down at the floor, as if an answer might be waiting for him in the soft weave of the carpet. Then he remembered Malcolm's advice: be straightforward.

He raised his head and saw that everyone was looking at him, waiting for him to speak. So he took a deep breath, looked back down at the floor, and began.

"I got up in the middle of the night to have some cereal," Charlie said. Surprisingly, his voice was steady, betraying none of the shame that he felt.

"When I got back upstairs, I saw your light on under the door. I could hear your voices. I shouldn't have stopped and listened, but sound carries from the heat vent in the hallway."

"I didn't know that!" Randall blurted, looking embarrassed.

"Keep going," Beverly said, ignoring her husband.

"I heard you two talking. About Diego and me. About ..."

"Oh no!" his aunt whispered, her hands flying to her face.

"What? What did you say?" Rita demanded, looking at Beverly.

"Charlie, what did you hear?" asked Randall.

He took a deep breath. He felt his resolve wavering. He didn't want to be having this conversation right now, in front of people he barely knew. He didn't even want to have it with his aunt and uncle. He wished he could be outside with Diego somewhere, looking at the Olympic Mountains. Not talking. Just sitting.

But he looked up again and saw the faces of the adults watching him. Save for Randall, they had all put themselves in mortal danger tonight. For him. It didn't matter that they had escaped relatively unharmed. He knew that one or more of them might have been killed. All because of his stupid selfish mistake.

He ran a shaking hand over his forehead, then rubbed hard at his eye sockets, trying to summon as much nerve as the witches sitting before him had shown when they had attacked Grace.

"I heard Beverly say she didn't want me to be gay."

"No, Charlie, that's not what I meant! I ..."

"It's okay. I don't want it either. I've tried for a long time not to be, but ..." His voice caught in his throat, and his eyes filled with tears. He looked down at his knees, at the color of the denim on his legs, at how the toes of his stockinged feet were digging into the carpet, trying to grab hold of something solid.

Don't cry, you big baby, don't be such a …, the angry voice chided in his head.

But he found that he didn't care anymore what that voice said. He was too tired to worry about it. Hiding things from everyone didn't work anymore. Even Grace knew his business.

So he cried. He just sat on the couch and cried. And blessedly, the others didn't rush in to hug him. They didn't try to cheer him up with their loud voices. They just watched and waited.

After a moment, he wiped at his eyes and coughed a few times to clear his throat. "I've tried for a long time to make it go away. But it never seems to work. Back home in Clarkston, I wasn't sure what to do about it. I ignored it. But the day that it all happened, when that dog, or that man or whatever, broke into our house, earlier that day," he exhaled, "I saw a story, a story on the news. There was this kid, this local kid who was … was found …"

He began to cry harder. He waited, letting the shaking wash over him. When it settled down, he wiped his nose on the back of his sleeve. He could tell that momentum was building, momentum that might help him get the whole story out, if he just kept talking and didn't listen too much to what he was saying.

"Some people beat him up and left him by the side of the road. They didn't kill him, but … but they almost did. He was a football player at this other high school, you know? And he had told his coach and his team that he was gay. They just … somebody just … the cops didn't know who …"

He paused, gulping for air, unable to get enough oxygen in his lungs. He could hear the breathing of the other adults.

"I don't want to be like that. Like him. But it won't go away, you know? I don't, don't really know what to do. And then, well, Mom and I came up here. It was all so fast and intense that I even forgot about it for a while. But then Diego, he saw me at the farmers market, and he thought I was, you know, he thought I was …"

He looked up at Rita, who was nodding, hanging on every word he said. Her face was gentle, not as ravaged-looking as his aunt's and uncle's. It was easier to focus on her.

"Diego's this kid at school who's gay, you know? He's open about it, to his mom and to people at school. Everyone knows about him. He's really popular and cool. A few kids hassle him, but most of them don't.

"I just thought he was nice, though I was surprised that he wanted to be friends with me. I mean, he's so popular and stuff. He invited me to this party, and then that night he told me he thought I was gay. I couldn't believe it. I mean, I don't do anything, I never ... say anything, I try to hide it ..."

More tears, more shaking. Someone handed him a tissue. He blew his nose, then kept going.

"When I met Malcolm the first time, he asked me who the girl was. I didn't know what he meant. Then he said, 'Oh, what's his name?' Malcolm knew too. He even knew more than I did. He told me that he didn't care, but that if I lied to myself, I wouldn't be able to be a witch. I wouldn't be able to hear the things I needed to hear, to, you know, concentrate, if I kept this big secret. He said I didn't have to tell anybody else, just myself.

"He told me he didn't use any witchcraft on me to find out. He just knew, you know? Even he could tell."

He took another deep breath. Tears were falling down Beverly's face, but he knew he couldn't do anything about it. He was tired of trying not to hurt people. It didn't work anyway. He just hoped she could forgive him for tonight. He didn't deserve her forgiveness. It wasn't an excuse for what he did, but maybe if she understood the whole story, then ...

"I don't know if I like Diego. I mean, like that. I don't know how it all works. I think he wants to be my boyfriend or something. But that's ... that's just ... that's just ... so gay."

Charlie heard someone guffaw. Everyone looked over at Morty, who turned bright red.

"Sorry. Sorry," he said, looking down at his lap.

Charlie continued. "I keep wishing everything would slow down. But it doesn't. I can't keep up with it all. It's like I'm in a race, like at track at school. I thought it was the hundred-meter dash, but then it turns into the four-hundred, then the eight-hundred, then long-distance. Somebody keeps pulling the finish line farther and farther away from me."

Charlie turned to his aunt. "I know I wasn't supposed to go out on my own like I did tonight. Even if you hadn't told me not to, even if Malcolm hadn't drilled it in to us over and over that time at his cabin. I know I shouldn't have done it. But when I heard you say you didn't want me to be gay, I just …"

He paused, thinking that he was going to cry again. But no tears came. Maybe he had cried them all out.

"I just gave up. Nothing seemed to work anymore. Maybe it never did. That's why I, uh, why I left. I couldn't figure out anything else to do. I just wanted to run away."

He stopped talking. Rita and Beverly were both crying. Daniel looked as stern as ever. His mustache twitched slightly. He and Morty exchanged a glance. Joan stared up at the ceiling, her teacup and saucer resting on her belly. Randall looked back and forth from Beverly to Charlie. Then he opened his mouth.

"Charlie, it sounds like you didn't hear the whole conversation between your aunt and me. Just in case you think everyone knows your secret, they don't. Beverly didn't. When I told her I thought that you and Diego might be more than friends, she was surprised. And yes, she said she didn't want it to be true. I got mad at her. I thought she was being closed-minded. But that's not accurate. She thought …"

"I thought," interrupted Beverly, raising her head and looking at Charlie, her eyes red and puffy, her cheeks wet, "that I really loved you and I was tired of all the things you were having to go through. It didn't seem fair to me that such a good kid had to deal with so much. This world doesn't seem very kind to people, people who …"

She paused, searching for words.

"People like me, Charlie," said Daniel, from across the room. "People who are gay. The world doesn't always like us."

Charlie's jaw dropped open. Daniel Burman was gay? That couldn't be possible. He looked so normal. Charlie couldn't imagine him wearing women's clothes, or running around fluttering his eyelashes, or whatever else gay men were supposed to do.

None of the other adults seemed surprised by what Daniel said.

"That's right," continued Beverly. "The world doesn't always treat gay people, people like Daniel and Diego ..."

"And Maureen," said Joan from the couch.

Randall rolled his eyes. "Uh yeah, Joan. Thanks. Charlie has no idea who you're talking about."

"Just trying to help. Jeez."

"It doesn't always treat gay people well. I wanted you to have a break. Charlie, you have to understand. It's not that I think there's anything wrong with you liking Diego or wanting to be more than friends with him. He's a great guy. I just got scared for you. I was worried that people would tease you or hurt you. I figured that I wouldn't be able to stop that from happening. I felt helpless. That's not a feeling I'm used to.

"Don't you see, Charlie? It's not you. What I mean is, it's not that there's anything wrong with you ... it's that I love you." More tears.

"I don't know how it happened. You've only been here for such a short time. I didn't know I had a nephew until a few weeks ago. I didn't even know if Lizzy was alive or dead. But then she comes here, you come here, and you're so, you're so sweet, and good, and I was scared I didn't have what it takes to be your guardian, or your aunt, or your mother, or whatever I'm supposed to be. I didn't know I if I could do it. And then this unexpected ... love ... slipped in and grabbed me before I saw it coming. It happened to both of us," she said, indicating Randall, who nodded back.

"And when Randall told me about you and Diego, I got even more scared. I didn't know if I could be the right kind of aunt for you. What if you asked me questions about being gay? I feel so clueless. I don't know anything about it. What if I said the wrong thing? I mean, look what happened tonight. I did say the wrong thing. Or at least, you took it the wrong way. And look how much it hurt you. I just, I don't know ... I want you to know how much I love you and care about you, and if Grace ever even thinks about getting her goddamn claws on you again …"

The couches began to shake as if in an earthquake, while the food platters rattled on the coffee table.

"Okay, okay, honey," said Randall, standing up. "Let's all just take a deep breath. No more broken furniture."

The shaking subsided. Rita laughed, and soon the others were smiling too.

"Sorry. What I'm trying to say is that I will come rescue you again if something happens. But I'm afraid. What if I can't be there next time? What if …"

Her words stopped, and she took a deep breath.

Charlie felt his own tears again as he heard what his aunt was saying. At first he thought she was just talking to say the right thing, but somewhere in there, as more and more of her words tumbled forth, he began to believe her. It was as if her words snuck into him—the same way that the "unexpected love" had slipped into her. He believed her. He believed his uncle, and he could tell that the other adults weren't disgusted or angry with him for liking Diego.

He still couldn't believe that Daniel Burman was gay. He didn't know you could be a detective and be gay at the same time.

But he believed Beverly. And this helped to calm him. The final vestiges of his desire to run away disappeared. He looked at his aunt and uncle.

"So you're really not mad if I, well, if I like Diego? Or if I don't like girls that much?"

"No, we are not mad, Charlie," said his uncle. His look was so earnest that Charlie could feel his own heart breaking open.

"No, we are not mad, Charlie," repeated his aunt. "We love you just the way you are. Oh my god." She crinkled her face as if smelling something foul. "That sounded really corny."

Morty broke out into song. "We love you just the way you are." The others joined in. It was completely embarrassing.

Charlie wanted everyone to stop singing, but he found himself laughing. Laughing because he had spoken out loud the biggest secret he had, so big he hadn't even been willing to tell himself. And nothing bad had happened. Nobody called him a dirty little fag. Nobody beat him up. Nobody got up and left. The skin on his face felt strange, as if it had been stretched out over his chin and down his shoulders. He wanted to touch it, to see if it was real. He wanted to look at himself in the mirror and see if he recognized the reflection. Maybe he would look like normal scared Charlie. Maybe he wouldn't look any different. But maybe, just possibly, he would look like someone brave.

CHAPTER 15

The Watering Hole

TONY, CLAUDIA, AND THOMAS the Dog Man sat together at a table in the basement of a dark elegant bar in Belltown. The décor imitated a 1920s laboratory, dimly lit by overhead rods pulsing blue with electricity. Hammered bronze tubing covered most of the walls, and each of the myriad sitting nooks pocketed throughout the bar displayed tributes to the spiritualism of the era, including crystal balls in glass cases and black and white photos of mediums with head-dresses holding seances.

The patrons that night were enchanted by the collective charm of the three witches and bought them round after round of bright cock-tails in vintage glassware. Plates of tapas continued to arrive at the table, courtesy of the chef, or a bartender, or a shy besotted member of the waitstaff.

Upon each delivery, the witches smiled, nodded their thanks, and then continued their conversation, not inviting a single person to join them. No one dared approach the table.

"Think she'll be back after midnight?" asked Claudia. She wore a purple flapper-era cocktail dress. The tassels shimmied as she breathed, raising the blood pressure of her many male and female admirers.

"Nah," said Tony, watching his reflection in the glass case of an exhibit featuring Nikola Tesla, the Russian electrical engineer. Stub-ble accentuated the sharp length of his jawline. He turned his head left, then right, looking at his face from different angles.

"She'll be here any minute. Knowing her, she went full out."

Thomas ran his hands through his curly blond hair. "Jesus, Tony, do you know how annoying you are? Believe me, your face hasn't changed since you looked at it five minutes ago."

"We Americans could learn more art appreciation, my friend. I'm just leading the way."

Thomas and Claudia exchanged looks.

"For some reason," Thomas continued, "I'm not feeling as confident in our leader as you two seem to be. The boy hasn't given us anything but trouble. His whole family, for that matter, has been nothing but ..."

"Such a doubting Thomas," said a soft voice from behind them.

Grace walked around the corner and sat down at their table. Her hair was smoothed and shaped into its usual chignon. Her peach dress, complimenting Claudia's period clothing, was soft and unruffled. Her elegance and beauty outshone all three witches. A collective intake of breath could almost be heard as the bar's patrons took in the newcomer.

Grace's companions examined her. Her usual glow seemed diminished. Her eyes shone with a predatory light, and there was a tiny cut on her right temple. It wasn't bleeding, but it was the first blemish any of them had ever seen on her.

That, combined with the fact that she arrived empty-handed, made them nervous.

"Are, uh, are you okay?" Claudia asked, trying to hide the worry in her voice.

"I'm fine. What does a girl have to do to get a drink around here?"

A waiter appeared at their table.

"What do you have that is especially perfect for an evening of revenge?" she asked. The waiter was tall and golden-skinned, his black hair oiled back from his brow. His eyes had the double epicanthic fold common in East Asia. He smiled, and two perfect dimples formed at his cheeks.

"Besides you, that is," said Grace.

The other witches fidgeted. Her light flirtation meant that she might have plans for him later. They hoped that her plans might include them too.

Grace's eyes lingered on the waiter as he walked to the bar to put in her order.

"The boy got away," she said, turning to face her underlings. "I had him. He was ready to follow me and learn what I had to tell him. But there was a surprise attack from Beverly and friends, and ..."

"What?!" said Tony, mouth agape. "But she's nothing compared to you. How could she ..."

His words were cut short as Grace balled her hand into a fist. He clutched at his chest. His eyes rolled into the back of his head and he made sharp grunting sounds.

"Don't!"

A grotesque expression of pain marred his perfect face.

"Question!"

Drops of spittle spilled over his lips.

"Me!"

Tony gasped, then wheezed in breath as Grace relaxed her fist.

He mumbled a quick "sorry" and grabbed for his martini. His shaking hands spilled some of the drink. Claudia took the glass from him and brought it to his lips so he could take a sip.

"You," Grace said, turning to Thomas.

"Grace?" the man asked, his voice thinner and reedier than before Grace had appeared.

"Ever think about all of this when you decided to get us involved?"

Thomas held his head in shame. There was no reason to play-act in front of Grace, and she wouldn't permit a defensive stance. He tried to think of a way to apologize.

"No matter," Grace said. "Now we know that Charlie might be able to help us, which makes it all worthwhile. Besides, we've all tried to catch him, and we've all failed. We're members of the Losers Club, apparently."

The three tried to laugh at her joke, but the quivering lips and the forced chuckles stopped once they realized she wasn't laughing with them.

"Here we are," said the waiter, returning with a tall champagne flute filled with a clear blue liquid, which he placed in front of Grace. "I hope this helps with your evening revenge plans."

The other three noticed how he stood a little too close to her, how his smile lacked a server's formality. How he seemed slightly drunk himself.

"Oh, I'm sure it will," Grace said, sipping the cocktail. "Lovely. Just lovely. Tell me, what's your name, handsome waiter?"

"Jason."

"Jason," said Grace, drawing out the word as if it were a good idea she was considering. "Wonderful. Tell me, Jason, would you like to join my friends and me for a little fun later tonight?"

He answered immediately. "Yes. Yes, of course."

"Excellent. We'll be leaving after I finish my drink. You'll come with us?"

It wasn't a question. The others knew that she sometimes liked to soften even the most vicious of blows with a façade of mutuality, or even subservience. This was when she was at her most dangerous.

"Good. Then wait over there in the corner against that wall, okay, Jason? Just stand there. No one else will know. It'll be our secret."

He nodded, then walked over to the shadowed corner where Grace had made her entrance and stood stock-still, facing the wall.

Tony, Claudia, and Thomas the Dog Man smiled their hungry smiles. In spite of the edge on which Grace always kept them, they were excited. Jason was a very good choice. They were eager to learn what she had in mind for him.

*   *   *

During the car ride to her house, Grace kept Jason bewitched enough to relax him, but alert enough so that he could respond to stimulus. He proved to be an excellent sport.

Grace's home was located on the shores of Lake Washington. Claudia had once said that it deserved to be described with a verb, not an adjective. "It sprawls," she had said. It was a far cry from the three-bedroom, mid-century house with the moldy basement that Grace had purchased in the nineties when she had been starting out.

Grace kept her hand on the small of Jason's back as they walked into the house. She needed to maintain contact with him in order to keep him docile.

Thomas started to gather bags from the trunk of the town car.

"Leave them be," Grace ordered over her shoulder. "The people will handle them."

"The people" referred to an entire class of workers, assistants, helpers, and in some cases, slaves, who inhabited the residence. Some of them were echoes who ran errands and such for Grace in the hopes of learning more about their stunted abilities. Others were paid workers who kept the grounds, cleaned the house (except the basement; they were never to go in the basement), and prepared meals. Another group of them were Grace's gofers. They were people like Mavis, kitchen witches who showed enough talent or seemed useful enough for Grace to pop and then use as her eyes and ears in the city≠. Most of them never came near where Grace lived, though occasionally one might be seen in the living room.

Thomas was always relieved when Grace referred to "the people." It meant that she still considered Claudia, Tony, and himself as a separate superior class. He also knew that her ranking system was capricious at best. The three of them were too far in to ever leave on their own, even if they had wanted to, so they had to be always on the lookout for ways to prove themselves useful to Grace. Being in her inner circle gave them status over the others, more power than they had ever imagined, and slightly more margin of error than, say, the ones who cleaned the toilets.

But the trio had no illusions that she kept them around out of the goodness of her heart. Grace had no heart.

"Go find out if the people know anything new. I want to see what Jason's made of before we, well, before you-know-what," Grace said, leading Jason upstairs.

CHAPTER 16

Park Bench

MAVIS SAT NEXT TO a sullen-looking teenage boy with a shock of pink hair on a bench up in the old-growth part of Seward Park. The sun was just starting to rise, turning the gray expanse of grass at their feet into a mint-green carpet.

"Don't be fresh with him the way you are with me, and don't ask him questions about what else you can do, and don't, well, just don't talk, okay?"

"Okay! Jeez, I'm not some little kid, you know."

"That's exactly what you are. So just shut up and ..."

"Hello, Mavis."

The woman jumped a foot, yelled "Whatoofy!" and landed with a jowl-shaking thud back on the hard seat of the bench.

The pink-haired kid started laughing at the older woman's reaction, then stopped short. A man with blond curly hair was standing a few feet away from them, dressed in a pale-colored fitted suit. He walked over to the park bench and sat down. The hairs on the back of the kid's neck stood up. Even in the faint dawn light the man's expression reflected that he was here for nothing other than business. And by the looks of things, it would be dangerous business. The boy had no trouble following Mavis's directions to keep his mouth closed.

"What's new?" asked Thomas.

"Why do you people always have to sneak up on me?" Mavis said, clutching at her heart.

"Because the results are so satisfying," the man replied.

"What do you know?" he asked, his words clipped and quiet.

"Not much," Mavis said, trying not to sound frightened. "Seems like there was a kerfuffle over at Beverly's house tonight. Witches coming and going. We can't get anyone close enough to scope it out, and there are so damned many cats!"

"It's all right. We don't expect you to get around the cats. What else have you heard?"

"The kid's gay," Mavis shrugged. "But Grace already knew that. The police report on Todd Laramie was filed 'missing persons.' No one has linked him yet with the two girls from Rainier Beach, or that punk out in Maple Valley. Russ Yamada at SPD moved some things around so the connections are harder to make. He has Daniel Burman to worry about, but …"

"Keep him on Burman. Bring in more reinforcement if need be."

"We got Gracie Guerrero downtown too, so we shouldn't have to …"

"I don't want to hear 'shouldn't have to,' Mavis. Track Burman and report his every move to us. She won't like it if she hears you've been lazy. And you won't like it if she doesn't like it. *¿Comprendes?*"

"Sí, comprendes."

"It's *'comprendo,'* for 'I understand,' Mavis. See, you even get to learn Spanish by associating with us, not just more ways to trick people into buying your hand creams."

"Gee thanks, Thomas. My world is expanding so broadly."

He was on her in a flash, sitting astride her, his legs surrounding her ample hips and squeezing tightly, his face inches from hers. The pink-haired kid scooted to the far end of the bench, his eyes wide.

"Don't be cute, Mavis. I don't like cute. Claudia may be more forgiving than I am. Trust me, you don't want to push it."

He slapped her hard in the face. Then he hopped off and punched her, once, in the gut. She doubled over and fell to the ground, clutching her stomach.

Thomas was behind the teenage boy before he could do anything. The man's hands clamped around his neck. The boy thrashed on the bench, kicking at the air, beating uselessly against Thomas's hands.

"You work for us, kid. End of story. All those fun things you can do now? They mean nothing. You do what we say, you do all of what we say, and maybe you'll live long enough to enjoy bossing people around with your new bionic superpowers."

Thomas released his hands from the teenager's neck. The boy fell to the grass next to Mavis, gasping for air.

The scent of wet wood surrounded them, and then the man was gone. In his place stood a large German shepherd. The dog walked over to where they lay on the ground, bared its teeth, and began to bark violently, its spittle landing in their hair.

The pink-haired boy started to cry and shake, unaware of the growing wet spot in the crotch of his pants. Mavis threw her hands above her head.

The dog turned and ran off into the woods.

A few moments later, a woman in a turquoise jogging suit, with a small poodle on a leash, ran over to them.

"Do you need help? Can I call someone?"

The poodle began a low series of growls, the fur on its back raising as it stood over the middle-aged fat woman and the skinny teenager, both of whom inched away until they were blocked by the park bench.

"Amber. Amber sweetie, stop that. You're never this mean. Stop it!"

"Get out of here! Get the hell away or I'll give you some real nightmares, lady!" Mavis wheezed through her clenched teeth.

The woman's horrified expression was small reward for the pain in Mavis's gut. All she could do was lie on the grass and watch as the stupid jogger pulled her snapping dog back down to the running path.

CHAPTER 17

The Bleachers

THEY WERE WAITING FOR CHARLIE. He had just walked out of the gym, hair still wet from showering after PE, and was heading up to the main school building for lunch. Julio, Dave Giraldi, Randy, and some other guy he didn't recognize. He had taken the shortcut underneath the bleachers.

"Hey, faggot boy, you been bumping it with the Diegster? He been giving it to you good?"

Charlie froze. They had him cornered in the perfect place. Nobody could see him from here.

He turned to walk away, but a hand grabbed his shoulder and jerked him around.

"Don't walk away from us, you shit. You California shit. We want to have a little talk. Rumor says you and Butt Pirate are an item. Maybe you give it to him?" Dave Giraldi said, raising his eyebrows and making a kissing shape with his mouth.

"Leave me alone," Charlie said, his voice shaking. He put his head down and tried to shove past them, but they surrounded him.

"'Leave me alone, leave me alone,'" Randy teased. "Look, faggot bitch, the minute you came to this school, you became our problem. You haven't left us alone with your goddamn googly eyes at Diegster. We're here to tell you to leave us alone."

"That's right," said the fourth guy. "You're disgusting. Your faggot-ness bothers us every day. You're gonna stop. You hear me?"

"He asked you a question, boy," said Julio. "Answer him."

"Just leave it, all right? Why do you have to make such a big deal out of …?"

Julio boxed him in the ear. Charlie stumbled back against Dave, who grabbed his shoulders and kept him from falling. White lights flashed across his eyes, and the hot pain on the side of his head was accompanied by a booming sound, then a dull ringing.

"Why do we have to make such a big deal? Oh yeah, right. As if we're the ones parading around school, going to GSA meetings, and wearing frickin' pink on Pride Day. You faggots taking over the world, marrying each other, and turning kids gay is making a big deal out of it. You make me sick, you know that? Doesn't he make you sick?" Julio asked the other boys, who nodded.

Then he leaned back and punched Charlie straight in the stomach.

The agony in his gut was singular and brutal, forcing him to bend over and clutch at his midriff as all the air whooshed out of his mouth. He couldn't catch his breath and was vaguely aware that his insides had sloshed together when Julio punched him.

"That's right, bend over. Bet you're real good at that," someone said. Charlie was having trouble seeing. The pain made him forget where he was, or even what was going on around him. He knew he was in trouble and was pretty sure he was supposed to be able to do something about it, but he couldn't remember what. Something about words. Saying words. Saying Words?

Someone grabbed him by the hair and yanked his head up. A face swam into view. He could smell rank swampy breath and heavy cologne. He saw something silver and realized the face had a hand and the hand had a knife. An image of Grace flashed in his mind, with her crazed expression while she choked him, a knife held above his head …

"You keep quiet about this, Charlie boy, or we'll make sure you stay quiet. It'll be our little secret, okay, faggot? Nod your head if you understand."

Charlie nodded. He felt wet lips on his cheeks.

"Atta boy. Remember, tell Principal Wang or anyone else about this, and you'll make things really rough for yourself."

"Yeah, Charlie boy. We'll come find you on Washington Street," someone else said. And then they were gone.

Charlie's legs gave out, and he collapsed backwards until he was lying flat on the ground. As his vision cleared, he could see strips of gray sky through the bleacher slats. The wet cement felt cool on the back of his head. He wished he could turn over so that the coolness would touch his stomach. But for the moment, he couldn't remember how to turn over. He stayed under the bleachers for a long time. If the pain hadn't been so terrible, he might have even enjoyed the quiet.

*   *   *

"Hold still. Let me look at you," Rose Patchke said, as she examined Charlie at home in the living room.

"Of all the godforsaken …" said Randall, walking in circles.

Charlie had managed to pull himself up into a standing position after lying under the bleachers for a while. He had started walking home, thinking that he could manage the short distance but had to sit down on the sidewalk several times so that he wouldn't pass out. He had called Randall, whom he knew had the day off. In the short time while he waited for Randall's car, no one had bothered him or asked if he needed help. He was glad. He just wanted to go to bed.

"Randall, please. I can't concentrate with you pacing back and forth like that."

Rose looked into Charlie's eyes. She held up a cup of something warm and asked him to drink it. The liquid was thin and tasted like raspberries. He drank it all in one large swallow.

"Good job. I think you're going to be okay. That tea will tell us if there's anything wrong with your head."

"Always something wrong with my head," Charlie said, trying to make a joke.

"Yes, well, I can't do anything about that," Rose smiled, winking at him. "Just sit back and rest on the couch, all right?"

"We need to go tell Principal Wang," Randall said. "That school has a no-tolerance policy. Which he upholds!"

Charlie shook his head. "They said they'd make trouble for me if I told."

"Trouble?! You think those boys could get away with causing trouble? Look who they're talking about! Look who surrounds you, Charlie. Witches who would be their worst nightmare, not the other way around."

"Randall," Rose chided. "You already know this. The witches will do no such thing. We won't interfere like that. It'll draw attention to us. If Beverly weren't out running errands, she would tell you the same thing."

"Yeah, yeah. I know, I know, I know! But what good is it all if you can't use it when you need to?"

"This isn't a case where we need to. Charlie's growing into a fine young man. You'll think of a way to deal with this, won't you? Without using the craft, I mean?"

Charlie nodded again, feeling like all he was doing today was following instructions. What he really wanted to do was to go to each guy's house, ending with Julio's, whisper Words, and make things happen that would scare them half to death.

But he knew he wouldn't. Not after his solo flight that had nearly gotten the other witches killed. He wanted to rationalize things, saying that this was a different situation, that these were just stupid seniors, not Grace, and that he could clearly handle himself with them.

But he was gun-shy of his witchcraft. He had used it improperly, with dangerous results. He didn't trust himself yet to try anything, let alone give payback to Julio and the other guys. Who knew what could happen?

CHAPTER 18

Folding Chairs

THE WITCHES CROWDED INTO Beverly and Randall's basement. Some sat on couches or on the folding chairs that Randall and Charlie had pulled out. Others stood around in groups of twos and threes. All told, there must have been over fifty people, including some of the kids who had been trained up at Malcolm's cabin. The atmosphere crackled with tension.

A middle-aged couple stood off to the side, surrounded by several witches offering comfort. Charlie watched as the woman alternated between wringing her hands and running them through her hair. The man stood stock still, his eyes dull, his mouth open, arms hanging at his sides.

"But what about all of our children? How do we protect them? June and I have two who are still unpopped. Who's to say they won't be taken too?" a stocky man asked. He wore a flannel shirt and jeans, the same thing that every man in the Pacific Northwest seemed to start wearing once the weather turned cold and damp.

"Bob, I understand your concern," said Beverly, standing with her back to the large flat-screen television mounted on the wall. "We're all worried about the same thing. But we honestly don't know what to do."

"That is not acceptable! You are our leader! Figure it out! In your father's day …"

"In her father's day," snapped Sean Crenshaw, crossing his arms across his chest and narrowing his eyes, "her father was busy giving away our secrets to Grace, so don't wax nostalgic on us, all right, Bob?" He paused, then winced and looked over at Beverly. "I'm sorry, I didn't mean to ..."

"It's okay, Sean. No need to tiptoe around the fact that my father did unscrupulous things. And I'm afraid that what he did has helped Grace to be able to infiltrate us today. That's why we're here. Grace has the upper hand, and we need to figure out how to get it back."

Randall had explained to Charlie what happened. The grieving couple, Les and Ginger Nickerson, called Beverly to report that their daughter Suzette had disappeared in the middle of the night. She had gone to bed when she normally did, but she wasn't in her room the next morning. Daniel Burman went over to their house and, upon investigation, discovered traces of witchcraft, which had him rule out a runaway situation. He sensed the presence of Grace and one or more of her witches.

The Nickersons had brought pictures of their daughter with them tonight. Charlie didn't recognize her. She looked to be about eight or nine years old. She had a mousy look about her and reminded him of the girl with the wispy hair and thick glasses from the warehouse the day they had been popped, the one who had asked how long it was going to take. Charlie wondered if Suzette was the girl's younger sister.

"I'm sorry, Beverly. He, uh, we didn't mean to be ungrateful," said the woman sitting next to Bob. "We're just worried is all."

Charlie watched his aunt. Warring emotions played across her face. She opened her mouth to speak, then shut it. Opened it again, then shut it again. Everyone waited, willing to let Beverly find her words. Finally she spoke.

"Les and Ginger, I am so sorry. You must be out of your mind with worry. Twice now there have been attempts to kidnap my nephew."

Several people in the crowd gasped. All eyes turned to Charlie. He dropped his head, wishing that he could be invisible. His hand automatically went to the cut on his neck, nearly healed, where Grace had cut him with her fingernails.

"What?"

"When?"

"How did …?"

"As you can see, Charlie is safely with us here today. But if he wasn't, I would be crazy with fear and worry myself. It's time for us to band together to protect our children. We cannot, will not, let any more of them be taken." Charlie wondered why his aunt hadn't said anything about the fight with Grace.

"But what's going on? Why is she trying to take our children?" someone in the far corner shouted.

Beverly looked around her, trying to find words once again. There was a shuffling from the back as Daniel Burman made his way to where Beverly stood.

"At first I wondered if Grace were doing it to try to get at us," Daniel said, "to use the kids as bargaining tools. But there have been other kidnappings in the greater Seattle area, and that tells me it might be something else."

"What do you mean?" asked Ginger Nickerson.

"Well, there have been four other teenage kidnappings in the last month. The higher-ups at the Seattle Police Department seem to think they're unrelated: one might be connected to drugs and gangs, another could be teenage prostitution, and the last one seems to be for reasons unknown.

"However," Daniel continued, his ice-blue stare holding authority over the crowd, "I believe that they're related. Or I'm suspicious that they might be. Kidnappings don't tend to happen as much at this time of year, when school is newly underway. Parents and teachers are more on guard. Kids too. Security is tighter. It's in the late winter and early spring that kidnappings tend to increase. So the fact that at least four teenagers have gone missing, or five, now that we're considering Suzette's disappearance in light of the others, has me suspicious. As I'm sure you all know, we have reports that echoes in the area have an increased skill level, and Beverly can attest to the fact that our local bookie and potions-and-lotions witch, Mavis, has considerably more abilities than ever before."

Daniel looked over at Beverly, who nodded back to him.

"I suspect that there are a few in the upper echelons of the Seattle Police Department who may be part of a local echo network, people who have somehow acquired new abilities and are in cahoots with Grace. And that somehow, the kidnappings are related. And that this network is trying to make it look like the they are random, individual events."

The basement was quiet as everyone digested this new information.

"I agree with Beverly. Grace has the upper hand right now. But we're working on finding a connection.

"In the meantime, I think it would be best if we applied new wards to our homes, used more talismans for our children's safety, and accompanied them to and from school. I don't think Grace would be stupid enough to attempt a public kidnapping during the day, while someone is at school or soccer practice. But the fact that she's able to get into our homes at night tells me that what we thought was effective at keeping intruders out isn't working."

"What I want to know is, where's Malcolm?" asked Bob, the flannel-wearing guy. Others nodded and voiced similar questions. "Shouldn't he be here?"

"You know him. He's out popping kids. I think this time he's in the Midwest somewhere," said Beverly. Charlie looked at his aunt. He knew her well enough now to know that there was something she wasn't saying, something she was keeping from the crowd. He watched the faces of those around him. No one else seemed to notice.

A few committees were formed. One of them took on the task of resetting stronger wards and other spells that would be used to protect people's homes from invasion. Another set about acquiring protective talismans for the children. A third agreed to help Daniel with his investigation. The meeting broke up soon after.

On their way out, several people asked Charlie about the kidnapping attempts. The first one was easier to talk about, since he had been in bed asleep when it had happened. The second one, though, made him uncomfortable to explain. Remembering how Beverly hadn't told the group about the fight with Grace, he left those details out too, though he wasn't sure why he was doing it.

"One of the witches tried to get me when I was out alone one night," he said, deciding that this was true, if only partially. "Beverly found out that I was missing. I guess she used a scrying bowl to find me, before, uh, before anything bad happened."

His answer seemed to satisfy people, and none of them asked if it had been Grace or someone else who tried to kidnap him. But it left Charlie with a hollow feeling inside. The fact that he had been out on a broomstick by himself because he thought Beverly hated him being gay and that the witches had been forced to come to his rescue, narrowly escaping with their lives, was still very painful to accept.

Charlie had begun to think of the attack beneath the bleachers as something he deserved, something that had happened to teach him a lesson. True, he had wanted it to stop when it was happening. But the more he thought about everything, the more shame he felt. His actions put people at risk. Maybe getting beaten up by the guys at school was something he had coming to him.

He wanted to help Beverly and Daniel stop Grace and find the kids who had gone missing. But he was worried that he would cause more trouble and put more people at risk.

He had also been thinking again about what Grace promised to tell him, about why that Dog Man had gone to all the trouble to come find him in California.

Why hadn't he told Beverly and the others about this, about the information she offered to him? Maybe he was worried that they would overreact and do something foolish, like go after Grace, all the while lacking the strength or ability to escape unscathed.

More likely you're ashamed of yourself for listening to her, for hoping that she could give you something good, he said to himself. This seemed true.

He was conflicted enough about it that he decided not to mention it for the time being.

Was it connected to the other kids disappearing? Why had there been two attempts to kidnap him? He couldn't really have anything that Grace wanted, could he?

These thoughts troubled him as he helped Randall and Beverly, as well as some of the stragglers, clean up after the meeting.

*　　*　　*

Later, Charlie sat in the kitchen with his aunt and uncle, eating leftovers. Amos slept by the blazing hearth.

"Where is Malcolm anyway?" Randall asked.

"I told you. He's out popping kids."

"Come on, Bev. You didn't look like you believed it when you said it to the group downstairs, and you don't look like you believe it now. What's up?"

Charlie watched his aunt's face, eager to hear her honest answer.

Beverly picked up her fork, and then set it down on her plate. She twisted her wedding ring back and forth, then scratched her palm lightly before speaking.

"I don't know. This is unlike him. I can usually reach him. But he hasn't been himself this week. He seems preoccupied. When Daniel told me about the other kidnappings, I called him to let him know. He basically brushed me off and said it probably wasn't anything related to our community. This, from the man who is so protective of our kids that he's basically gone ninety percent of the time, from one city or town or hamlet to the next, popping and educating and overseeing everything kid-related?

"'Why would I want a kid of my own?'" Beverly said, doing a very good imitation of Malcolm's gruff voice. "'I already have so many all over the world to parent.'"

"What do you think is up?" asked Randall, his forehead crinkling.

"I haven't the slightest. I asked him about it but he just told me he's extremely busy, even more so than usual.

"Another thing," she said after a moment, "I wish he were here to talk to the community. They trust him. They rely on him. He has more of a global vision, and I know how much they relax when he's back home among us."

"Bev, you're the heart of leadership for these people. Don't think they don't trust you. They're wild about you, and you know it."

"I know they appreciate me, Randall. And many of them respect me. But I wouldn't say they trust me. They trusted Dad, and look where that got them. I think it's hard for them when they know that I'm his daughter."

"Don't you think they're passed all that now? That they can separate you from him?"

"In good times, sure. But when the shit hits the fan, like it is now, I don't know," she said, looking at the window at the dark night, scratching her palm again, this time with an absent-mindedness that Charlie found to be a little spooky. "I just don't know."

CHAPTER 19

Creek Talk

THE TWO BOYS WALKED along the trails at Carson Park. There was no dog yanking them along. No late summer sun to warm their backs. Just the two of them wearing boots and waterproof jackets as the rain drizzled down on them. Beverly had agreed to let Charlie go to the park with Diego on the condition that he wear his new talismans (two bracelets, a necklace, and a ring), all of which had been newly charged for protection and identification, should something happen. That, and the fact that the whole park had been newly fortified with wards of a much higher caliber than the community had ever used before, seemed to satisfy his aunt.

Diego was upset. He had been mostly silent when he had picked up Charlie, other than a few questions about his new jewelry, which he had asked without really listening to the answers. But as soon as they entered the park, the boy looked around to make sure no one was listening, then turned to face Charlie.

"What are you hiding?" Diego asked.

Charlie looked at him in disbelief, which was genuine. Of course he was hiding things from him, but he couldn't believe that the boy knew Charlie was lying. Diego talked about how strange Charlie seemed the last few days: quieter than normal, looking over his shoulder, not replying to voicemail or texts right away like he usually did.

Finally Charlie responded. "Look, Diego, I don't know how to tell you about it. Can we just walk for a while and then I'll say something?"

The boy had agreed, but the look on his face changed from suspicion to worry.

Back in California, Charlie loved going on quiet hikes in the hills behind his house with Mike or another friend from school. They didn't talk much. He enjoyed the quiet, enjoyed hearing the sounds of nature around them. But today, the silence between Diego and him was nearly unbearable.

Charlie looked around him. More of the trees were changing color. Even though the wet weather dampened the fiery display of autumn leaves, the change was still noticeable. The ferns and the conifers retained their bright green hues, of course, but the deciduous trees seemed to be changing into their October coloring before September even finished.

He felt a sense of foreboding. He had no idea what was going to happen with Grace or the others. He only knew it would probably happen soon. Of course he couldn't tell Diego any of this. But there were some things he could confide.

Charlie's jeans were wet at the knees and the sides of his legs by the time the boys stepped out from the narrow wooded path and saw the clearing in front of them. He smelled the saltier, cooler air and saw the familiar expanse of the bridge above their heads.

Without talking, they walked over to the bench and sat down. The light rainfall mottled the surface of the creek.

Finally, Diego spoke. "Look, if you want to stop hanging out with me, just tell me, okay? I mean, this whole keeping-your-distance thing is really pretty awful. I'd rather know, instead of …"

"What are you talking about?"

"… have you sort of fade away, like a ghost or something."

"Diego, I don't want to stop hanging out with you. Why do you always assume that's the case whenever I'm upset or something?"

"I don't know. It's just that you seem so, not into it that much, is all."

"Believe me, what I'm going to tell you doesn't have anything to do with not wanting to hang out with you."

"Is it about the, uh, the kissing?" he asked, whispering the last word and looking around to see if anyone could hear them. "Because if you're feeling too much pressure ..."

Diego's face looked so earnest, his eyelashes blinking so rapidly under the hood of his raincoat, that Charlie couldn't help giggling.

"What? Don't tease me. Why are you laughing?"

"I'm sorry. You just look so cute," he said, then leaned in and kissed him softly on the mouth. He kept his eyes open, watching as Diego's nose doubled and his eyes blurred together from the close-up vision.

"That's the first time you've ever called me 'cute,'" said Diego as their lips parted, his voice soft. "I like it."

"I've told you before that you're cute."

"No, you haven't."

"Seriously?"

"Seriously."

Charlie felt badly. He knew Diego needed more reassurance than he gave him. But he wasn't used to giving it. For one thing, Charlie hated the encouragement he had been given his whole life, by his mother, by teachers, by his friends' parents, to open up more, to not be so shy. He knew it was well-intended, but it always left him feeling like there was something wrong with him. He didn't want to do the same thing to Diego. And secondly, it was still hard for Charlie to believe that Diego, so self-assured and independent, needed to hear from someone else about his good characteristics.

Charlie wanted to do better. Even now, by asking Diego to wait for him to disclose what he had been holding back, he was making the boy anxious and worried.

"Okay, I'll tell you what I was going to tell you. But you have to promise not to get mad. Or to do anything about it, okay?"

"Okay, I promise."

"Well, I want to tell you two things," Charlie said. "I don't think you'll be mad at the first one. But don't be mad at the second one, okay? You'll probably want to go rush off and ..."

"Will you just freakin' tell me?"

Charlie explained that he came out to his aunt and uncle. Diego's smile grew so large that the corners of his mouth expanded beyond the edge of his hood. In spite of himself, Charlie smiled back.

"How did it go? What did they say? Why did you decide to tell them?"

Diego's enthusiasm was so great that he didn't seem to notice the holes in Charlie's story. He told him about overhearing his aunt and uncle talking, about misunderstanding what Beverly meant when she said she didn't want Charlie to be gay. He then lied, explaining that he stormed off in the middle of the night and that Beverly drove around until she found him. That he and his aunt and uncle had a huge talk about it all, and that they were supportive.

"Oh, and they really like you, Diego," Charlie said.

Diego looked as excited as a little kid with a new toy.

"This is totally cool. Hey, they can go to PFLAG meetings with my mom if they want to."

"What's a pea flag?"

"PFLAG. Parents and Friends of Lesbians and Gays. It's a nation-wide support group for people who love queer people. They have a local chapter, and I bet they'd …"

"Uh, I don't think that my aunt and uncle are support-group kind of people."

"Oh. Well, if they change their minds, maybe they could go with my mom. She likes to go sometimes when she doesn't have to work late. I think it gives her some peace of mind and helps her overcome her own homophobia."

Diego went on to explain about how everyone was homophobic, that you couldn't not be in this culture, that gay people's homophobia was called internalized, that …

Charlie stopped paying attention. He knew at times that Diego, who was very smart and had many thoughts running in his head at the same time, needed to talk things out to calm himself down. Usually Charlie just listened, knowing that it helped the boy to say things out loud. But today he had too many other things on his mind to be able to concentrate on the chatter.

Eventually Diego stopped talking. Together they watched leaves and twigs float down the creek toward Puget Sound. The drizzle had stopped. The clear water eddied and swirled in places. At a slight bend in the creek, several small leaf-covered branches had bunched together. A yellowish foam gathered around the branches, adding froth to the leaves' surfaces.

"What's the other thing you wanted to tell me?" Diego asked. "Is this the part where I'm not supposed to get mad or go do anything drastic?"

"Yes. Although I didn't just say drastic. I don't want you to go do anything at all. Except listen."

"I'm all ears."

"Well, promise me again."

"I promise. I won't do anything except listen. Just tell me."

Diego's lips were parted, and his breathing increased slightly as he waited for Charlie to speak. In that moment Charlie wished he hadn't decided to disclose anything. He knew Diego would get upset. Charlie was enjoying his friend's companionship on the bench after their hike in the damp woods, away from school, and witchcraft, and worry. He didn't want to ruin it. But it was too late. Diego was expecting something and wouldn't leave Charlie alone until he knew. So he began to speak, marring the calm the way the rain had disturbed the surface of the creek only moments ago.

Charlie told Diego what happened under the bleachers with Julio, Dave Giraldi, Randy, and the boy he didn't recognize. He watched as Diego's mouth went slack, how the caramel color of his skin paled to light beige, how the light in his dark brown eyes dimmed.

He told Diego what they had said to him, how Julio had hit him in the head and the stomach, how they had threatened him with a knife.

He expected Diego to become angry. He thought he would yell at Charlie for not telling him. He figured Diego would run off and call Principal Wang and Ms. Barry immediately, to hold meetings, to put together something he called a task force.

What he didn't expect was to see Diego's troubled eyes start to glisten, to fill up with water until the tears spilled over the rims and ran down his cheeks in twin tracks, leaving droplets of moisture on his eyelashes.

He didn't expect Diego to put his head in his hands and whisper, more to himself than to Charlie, "Damn it. Damn it. I knew this would happen. Damn it ..."

He wasn't crying so much as mumbling to himself as the tears flowed from his eyes.

"Charlie, I'm so sorry. I didn't know, I'm so sorry."

Charlie was dumbfounded. What was he sorry for? He hadn't done anything. It was Julio and his gang who'd threatened him.

"What do you mean, 'sorry'?"

"I got you into this. It's my fault. If I hadn't asked you about being gay, then maybe ..."

"Diego, that's ridiculous. You didn't make me gay or turn me into a homosexual!" Charlie said, hoping it would sound funny, hoping it would make Diego smile.

"I know, I know! But I did rush you into coming out."

"No, you didn't, you ..."

"Yes, I did! I came after you at the farmers market, I invited you to the party, told you I thought you were gay, all because I thought you were cute, and I was lonely and tired of not having a boyfriend, and you just showed up, so nice and handsome, and I wanted you. I wanted you to be my friend, my boyfriend, my, I don't know what. I've been selfish and stupid, thinking that we could just parade around school, showing off in front of everybody."

He stood up. Protruding from the sleeves of his rain jacket, his fists were bunched so tightly that he squeezed all the blood from his hands, turning them nearly as white as Charlie's.

"Diego, no you haven't been! Come on, I wanted to be your friend, I ..."

"That's just it. You wanted to be my friend. I pushed for more, I flirted with you, I manipulated you, I ..."

"You did not!"

"I did too! I knew what I was doing when you came over to my house that first time. I wasn't being nice or friendly. I wanted you to come over to the bed, to take, to take off your clothes, and ..."

A choke stopped his words short. He shook his head and wiped his nose with the back of his hand as he looked out over the creek bed, all the while avoiding Charlie's eyes.

"I wanted you so badly, Charlie," he whispered. "I couldn't stop thinking about you, about kissing you, touching you. I thought this time it could work out, that maybe it wouldn't be just another stupid crush that wouldn't turn into anything, where I'd have to smile and pretend that I wasn't totally in love with somebody yet again."

"Diego, it is working out. I mean, I know it's maybe slower than you want, but …"

Diego spun on him, the hood of his jacket slipping from his head, exposing his dark hair, the wild look on his face lit by the faint afternoon sun.

"Working out?! Are you crazy, Charlie? You call this working out? You basically have to fend me off, and yet I still keep throwing myself at you. And now this? This crap Julio and Dave did to you …"

His voice caught. He gritted his teeth and squeezed his eyes shut.

"If I hadn't started this with you, you'd just be a quiet kid at school who everyone left alone. But no, loudmouth Diego had to pull you into all of his drama, and now …"

Charlie hadn't seen Diego like this before. He knew that beneath his friend's confident demeanor was worry and fear, but he hadn't seen the boy spin out like this, as if he were on an icy slope and, having lost his footing, was slipping and sliding toward a huge crash. Diego wasn't listening to Charlie, didn't hear how stupid he sounded. Charlie couldn't stand how lost and off-base his friend was.

"Shut up! Just shut up!" he yelled, standing up and facing the boy.

Charlie hadn't been sure why he had wanted to tell Diego about the incident beneath the bleachers. He knew it would upset him and hadn't been sure it would be a good idea. Now, with a sudden burst of clarity, he knew why.

"You know what? You are so wrong right now I can't believe it. You not only didn't make me do anything I didn't want to do, you gave me a nice slap in the face and told me to stop hiding, to stop being afraid of everything all of the time. My mom is like that. Worried all the time, scared to do anything, afraid of people and what they might do to her. Afraid of her own shadow. I don't want to be like that anymore, the scared shy kid. I'll never be like you, so talkative and friendly with everybody all the time, but still. I don't want to be scared anymore. I don't have to be."

He took a deep breath. Diego watched him, lips closed, eyes bright, a look of surprise on his face.

"So quit telling me that you made me do anything. I did it, okay? It's what I wanted. I wanted you. You just helped me see it."

Diego lunged for him, throwing his arms around Charlie and taking them both to the ground.

"What are you doing?" Charlie grunted, barely able to talk as most of the wind was knocked out of him.

Diego's mouth found his. And he tried to talk, tried to laugh, even tried to cry as his lips pressed over Charlie's.

Charlie pulled his head back and looked up at the boy, whose face was cast in shadow from the bright gray sky above them, which had started to rain again.

"I can't understand what you're saying. You're ..."

Diego lifted his upper body away from Charlie.

"I said ..."

"Ow! You're crushing me!" Charlie yelled, as the boy's full weight rested on his ribs.

"Oh god, oh god, Charlie, sorry!" Diego said, putting his hands on either side of Charlie to distribute the weight.

"I said ..." the boy continued, looking into Charlie's eyes.

"I said this," he whispered, then bent down and placed his full sweet lips over Charlie's mouth.

It was all Diego needed to say. Charlie could tell that the boy had calmed down, and he was so glad that he forgot for a moment about all the dangerous things happening around him and simply let himself be kissed, let himself want Diego without holding back.

All the while the rain fell lightly on them, and the sun stayed hidden behind the clouds.

CHAPTER 20

Myths and Legends

CHARLIE STEPPED INTO THE FOYER and closed the door behind him. He hung his wet jacket on the coatrack mounted on the wall, then took his boots off and placed them in the corner near the others.

"Hey, buddy," his uncle called from the kitchen. "Wash up and come help me set the table, will you? We're having lamb burgers for dinner."

Charlie set his backpack near the foot of the stairs, washed his hands in the first-floor bathroom, then walked into the kitchen where his uncle was sprinkling spices in a large mixing bowl filled with ground meat. Several buns, fat as hens, sat on a baking sheet. A tossed salad layered with bright vegetables filled a white ceramic bowl.

"This is the way I defy the end of summer," Randall said, smiling at him. "Grilling in the rain!"

Charlie thought about how much he liked his uncle's face. His eyes were nearly always twinkling, except when he was mad and ready to explode. Nothing was hidden from view.

"Your face is like a cocker spaniel," Charlie heard Beverly say once to her husband. "Everything happening on the inside shows up on the outside."

"Are you saying I have to bid adieu to my poker career?" Randall had laughed.

Even though his mouth smiled most of the time, his dark mustache and eyebrows gave his face some weight. Lines that etched across his forehead thickened when he questioned something. Crows feet marked the years of laughter at the corners of his eyes. Slightly larger than normal ears added a boyish look to his overall appearance.

He liked Beverly's face too, though it was different. It was more like a deep river. You could make out what was happening on the surface, but you had no idea what might be churning underneath. Smooth, mostly unlined, Charlie thought that she could be the queen of poker if she wanted to be. He had seen emotions on her face from delight, to hurt, to rage. But mostly she held an inscrutable expression, which at times made him nervous.

"I feel different today," Charlie announced to his uncle.

"You don't look any different," Randall replied, wiggling his hand near his mouth as if he were holding a cigar in a Groucho Marx imitation. Then his smile faded.

"Oh, you're serious. Tell me," he said.

Charlie went over to the cupboard and pulled down three plates, then began opening drawers to gather the silverware and glasses for the dining room table.

"I'm tired of being afraid all the time. I don't want to be afraid anymore."

Randall's hands, which had been mixing the ground lamb meat in the bowl, stopped moving.

"Afraid of …?"

"Afraid of everything. Of saying the wrong thing. Of looking stupid. Of worrying about what other people think. Of liking boys. Of Grace. My mom was always shy and hiding out, afraid of everything. I think she taught me to do that. But maybe that's not really me, you know? I think I just I learned to do it. Like maybe, I was born speaking, uh, Spanish, but she taught me how to speak …"

"Swahili?"

"Yeah, Swahili. And even though I can, it's not my native language. I want to speak Spanish like I'm supposed to."

"That's a pretty amazing realization, Charlie."

He shrugged. "After what happened the other night with Grace,

I started to feel really bad about Joan and Beverly and the others who saved my life. I mean, I felt really guilty."

"I know."

"You knew?"

"Charlie, you started moping around here with a hangdog look on your face. It was obvious. But I also thought it might be about … coming out to us."

"Yeah, it was. But I just got scared too. I mean, I started thinking about what I did and how it hurt others. And how witchcraft got me into trouble. It freaked me out. But then Diego said some stupid stuff today that made me think."

He explained about his conversation with Diego.

As Randall listened, he washed his hands in the sink, wiped them dry, then sat on the edge of the counter.

"It's pretty amazing that you told him that, Charlie. Most people never fess up to all that stuff."

"I'm just tired of hiding all the time, of hoping no one will notice anything. I thought I was good at it. But even Grace knew about Diego. So why bother? Why not just keep up with what's really happening instead of pretending that it's something else? I mean, what I still feel bad about is sneaking out on my own and putting others at risk. But not that stuff about who I am."

Randall paused, then shook his head slowly. "Charlie, you are destined for greatness. Most people never in their whole lives figure out what you just did."

"Well, most people don't have all this creepy stuff happening to them."

"True. I guess if everyone were hunted down by Grace, they'd all admit to having crushes on Diego," he said with a mock stern expression before winking. Then he slid off the counter and walked over to Charlie.

"I'm proud of you, son," he said and wrapped his arms around him.

Charlie used to feel shy when Randall hugged him. But today he let himself enjoy being enveloped in his uncle's strong arms, the smell of Beverly's homemade laundry detergent on his shirt, the way he felt safe and comfortable. Even the way Randall had used the word "son."

But something distracted Charlie. Something Randall had just said ...

He pulled back, breaking the embrace, and looked up at his uncle.

"Why did you say 'if everyone were hunted down by Grace?'" Charlie asked.

"I don't know. What do you mean?"

"Beverly and everybody keep talking about how Grace is kidnapping kids. But you said, 'hunting.'"

"You're right. I did. What's the difference?"

"I don't know. Hunting."

Charlie paused, trying to find the words. "Well, when you hunt something, it's to kill it, right? To kill it and to eat it."

"Yeah. You think Grace is eating kids? Like some fairytale witch?"

"No, not exactly. Well, I don't know. But ... hunting is different from kidnapping, isn't it? Maybe she is hunting them down. Maybe she's ..."

They heard the front door open and Beverly's voice carry down the hallway toward them. "I'm home. Sorry I'm late. Traffic on Aurora was backed up."

She walked into the kitchen, smelling of the outside rain mixed with something floral.

"What's for dinner, honey?" she asked. Then, looking from Randall to Charlie, "What? Did something bad happen?"

"No. Just a chat. And something that can be continued once I get dinner finished."

"Great, I need a shower. Don't say anything interesting until I get back."

Randall walked out onto the back deck to get the grill ready. Charlie set the table in silence, trying to grasp some of the vague ideas floating around inside his head.

"So, what were you two talking about?" Beverly asked as they sat down to eat.

The lamb burgers were delicious. Randall had spiced them with garlic, cilantro, cumin, then added feta cheese. They were thick and meaty.

Charlie and Randall both spoke at once.

"Charlie isn't afraid anymore!"

"What if Grace is hunting kids!"

"Whoa, whoa, slow down."

They explained to her how Charlie didn't want to hide anymore. Beverly listened with growing excitement, and when they finished, she smiled so brightly that Charlie felt a thrill in his stomach.

"Honey, that's just beautiful. Really. Even people twice your age have trouble with that one."

"That's what I told him," added Randall. "Though I think it's safe to say people eleven times his age have trouble with it."

"Now what's this thing about Grace? And hunting?"

Charlie finished chewing, then explained.

"Everyone talks about how Grace is kidnapping kids, but they don't know why. Daniel said the other night that there have been more kids taken than just from this community and that he thinks it's related, but that it's not to use them as bargaining tools."

Beverly interrupted. "He isn't sure, Charlie, though he hasn't thrown out that idea. He's trying to look at this from as many different angles as possible."

"Well, when Randall said the word 'hunting,' I pictured a guy with a gun and a dead deer at his feet. People hunt animals to kill them, right? To eat meat, to use the skin, or whatever."

"What does this have to do with Grace?"

"Well, it's not like a hunter traps an animal to, you know, get at its parents, or the herd."

He paused, looking out at the sunset and the sky growing darker.

"What if Grace and those other witches are using the kids somehow?"

"You mean, like eating them?" Randall asked, incredulity thick in his voice.

"I don't know. Maybe. Or maybe something like that. Is there a way to eat someone? Or some kind of witchcraft where you kill people because it sort of feeds you?"

Beverly's face darkened. "Who told you about that?"

Charlie felt the water in his throat evaporate under her gaze. He thought of how he had compared his aunt and uncle's faces, about how Beverly's could seem so inscrutable. And at other times, deadly serious. Now was one of those times.

"N- … no one, Beverly. Nobody said anything. It was just how Randall talked about hunting. It made me wonder, is all."

Beverly stared at Charlie, her eyes narrowing as if they were lie detectors scanning him for the truth. Finally, she looked away, casting a sideways glance at Randall. Charlie felt like he had just passed a test. Barely. He exhaled.

"You remember when Mavis grabbed you by the arm and sucked energy from you?"

Charlie nodded.

"That's certainly one way. Witches try to do it to each other when engaged in hand-to-hand combat."

Charlie waited. There was something his aunt wasn't saying.

"But that's not what you meant when you said, 'Who told you about that?'"

Beverly looked down at her plate and the unfinished salad. The dressing had blended together with grease from her lamb burger, leaving a small gray pool on the side of her plate.

"No, it isn't."

Randall interjected. "Okay, is this one of those moments where you go into mystery mode and your listening audience is left creeped out?"

"I do not go into mystery mode."

Randall rolled his eyes and looked over at Charlie. "Do you know what I mean about mystery mode?"

"Uh, well, yeah."

Beverly's eyebrows furrowed, until she gave in with a smile. "I do not."

"Oh puhleez!"

"Okay, okay, okay, so I'm a woman of mystery. As I was saying … Charlie, there is so much to talk about. So many things you don't know about yet in the witching world. It's not my intention to keep secrets from you. But sometimes I don't even know where to start. Filling your head with a bunch of history, or even esoteric spells when you're still learning the basics," she said. "That's not a good idea."

Charlie waited.

"Anyway. We witches tend to carry around a lot of fables about our kind. I say 'fables' because most of them are a load of hogwash. One of them concerns a legend where witches of old gained power and strength by killing people. It fits right in with all the demon worship and baby sacrifice myths that are out there about us in the normal world.

"It's a fable because it's never been proven to be true. It's like one of those urban myths. So-and-so said that in Ireland, hundreds of years ago, people did it. Then it changes to the Congo, a thousand years ago. Then Peru, five hundred years ago. Sometimes it's a zombie story. Sometimes it's more like Jack the Ripper.

"Now," she continued, "I wish I could say that the reason these stories are a myth is because no one would be evil enough to try it. But don't forget, witches are humans first and foremost. And some humans will try anything to gain power.

"The reason they're a myth is because it doesn't work. Our historians in Europe have researched cases where witches were tried for committing such crimes using their craft. The accused killed people and attempted to amass power. It never worked. No one has been able to crack the code of using someone else's death as a way to boost their own strength."

"You make it sound like it's a goal or something, honey," said Randall.

"No, what I'm trying to say is that it has been tried throughout history. But it has always failed. Nature is nature, thank God. When something dies, whatever force gives the creature life, goes away. It cannot be harnessed. We don't know where it goes. On that count we're no closer to knowing if there's an afterlife than non-witches.

But we do know that we witches haven't been given the ability to use someone else's life force when they die."

*   *   *

Charlie's mind rushed with thoughts of the day as he lay awake in his room that night: telling Diego to shut up when he continued to apologize, finding the desire in himself to stop being afraid, hearing Beverly's stories about witches killing people to bolster their witchcraft.

There had to be a reason why Grace and the other witches were kidnapping young kids. Or hunting them down. What had she said to him? That there were other things she wanted to tell Charlie, things that Beverly and the others were hiding. He had no illusion that Grace had his best interests at heart or that she even wanted to help him.

But he did believe that she knew things, that she held the key to certain secrets. And maybe there was a way to find out what those secrets were.

CHAPTER 21

Something Like Normal

SEPTEMBER CAME TO AN END, and Charlie dove into his witchcraft studies with fervor. Part of not hiding out anymore meant studying as many aspects of the craft as he could. He had temporarily lost his drive to embrace witchcraft after his solo ride caused so much trouble. But one of the side effects of his talk with Diego was the realization that he couldn't hide from Grace anymore. And that meant he knew she would probably come for him eventually, or at least come for someone else in the community whom he would want to protect. He needed to be well-prepared and well-armed.

So every afternoon when he came home from school, he diligently finished all of his homework. Some days he spent an hour or two with Diego. But he always made sure that he had at least a few good hours in the evening for expanding his craft.

He spent some of those evenings with Beverly, down in her workshop. She introduced him to the uses of plants and herbs, how to make a simple magical object so that it would hold a spell and how to deepen his concentration.

Some evenings were spent with other adult witches. Rose and Sean took him out at night, which came much earlier now that it was October, showing him the finer skills of broomstick riding in the dark. Charlie could barely remember what it felt like to be as wobbly as he had been on that first day in Malcolm's field. The broom had become second nature to him.

Rita Jostich and Daniel Burman worked with Charlie to develop skills in hand-to-hand combat. This was completely daunting at first. He didn't know enough spells to actually do anything if someone attacked him.

"All I can do is make a Ping-Pong ball float around!" he complained.

But they showed him that a lot of fighting was about keeping a cool head and staying resourceful. They built on what he had learned in his broom-riding lessons, showing him how to mount the stick and still keep his hands free for attack. They taught him how to fight with bewitched knives, how to blast beams of light that were stronger than hitting someone with your fists, and how to surround himself with a protective glow.

"Because the best offense is a good defense," said Daniel, feinting a jab at him as they circled each other in Rita's basement one day after school.

"Isn't it supposed to be the other way around?" asked Charlie.

"Not for you it isn't," Daniel answered, his intense gaze cutting off any retorts from him. "Don't ever forget that in a fight."

Is he really gay? Charlie wondered for the hundredth time. *Does he have a boyfriend? When did he first tell someone? Does he …?*

Pow! Charlie felt a sharp stab of pain in his shoulder, and he found himself lying on his back on the hardwood floor.

"Don't lose focus," Daniel admonished, standing over him.

There were so many things to learn. On the one hand, Charlie was extremely excited by how much he was accomplishing. On the other hand, he felt overwhelmed because of how little he actually knew. Things that had seemed impossible at Malcolm's cabin now seemed easy. Yet he still felt like a kindergartner compared with his adult teachers.

"I've been doing this for years, Charlie. Give yourself a break," Beverly liked to say to him.

"Yeah, I know, it sucks. Just keep going," Jeremy Lostich said one rainy afternoon when Charlie was having trouble mastering a tracking spell.

"Are you going to let that stop you?" Daniel asked one night as he pinned Charlie to the ceiling with a wispy cloud of smoke vaguely resembling a large hand. "Grace could be here any day. You need to be ready."

Charlie went to bed so tired every night that he didn't even remember turning off his bedside lamp. His muscles were constantly sore from either fighting or hunching over scrying bowls and miniature cauldrons every day, not to mention all the late-night flights on his broomstick. "You get used to it. Like Lance Armstrong," Joan said one evening. Charlie had trouble believing her.

Charlie was finishing his schoolwork on time. It had become a game for him; he would crack his books as soon as he got home and race to finish everything before dinner, knowing that if he did he would have more time to learn witchcraft. However, being in school was another issue altogether.

"You look tired," Diego said more than once as Charlie wandered down B-wing, momentarily forgetting where his next class was.

"Stay awake, Mr. Creevey," his sophomore English teacher said while tapping him on the shoulder. They were reading *The Haunting of Hill House* by Shirley Jackson. All of his classmates were glued to Jackson's prose and the terrifying ghost story. Charlie had been fighting to keep his head from dropping.

"Tongxue," Chen Laoshi said to him one morning as the other students were leaving the classroom. *"Ni de gongke zuo de bu hao."* Charlie stared at her, knowing that she was saying that something wasn't good but having no idea what the subject of the sentence was.

"Shenme?"

"Charlie, you don't say *'Shenme?'* when responding respectfully if you don't understand something. You say, *"Qing zai shuo yici."*

"Qing cai zuo yizi," he mumbled.

"Budui," she said, correcting him. *"Qing zai shuo yici."*

"Qing zai shuo yici."

"Hao. Ni de gongke." She held up a piece of paper showing the Chinese characters that Charlie had handed in for homework the day

before. Half of the page was covered in red ink corrections. *"Zuo de bu hao."*

"Oh, *duibuqi Chen Laoshi, wo … wo …"*

Chen Laoshi stood up and looked over at the doorway, cast her glance around the classroom, and then spoke in a lowered voice.

"Charlie, I know you are studying other things late at night. And I understand that you are under tremendous pressure to learn as much as you can before the next attack."

Charlie winced at her words. A part of him still hoped that the next attack might not happen. He knew it was a ridiculous thought, but he couldn't help himself. When he heard the adults talk about it, it wasn't a matter of if, but a matter of when. And when seemed to be swiftly approaching, at least in their eyes.

"But you must keep up with your schoolwork and your attendance here at Puget Academy." Chen Laoshi continued. "If you don't already know this, we have the double burden of maintaining both sides of our lives, the public side and the community side, which of course must remain private. Do not let your public life suffer, Charlie, or it will cast aspersions not just on you, but on all of us."

He didn't know what "casting aspersions" meant, but he figured it must be something bad.

As Charlie nodded and turned to go, Chen Laoshi took him by the arm.

"I know it's hard work, Charlie. Hang in there." Then she winked at him. It was very uncharacteristic for her to break her formality and do something like that. He felt kindness from her, and understanding. Her gesture emboldened him, and he took her words to heart, more determined than ever to do his best to maintain his school life and his witch life.

CHAPTER 22

Right as Rain

ON A SATURDAY IN MID-OCTOBER, Charlie awoke late and lay in bed trying to decide how to use the day to catch up on everything, when he heard a knock on his door.

"Come in," he said, his voice still groggy.

"Hey, bud." Randall opened the door halfway and peeked his head in. "I asked Beverly if I could kidnap you for part of the day today. She told me I shouldn't use that word, since it's a little 'sensitive,'" he smiled, adding his ubiquitous air quotes.

Charlie smiled back. His uncle's enthusiasm, as well as the way he teased his wife, was infectious.

"To do what?" he asked, yawning and stretching.

"Well, if Diego's free, I thought I'd take you two over to the East-side. There's a place over there that looks really fun. I don't want to tell you what it is, but I will say you'll need to wear something comfortable. Like gym clothes. What do you say?"

*   *   *

Diego rode up front with Randall. Charlie listened to the two of them chatting away like old friends. He enjoyed their banter. It was a nice distraction from the worry that he wouldn't get enough done today.

"I know, right? And then she's all 'whatever,' and then he was all like, 'whatever.'"

Randall laughed. "Yeah. But I still like the show."

"Okay, me too. I think it's rotting my brain, but I can't help watching it."

"Have you seen the trailer for that new reality show where they make some bozo millionaire live in a poor rural area like a local, and then at the end it's revealed that the people have a millionaire living among them?"

"Totally!" cried Diego. "And then the rich guy cries, and everybody cries, and he donates all this money to the town to like build a library or something?"

"My thoughts? Cheesy."

"Cheesatoidinal!"

"But I'm still going to watch it."

"Me too! I'm gonna record the whole series!"

Diego looked in the back seat. "You're kinda quiet back there, Charlie. Even quieter than normal."

"I'm just enjoying you two gossiping about every TV show ever made."

"Charlie!" Randall gasped, pretending to take offense. "It's not gossip. It's artistic critique."

"That's right," Diego chimed in. "We are refined minds here, speaking of refined things."

"Oh, you mean like who sleeps with who on *Bachelorettes Gone Bad?*

Randall exited off the main road and pulled into the parking lot of what looked like a large business park.

"Where are we going, anyway?" asked Diego.

"I thought you two boys might like ..."

"No way!" yelled Diego. "I've wanted to come here for like ever!"

The place was a huge gymnasium-like structure filled with trampolines. After paying an entrance fee, they were given a short tour of the facilities. There was an open floor with segments of six-foot-by-six-foot trampolines, bordered on all sides by padded dividers. As the guide explained how things worked, they watched little kids running and jumping from square to square, as older kids did flips, and even ran up the sides of the padded walls.

In another section, two large trampolines were split down the middle and separated by a long strip of hanging mesh. Teams on either side threw balls at each other while trying not to fall as they bounced around. The kids here were older, and even though they tried to be serious, most couldn't help laughing at their failed attempts to stay upright.

"Dodge ball, trampoline style," said the guide.

"Awesome!" Charlie, Diego, and Randall replied in unison.

The last section had five long runs of trampolines, running parallel to each other, which ended in a pit filled with huge pieces of foam. People were throwing themselves off the end and flipping into the pit with varying degrees of klutziness and skill.

Diego started jumping around on the floor. "Can we, can we, can we?"

The three of them put their wallets and cell phones in a locker before walking over to the open floor filled with the trampoline squares.

"I haven't been on one of these in a long time," Randall said. He took a few small jumps, smiled at the boys, and then performed a perfect back flip.

"Whoa! Dude! Where did you learn how to do that?" Diego exclaimed.

"I was a diver in high school. Sometimes we trained on trampolines instead of at the pool." He gave them a mischievous grin. "Beverly made me promise I wouldn't do anything too wild."

The boys joined him, and soon they were bouncing, dodging kids, shouting to each other, and laughing.

Charlie enjoyed the weightless feeling at the apex of each jump. It wasn't like flying on a broomstick, but he imagined he felt more comfortable this high off the ground than he would have before he learned how to ride. He remembered Beverly telling him that some witches don't use brooms, that they had the inherent ability to fly through the air on their own. Knowing how hard he had to work to master even the simplest of witchcraft skills, the idea of learning how to fly without a broom made his head hurt.

Just then, Diego did a spinning twist in midair and bumped into Charlie, knocking them both down.

The boys fell back on the trampoline floor and began giggling, unable to regain their footing. Randall tried to jump onto their square right at the exact moment a young girl in pigtails and pink barrettes ran past him. He let out a yelp, spread his legs to let the girl pass underneath him, then sailed over the square and crashed into the padded wall nearby.

This sent the three of them into such guffaws of laughter that one of the young employees, dressed in a baggy polo shirt uniform, cheeks bright with acne, came over to tell them that they had to either keep jumping or leave the floor.

After recovering from laughing so hard, they tried their hand at the dodge ball game. Randall and Charlie were both fierce throwers and very competitive. Diego didn't like it as much. "I can't throw very hard," he complained, sitting out.

"I'll help you if you want!" Randall yelled as he bounced up into the air. Just then a ball launched by Charlie hit him hard in the gut. "Oomph!" he grunted in midair.

They moved over to the third area with the foam pit. Charlie jumped on the three successive trampoline squares then flung himself high before landing on the soft wedges of foam. He was surprised how difficult it was to pull himself out of the pit. The softness of the wedges was perfect for a safe landing, but gave no support when climbing out.

"This is hard!" he yelled to the other two as he tried to reach for solid ground.

Diego leaped into the air when it was his turn, swiveled his hips so that he could grab both of his feet with his right hand, then disappeared into the waiting foam pit. He had his own challenge climbing out.

"What are you going to do?" Charlie asked Randall, as his uncle stepped up to the trampoline.

"A double," he said, giving him a wink.

One bounce, two bounces, three bounces, and then he soared straight up, tucked into a somersault, spun around twice, and landed feet first on the soft wedges.

"Oh my god! Oh my god! Your uncle is amazing!" Diego yelled.

Although jumping into the pit was great fun, all three were exhausted by the time they could finally climb out. They were only able to complete a few more rounds of jumps before they found themselves standing off to the side, bent over with their hands on their knees, trying to catch their breath.

"Okay, guys, I'm hungry," Randall said, panting. "One more jump for me, and then let's say we get something to eat."

They watched as he launched himself into the air, spun around two and a half times, then landed hands first as if he were diving into a pool.

"Shit!" they heard him yell as he climbed up to a kneeling position on one of the foam wedges. He stayed there for quite some time, not moving, only holding up his left hand and looking at it.

"Sir, you all right?" asked one of the employees.

* * *

They sat in the first aid room as the facilities manager applied ice to Randall's wrist.

"Sir, I'm pretty sure it's broken," he said. "I mean, there's a bone nearly sticking out."

Randall laughed once before shaking his head. "Your aunt is going to kill me. Anyway, glad I'm right-handed." In spite of his attempt to be funny, the skin around his eyes and forehead had turned pale, and he was sweating.

They decided that Diego would drive them to the emergency room. Once Randall had been seen by a doctor, they would call Beverly. Not before.

* * *

The boys sat under the bright lights of the waiting area, worrying about Randall, while the physician's assistant put a cast on his broken wrist in the examining room.

He had been right. Beverly was furious.

"I told him not to show off!" she had yelled when Charlie called her. He had to pull the phone away from his ear. After much discussion, Beverly finally agreed not to come all the way over to the Eastside hospital. Diego would drive them home.

A young orderly came out of one of the storage closets pushing a cart of supplies. She glanced at Charlie, stopped her cart, then looked at him again before moving on.

"That chick was totally cruising you!" exclaimed Diego.

"What does that mean?"

"You don't know what 'cruising' means? It means she was checking you out. She thinks you're hot."

"Na-ah."

"Uh-huh!"

Diego punched him in the shoulder. Charlie tried to laugh it off, but something about the way the orderly had stared at him seemed strange.

After the physician's assistant finished with the cast, Randall signed a stack of paperwork, making more right-handed jokes. Diego went to get the car, and Charlie waited near the nurse's station.

"I have a message for you," a voice said behind him.

He spun on his heels only to find the same orderly staring at him from less than a foot away. She was bird-thin and quite short, and her eyes were caked with blue makeup. She looked to be about twenty years old.

"Can I show you?" she asked, gesturing to a patient room.

He turned and walked across the hallway after her.

Don't go in that room! a voice inside his head screamed. Ignoring it, he followed her through the doorway.

Once inside the room, she closed the door. Her mouth lit into a strange smile, exposing tiny plastic-looking green braces on her teeth. Charlie looked around. The two hospital beds were empty.

There were machines plugged into the wall, and an IV stand stood in the corner. On the far wall, a window was open and the blinds swung in the afternoon breeze, repeatedly hitting the window frame.

Slap. Slap. Slap.

"Grace said to say hi," the orderly whispered. Then she threw herself at Charlie.

Before he could react to her attack, her bare fingers grasped his forearms and began to squeeze. She hissed her hot breath on him, and immediately he felt disoriented. He had the sense that he was falling even though he was leaning back against the closed door. Darkness began to seep in around his eyes, and he thought he was going to pass out.

"Defend yourself!" he heard Daniel Burman's voice shouting in his head.

Another voice answered, prim and reprimanding. *You're not supposed to hit girls.*

He knew he should do something, but dizziness covered him as if someone had thrown a thick blanket over his head. He couldn't think clearly.

The woman inhaled, preparing to breathe on him again.

"Now!" Rita Lostich screamed at him.

The Words came from nowhere, finding his mouth, moving his lips. He bared his teeth and shoved forward with all his might. Light from his hands flashed up into the orderly's face, and her head jerked back as if she had been punched in the chin.

Her grip on his arms, however, remained vice-like. She fell backward and pulled Charlie on top of her. He could not free his hands. As they tumbled to the floor, the woman opened her mouth and lunged at his face, trying to block his Words. Without thinking, he jerked his head to the side and pulled back. Her teeth, snapping at his neck, missed their mark and instead sank into Charlie's right shoulder, biting through the cotton of his sweatshirt right down into his flesh. Her head shook and she made grunting noises as she tore at his skin.

Nausea and blackness. The pain was all-encompassing, as if it were a sound blasting through his ears, rendering him helpless. He opened his mouth and made a gargled screaming noise, which quickly faded as his remaining strength disappeared.

He knew that if he didn't do something soon, she was going to kill him, this stupid, skinny orderly in an empty hospital room while his uncle waited for him out in the hallway. But the paralyzing effect of her spell, combined with the horrific pain of her teeth clamping onto and tearing at his shoulder, overpowered everything.

He tried to let the Words find him again, tried to concentrate the way Beverly had shown him. But the orderly's grotesque biting, her grunts, her fingers draining his energy from him, the pain and shock blasting through his body, all of it rendered him helpless.

Then the door to the hospital room opened.

The orderly jerked her head away from his shoulder.

"Charlie, what are you …?" he heard Randall say behind his back as the man stepped into the doorway.

The orderly released her grip on Charlie's forearms, slid out from underneath him, and shot four feet into the air, her body twisting and coiling like a rope tossed from a boat. She flung herself at Randall, who stood with his eyes wide open and mouth agape, unmoving, his left arm with its blue cast hanging at his side.

The nanosecond her fingers released Charlie's arms, his mind cleared. Words found his mouth, and he felt a surge of white heat course through his body as his arms extended outwards from where he lay on the floor.

Just before the orderly's outstretched fingers could grab Randall, the IV stand from the corner lurched forward and struck her in the hip, stopping her trajectory and sending her spinning into the far wall.

Charlie hopped to his feet and reached for Randall, pulling him inside the room and shutting the door.

The orderly's body rebounded off the wall and shot headfirst toward Charlie's chest.

More Words. Her body rose above their heads just before her shoes could crack into Randall's skull. She was thrown against the opposite wall, toppling one of the bedside machines with a loud crash.

"What the ..." Charlie heard Randall exclaim from behind him.

The orderly tried to stand, but her legs wouldn't function. A gash above her right eye bled, sending a thin red line down her cheek.

Surgical tape from a nurse's tray sped through the air as Charlie's lips continued to move. It made a loud ripping sound. In seconds, several lengths of the tape wrapped themselves around the woman's hands, then bound her feet.

She screamed at him. "You bastard! We will eat you alive!"

More ripping, and the tape stuck itself in crude loops around her mouth, pinning her limp hair to the back of her head.

Charlie remembered something Rita had taught him. "It's a good way to render someone helpless without hurting them," she had said.

The orderly's voice now muffled by the tape, Charlie walked over to her and touched her pink-soled shoe the way Rita had taught him. Her body jerked once, then she sighed through her nostrils and fell unconscious against the bed.

"Charlie!" Randall said, his voice loud. Charlie turned to see him leaning against the doorframe, staring in disbelief.

"Quiet!" He shushed his uncle. "We're leaving. Stay close to me as we walk down the hall. Don't say anything to anybody."

"But ... but ... where's Diego?"

"He went to get the car. Follow me and don't say a word!"

Charlie pulled his uncle behind him, opened the door, and looked out. He briefly wondered if Randall would protest Charlie taking charge, but then tossed the thought aside. Three nurses sat at their station, chatting and reading charts. They did not look over at the doorway. It appeared that no one had heard the crashes inside the room.

Charlie reached behind him and grabbed onto Randall's good arm, pulling him swiftly from the room and its odor of musty wood. They walked down the hallway in the opposite direction of the nurses' station.

Avoiding the elevators, the pair snuck through a door marked "exit" and walked down the back staircase, the squeaky sound of their sneakers echoing off the walls. The smell of fresh paint in the stairwell nearly made Charlie gag. It seemed like the flights of stairs would never end. Step after interminable step, his senses buzzed on high alert for any sound or movement ahead of or behind them. Charlie was sure that at any minute a group of witches would jump from around the corner, teeth bared, biting and tearing into Randall's and his shoulders until they were reduced to bloody corpses on the floor. It took all his willpower not to run screaming down the stairs and out of the hospital.

But Randall's heavy breathing behind him helped him to focus and reminded him of his main responsibility: to get his uncle safely out of the building, to make sure Diego was all right, then to get the three of them in the car and back to West Seattle as quickly as possible.

The relief he felt when they stepped outside into the gray afternoon light was so great that he gasped.

He pulled Randall forward until they were walking side by side.

"Just keep moving. Look normal. Stay by my side and we'll find Diego," Charlie muttered to his uncle, who nodded.

They walked along a cement path that led through a small garden and then rounded a corner to the emergency entrance.

Diego leaned against Randall's parked car, tapping his foot and looking up at the hospital's upper floors. One of his arms was crossed over his chest, while the thumb of his free hand pressed keys on his mobile phone. He appeared to be completely safe.

More relief. A part of him wanted to run to the boy and throw his arms around him. But he knew he couldn't arouse any suspicions, and so far in their relationship, Charlie had never run to Diego and begged for a hug like a frightened child. It would definitely look strange. Instead, he scrunched up the shoulder of his sweatshirt to hide the hole that the orderly had made and walked to the car.

"What took you guys so long? I've been texting you. Why are you coming out the side door?"

"Oh, uh, Randall had a strange reaction to the medicine," Charlie said. "It made him start groaning and shaking."

He looked at his uncle, who was staring straight back at him. Charlie nudged him in the side.

Randall's face, which looked shell shocked, softened. He made a semi-convincing groaning sound, then moved his shoulders in a way that Charlie supposed could have looked like a shudder.

Diego bought it hook, line, and sinker. "Oh my god! What are you doing outside the hospital? Shouldn't a doctor be looking at you?"

"No, it's all right," Randall said. His voice was actually shaking for real this time, adding authenticity to the charade. "They, uh, told me to go home and …"

"And rest. They told him to go home and rest," Charlie continued. "They said it's normal, and he'll be, uh … ."

"Right as rain," Randall finished.

Diego drove them home, mostly in silence, though he told a few family stories of uncles or cousins who had broken arms and legs while working on the farm in Yakima. "You should be fine," Diego said at the end of each story, as if the fact that his own family members had survived meant a sure recovery for Randall.

"Yeah, should be just fine." Randall's face clouded as he watched the trees going by.

CHAPTER 23

Another Dream

THE PAIN IN CHARLIE'S SHOULDER lessened as Beverly fed him a hot broth and rubbed his skin with a pale-colored unguent. "She did break through the skin, but there's no bone showing, and I don't think she tore any muscle. This stuff will stave off infection, as well as rabies. You should be okay," she said, peering closely at his bare chest.

Charlie was relieved. It felt like the orderly had ripped his shoulder to shreds. Beverly placed her hands on the sides of his head and shut her eyes.

"Other than draining you some, she didn't leave a trace of anything in you. This broth will help you regain your strength and take away most of the pain."

In a way, Randall was lucky. The attack on Charlie diverted Beverly's attention to her nephew. She seemed to have momentarily forgotten about her husband's antics and how they resulted in a broken bone. All she did when they arrived home was give him a quick look, touch his arm with her hands, then nod.

"The doctors did a good job," she said to her husband, her tone icy, before turning her back on him and ministering to Charlie's injury.

When Charlie finished his soup and put his shirt back on, the three of them talked about what happened at the hospital. Beverly was most concerned with how the orderly flew through the air, bouncing off walls without seeming to be injured.

"It's not like witches have indestructible bones," she said, glancing at Randall's wrist with narrowed eyes. "We're just like you in that regard."

"But I thought you told me certain witches could fly," said Charlie. "Why does this surprise you, then?"

"Because witches like that are quite powerful in their own right. They tend to live clustered together, or far away from most humans. Their abilities far surpass just being able to fly. They wouldn't be working in a minimum-wage job at a hospital.

"Besides," she continued, glancing at Charlie's shoulder, "if she really were that powerful, you would have been no match for her."

"So she must be one of the echoes in Grace's network," Randall said.

"That's what I think too. And," his aunt took a breath and turned to her husband, "if you hadn't broken your damned wrist, you wouldn't have put the boys and yourself in harm's way!"

They began to argue, which Charlie took as a cue to go upstairs and lie down on his bed. He was tired from the afternoon's activities, in more ways than one. His eyelids felt heavy.

He had had his first real fight with someone. It was terrifying. But he had to admit that it was exciting too. He wish he had been faster when she lunged at him but was glad to know the reason his reactions were slow was because she had drained him, not because he choked in fear. He could still feel how his instincts kicked in once she let go of his arms and stopped the drain. All that training he had been doing in the last month had paid off.

Beverly thanked him profusely for saving Randall's life and for fighting so well. Her praise was tempered by her concern for any injuries he might have sustained. But it was good to hear. He couldn't wait to tell Rita and Daniel how he fought the witch and eventually subdued her, and how their voices were in his head, helping him. Well, he would tell Rita anyway. He could imagine her giving him high fives and making the "Woot! Woot!" noises she did to encourage him. Daniel, on the other hand, would probably just stare him down before saying, "You were lucky. Next time there might be five attackers. What will you do then?"

He yawned and stretched out on his bed, letting his eyes close.

In the dream, he stood in the doorway looking in at his first-grade classroom back in Clarkston. His uncle Randall was the teacher, though his face kept changing, turning into Mailman Bob who used to deliver to their house when Charlie was little. Bob used to slip Charlie a candy or two from his pocket whenever his mom wasn't looking.

Randall/Mailman Bob walked over to him and invited him into the classroom.

"But the desks are too small," Charlie said.

"No, they aren't. See for yourself."

Charlie poked his head inside and saw many adults from the witch community sitting at full-sized desks, taking notes and looking very serious. But somehow Charlie knew it wouldn't work for him.

"Don't be so shy," said Randall/Mailman Bob, handing him a green apple candy.

"I'm not shy anymore," Charlie answered, popping the candy in his mouth and stepping into the classroom. As the sweetness spread out along his tongue, he moved to an empty desk in the back. When he looked down at his feet he saw that he was wearing roller skates.

"It's a good way to get around school," said Diego, who was sitting in a desk to his right. He wore nothing except for a pair of white underpants. Charlie wanted to tell him to put his clothes on, but the candy had stuck to his tongue, preventing him from opening his mouth.

He tried to sit down but, just as he had feared, the desk was too small. His knees wouldn't fit under the table. He ended up sitting atop the desk with his legs hanging over the side.

When he looked up, he saw that all the other students in the classroom, except for Diego, had become little kids. They were taking a test.

"Keep your eyes on your own paper, only answer questions in Sections Three and Four, and whatever you do, no witchcraft," said the teacher from the front of the room.

The teacher was now the orderly from the hospital, her braces gleaming bright green under the fluorescent lights. Randall/Mailman Bob was nowhere to be seen. The orderly walked up and down the aisles, watching the children as they filled in little circles on their exam papers with number two pencils. Occasionally she would bend over and bite one of the kids on the shoulder, causing them to burst and then deflate like a popped water balloon. Each time a kid exploded, all the other children would laugh and point at the pile of wet, deflated skin on the floor.

Horrified, Charlie wanted to do something, to somehow protect the kids, but the sticky candy prevented him from opening his mouth to find any Words. Furthermore, he found that he had sunk down into the seat of the desk and had become completely entangled. He couldn't move his arms or his legs, and the roller skates on his feet kept sliding out from under him each time he tried to stand up. He wiggled back and forth, trying to break free.

Hearing a noise to his right, he looked over and saw the orderly with her mouth locked on Diego's. They were kissing. Charlie could see their tongues going in and out of each other's mouths. Diego pulled his head back and looked at him.

"I'm not gay anymore," he whispered to Charlie, just as the orderly sank her teeth into Diego's shoulder. Charlie watched in terror as he burst in an explosion of water. His skin shrank and slithered to the floor like a wet plastic bag.

"Now we can talk," the orderly said to him.

Charlie bolted upright in bed. He looked around for the biting witch, but he saw only his bedroom. As the details of the dream began to fade, he tried to hold on to them. He had seen something, or nearly seen something. Something important. It was like the dream he had had about the kids on the truck being chased by the German shepherds. Something was going to happen, but he didn't know what.

"Ding-dong," rang the front door. He heard voices in the hallway downstairs.

CHAPTER 24

Saturday Night

"WHAT I DON'T UNDERSTAND IS where the hell you've been!" Beverly was saying as Charlie stood inside his bedroom doorway and listened to the voices in the foyer. He wondered who she was talking to.

"Beverly, I'm sorry, but there isn't time for this. There's been another break-in, at the …"

Charlie recognized the deep voice right away. It was Malcolm!

"I don't care! I want some answers before you start ordering me and everyone else around! And why does your voice sound so strange?"

"Look, Bev, I really am sorry. There has been a lot of popping to do lately. More than ever before. I haven't even been able to get to Asia or Europe. It's all been the States and Canada. Maybe my voice sounds strange because I'm so tired."

"But why haven't you called? Or answered my texts? I've been covering for you, Malcolm. You left me alone here to defend you and run things all by myself!"

"You're the real leader here, Beverly. You don't need me to …"

"Do not patronize me!"

Charlie jumped as a pine branch slapped at the side of the house and raindrops pelted the window above the front door. He wasn't sure if it was the mounting weather or Beverly's anger that caused the noises.

"I've got a husband in bed upstairs, drugged out on painkillers, and a nephew who was attacked today ..."

"He handled himself fine from what I hear."

"Attacked today," Beverly continued, ignoring Malcolm's words, "by a hospital orderly. These break-ins are happening more and more and ..."

"Beverly!" Malcolm's voice barked, ringing with authority. "I'm cutting you off. I'm sorry, but listen to me. We do not have time for this. Someone or someones broke in to the Mossmans' house tonight. You're going to have to go over there and investigate with Daniel. They didn't get anything, but it just happened, and there's fresh evidence."

"Why aren't you going over there?"

"Because! As you so clearly pointed out, I haven't been around to help. The community is going to get all worked up about me being absent and demand answers. We need to act fast to get evidence. I'll do damage control later. Plus, you and Daniel have been following all of this, and you know the wards and protections that are up now much better than I do. You'll be able to figure out how they got in to such a well-fortified home. I'll stay here and watch over Charlie and Randall."

"What? But what if someone tries to ..."

"I'll call you, I'll call Jeremy and Rita, I'll bring in reinforcements. Now come on, get going. We're losing precious time."

Charlie held his breath, listening for his aunt's response. At first, he heard nothing. Then there was a quiet muffled sound, like an animal whimpering.

"I know, I know, honey. You've been under a helluva lot of pressure lately," said Malcolm, his voice tender. "I'm sorry. I really am. I've been an ass. I promise when this is all over you can call me every name in the book. I'll make it up to you, really I will. But you gotta get going."

"All right. Let me talk to Charlie first. He's heard all of this anyway," replied Beverly, her voice shaky.

Charlie stepped back into his room and closed the door, embarrassed to have been caught spying on their conversation.

He walked into his bathroom and began to brush his teeth. Another branch slapped against the house, this time over his own window. Amos, who had been curled up asleep in the corner of Charlie's room, got to his feet and hopped onto Charlie's bed.

There was a soft knock on his door. Charlie spit into the sink.

"Come in," he said over his shoulder.

His aunt walked into the bedroom. Amos hopped down from the bed and pressed into her legs.

"That's a good boy," she said, rubbing his fur.

"Honey, I know you heard the conversation below."

"Sorry, I, uh, I didn't mean to …"

Beverly smiled at him, her teeth reflecting the light cast from Charlie's bedside lamp.

"Don't worry about it. Listen, I'm gonna head out soon. I've got to meet Daniel at the Mossmans'."

"Was anyone kidnapped?"

"No. They broke into Ginny's bedroom, but she's fine. She's not popped yet. Her parents, however, are not fine. They're really scared and angry. We'll go over to investigate but also to reassure Mr. and Mrs. Mossman that we're doing all we can. Malcolm'll stay here to watch over things. It'll be better that way. The community is mad at him, so I think it's better if he keeps a low profile for the time being."

"Are you mad at him?"

Beverly paused, looking down at the floor before answering. "Yes. No. Sort of. But he looks terrible, like he hasn't slept in days, so I guess it's hard to stay mad at him. He's back, I've got this thing to do, and when it's all over Malcolm and I can duke it out."

"Can I come with you?"

"No. Stay here. You'll be safer here."

"It's not that. I want to see …"

"No. Look, you were very brave today. You saved your uncle's life. But Daniel and I need to do a bit of public relations with the Mossmans, not just police work. If not, the community might stage an uprising. It'll be easier if it's just the two of us."

Charlie sighed, then nodded his head. "Okay."

"Malcolm said he has some phone calls to make. He'll be down-stairs. We won't be long. Two hours tops, okay?"

He nodded again.

Beverly looked like she was going to say something else, then changed her mind.

"Get some sleep. You need to rest up after today."

She turned and walked out into the hallway, closing the door behind her.

Charlie sat down on his bed, then gave Amos a good head-scratch-ing before turning off the bedside lamp and lying back against his headboard. Even though he had taken a nap earlier, he doubted he would have trouble falling asleep.

He watched the shadows of tree limbs scurry across the carpet, just like the tiny crabs at the bottom of the tide pools at Lincoln Park.

He wanted to remember what seemed like an important element from his dream earlier. Something about Mailman Bob? Diego in his underwear? The orderly? What had it been? He was sure that it was an important detail, but it danced just beyond the limits of his memory.

*   *   *

"Hey, kid," a voice whispered. Charlie jerked awake, wincing at the crick in his neck from where he had fallen asleep against his head-board. Light from the hallway shone in his eyes, making it difficult at first to make out the shadowy figure standing halfway in his bedroom.

"Malcolm! Hi. You scared me," Charlie said, wiping at the stream of saliva hanging from his chin.

"Sorry, kid. I was trying to be quiet. I didn't want to wake Randall."

"That's okay. It's, uh, it's good to see you."

"You too. Sorry I've been gone so much."

Charlie shrugged his shoulders, still not used to adults apologiz-ing to him.

"There was another break-in? At the Mossmans?"

"We think so," said the man, walking over and sitting down on the side of Charlie's bed. Light from the streetlamp near the side-walk outside illuminated half of Malcolm's face. Raindrops dripping down the windowpane cast squiggly lines of shadow running over his left shoulder and across his collared shirt. Charlie's vision was still too blurry from sleep to find evidence of the fatigue Beverly had mentioned.

"You aren't sure?"

"Well, Daniel said that, even though someone got through the wards at the house, no one was attacked. He wasn't sure if it was a bungled kidnapping attempt or if they were looking for something."

His voice trailed off, and he sighed, looking down at the floor. "But we all do what we can, right?"

"Right," Charlie said, not sure what Malcolm meant.

"I mean, we all do the best we can with what we've been given," Malcolm continued, leaning in closer to Charlie. He had the sudden impression that the man was going to tell him a secret. Instead, he turned his head and said, "Come here, Amos."

Charlie heard the dog's paws pad across the carpet. The mattress sank as Amos put his forelegs up on the bed.

"Atta boy," Malcolm said, rubbing the dog's back. "Atta boy." Amos's tail wagged as he rested his large head on the man's leg.

Charlie watched as something seemed to pass over Malcolm's face, the way the shadow of a cloud passes over the land below. Charlie's nerves prickled on sudden alert, and a cascade of tingles showered down the back of his neck.

Malcolm blew out his breath, gritted his teeth, and made a jerking motion with his arms. Amos yelped once, then fell silent. The front half of the dog's body slumped onto the floor and began to twitch and shake as if inflicted with St. Vitus's Dance.

"What are you …?"

Malcolm's hands clamped down on Charlie's mouth before he could say anything more, and he felt something sticky cover his lips. Then the man pressed his knee against Charlie's chest, pinning him down on the mattress. Charlie reached up to try to push Malcolm's knee away. He heard a tearing sound. Before he could do anything else, Malcolm grabbed Charlie's hands and bound them in the same tape he must have used on his mouth.

Malcolm stared down at Charlie as if from a great distance, as if Charlie were nothing more than a piece of lint down on the carpet near his feet.

Charlie's mind spun with panicky questions. What was happening? What was Malcolm doing? What had he done to Amos?

He wriggled on the bed, trying to kick himself free. But Malcolm leaned over him, pinning Charlie to the bed. He then turned to the window and mumbled several Words. A loud pop sounded in the air, accompanied by a flare of white as brief and sudden as a camera flash. The windowpane opened by itself. A sleek black shape slunk into his bedroom, followed by another.

Charlie recognized the woman with the tightly wound black curls as the one who had broken in several weeks ago. Her jade green eyes glowed in the half-light. She smiled at him.

"No!" he tried to yell, but the tape at his mouth muffled the noise, diffusing it to a low grunt.

The other shape, much lower to the ground, came closer to his bed. Charlie could make out pointed ears, then the unmistakable muzzle of a large German shepherd. And not just any shepherd. Charlie would have recognized the steely glare of the eyes anywhere. It was the same dog who broke into their house in Clarkston. It stared at him, as if daring him to speak through the tape.

Charlie attempted a scream, then strained underneath Malcolm's weight, trying to scramble to the far side of the bed.

Unable to do anything, his mind ran with more thoughts. Why would Malcolm let that woman into his bedroom? Doesn't she work for Grace? And why the dog? Why would he …?

"Hello, boy," a voice said near his ear. Instead of the German shepherd, Charlie saw the tall man with the blond hair bending over the bed, the same man who had pummeled his mother in the heat of their kitchen. "You sure are a feisty one, aren't you?"

The man smiled and ran a hot dry finger along Charlie's cheek. Charlie jerked his head away from the man's touch.

Malcolm rose and stood next to the man and the woman. All three adults looked down at him. Charlie felt their cold, neutral stares. He wanted to run, to kick them, to find the Words to send bolts of light and bedroom furniture at them. He ran through the exercises Rita and Daniel had taught him for fighting off attackers. But none of his lessons included what to do when you were completely subdued. All he could do was kick and wiggle.

"Handle those feet," the Dog Man said. Charlie heard more tape being ripped. He watched as Malcolm yanked the covers off the bed.

The woman leaned down over his legs. She turned her head and looked at him, holding up a large pair of scissors.

"Go ahead, gay boy. Kick me and give me a reason to cut you."

Charlie froze. She ran loops of tape around his feet.

"Let's ride," the Dog Man said. Fingers dug into his skin as Malcolm slipped his hands beneath Charlie's arms and the woman picked up his feet. Together they carried him over to the window.

Where were they taking him? What about …

Charlie suddenly remembered Randall. Where was he? Had Malcolm done anything to him? If he had so much as touched his uncle, Charlie would make the man pay.

He swiveled his hips, managing to bunch up the lower half of his body and kick his feet hard against the woman's shoulder. She fell back with a groan, letting Charlie's legs slip to the floor. He pushed off the ground, driving Malcolm back against the wall, relishing the sound of the air being forced from the man's lungs.

Something hard struck Charlie in the head. Light, as intense as a doctor's scope, shot behind his eyes. A crunching pain made his vision blur and his body slacken. The last thing he remembered was the Dog Man peering closely at him with a strange smile on his face, then the vague sensation of being passed through the windowpane and slung over someone's shoulder. Then, nothing.

CHAPTER 25

The Basement

CHARLIE CAME TO, LYING on his side, surrounded by a thick moldy smell. He moved his head, then wished he hadn't. Pain bit at his forehead like teeth, and for a moment he thought he would vomit. Then he panicked when he realized that his mouth was still bound with the tape. Vomiting would make breathing impossible and would most likely choke him to death.

He sucked air through his nose and tried to hold his head steady. His heart slammed in his chest like a gorilla against the bars of its cage. Before he could even form a plan, instinct kicked in, and he found himself emptying his mind the way Beverly had shown him. Almost imperceptibly at first, he could feel his heart beat slow to a steady thump, thump, thump.

He opened his eyes and for a moment thought that his eyelids had also been taped shut. He was lying somewhere completely dark. No light creeping under a doorway, no window high up letting in sunshine. He stopped to consider what time of day or night it actually was. And he wondered just how long he had been in this place.

He wasn't sure how big it was, but it seemed to him that there were walls nearby.

Doing his best not to move his head, Charlie took inventory of the rest of his body. Tape on mouth: check. Hands bound behind back with tape: check. Deep pain in shoulders from hands behind back: check. Feet bound by tape: check.

Well, it could be something else besides tape, Charlie thought. *I mean, can I even see anything? Maybe it's rope.*

A useless thought. Who cares if it's rope or tape? The important thing was that he couldn't move his hands; couldn't find the Words that might let him unleash his craft and save himself.

Is that what it was down to? Saving himself? Saving his own life?

He remembered Malcolm's quick arm movements and the way that Amos had fallen to the floor. Had he killed the dog? Or only knocked him out of commission? His gut clenched, imagining Amos dead.

Then he thought of Randall, lying in his bed, sleepy from his pain medication. Had Malcolm done something to his uncle? Had he hurt him? Had he killed him?

His thoughts exploded into a starburst of anguish.

"If you even touched him!" Charlie tried to scream through his taped mouth. He strained at his bindings and shook his head as panic and helplessness overwhelmed him. Several long stretches of time followed where physical torment and emotional agony took him as if he were being dragged along under the surface of a raging river. No air to breathe, slamming into unseen boulders, jerked about in competing currents.

Empty your mind, Charlie. Beverly's voice called from somewhere on the river's bank.

"I can't, I can't, I can't, I can't … if he … if he hurt Randall … I … Amos … I can't … Randall … no … no … no …"

More moments passed with Beverly's words bubbly and gargled as they bounced along the surface of the angry water above his head. He tried to reach for them, but they slipped away. More agony. More time passing.

Yes, you can. You can, Charlie. Empty your mind. The words were clearer this time, but he still couldn't grasp them.

He was sure he was going to die. There was no air to breathe at the bottom of the river. Just sediment and water, rushing over him, drowning him. Then something that sounded like his own voice, but colder, more detached, reached him.

What's done is done, Charlie. If Amos and Randall are dead, then there's nothing you can do about it. You have to calm down so you can think things through.

The voice's chill passed from his scalp down his back to the bottom of his feet, sobering him.

What it said was true. Even if the truth was terrible. Even if it was beyond imagining. There really wasn't anything he could do about … he wouldn't let himself think about it anymore. He had more pressing needs to attend to.

He waited, letting his mind empty some more, letting himself relax.

He waited until he stopped shaking, until he could breathe almost normally again.

Better. Not great, but better.

Okay, Charlie, he said to himself. *Think things through. Try to figure out what's going on.*

And with that thought, an image of Malcolm arose in his mind.

Good. Now what do you think is going on with him? he asked himself.

Malcolm. Charlie pictured the man in his mind's eye sitting on the bedside with the reflections of raindrops running across his face.

Malcolm. The man who was the community's main trainer. Who traveled the world, popping young witches. Whom Beverly leaned on for leadership and emotional support. He had encouraged Charlie to be true to himself if he wanted to become a full-fledged witch. The irony of it all made him want to scream.

No. Now's not the time for screaming. That can be later. Just keep going.

A traitor. Charlie could barely get his mind around the idea that Malcolm had double-crossed Beverly and everyone else. How could he do such a thing? Didn't he know how bad Grace was?

Charlie couldn't make sense of any of it. Had Malcolm been on Grace's side all along? Had everything been a lie? Why would he have encouraged Charlie to be brave enough to admit that he might be gay? Why would he have brought all the kids up to his cabin to train them to use witchcraft if he was a sellout? Why would he have popped the kids in the first place?

Had there really been a break-in at the Mossmans, or did Malcolm just make that up to get Beverly out of the house? So he and the other witches could kidnap Charlie?

"I mean, we all do the best we can with what we've been given," Malcolm had said. What did that mean? That this was the best he could do? Letting Dog Man and Scissors Lady into the bedroom so they could steal Charlie away in the middle of the night?

His hard-won calm vanished as frustration and anger built inside of him at the thought of Malcolm turning against the community.

Red with rage, he kicked at the floor and then regretted it as waves of pain and nausea crashed over him. His nostrils sucked at the air in desperation, panic trying to take over again.

Charlie, knock it off. Get a hold of yourself.

An image of Rita Lostich swam before his eyes. He thought about how she encouraged him, how she would wink at him when he had mastered something new. He thought of how Beverly reminded him to breathe when he was about to try some new form of witchcraft. How Randall's eyes danced when he joked with him.

Diego. He thought of how Diego smiled after they kissed. Charlie felt warmth fill his chest.

These were good thoughts. They didn't necessarily tell him what to do, but he could see each person, almost as if they all stood in front of him, supporting him, loving him, wanting things to go well for him.

I want to see them again. I don't want to die here.

The strength of this realization ran through his veins, emboldening him.

I am not going to die. I will see these people again. Neither Malcolm nor Grace will take these people away from me.

He wasn't sure if it was true, but the courage these thoughts brought him was much better than the panic that sat almost like a bird perched on his shoulder, ready to peck at his eyes and his head.

He needed a plan. If he could somehow free his hands, he could remove the tape binding his mouth shut.

He pulled at the tape around his wrists, doing his best to keep his head still. Nothing happened. No wiggle room whatsoever. Then he tried his feet. The same results for the tape around his ankles. Maybe it was bewitched tape. All he knew was that he couldn't get it to budge.

He tried to move his mouth, to find a way to get the tape away from his lips. But it only made it bind more tightly. And it made him breathe harder, which caused him to break out in a cold sweat, inviting the bird on his shoulder to start pecking, pecking ...

Come on! Charlie told himself. *You've got to do something.*

He ran through the things he had learned in combat training with Rita and Daniel. They had taught him how to use weapons, how to call up spells that would protect or attack. Even ways to cloak himself, which could come in handy if he had to sneak around somewhere.

But they hadn't taught him what to do if he found himself tied up in a dark room, nor had they said anything about his mouth being bound. Knowing that the Words were crucial for most forms of witchcraft, wasn't this a gross oversight? Maybe they figured that if you found yourself unable to move your mouth you were, as he had heard Randall once put it, "Up shit creek without a paddle." ("But don't tell your aunt I told you that," he could hear his uncle saying.)

What could he do to get out of here?

Any way he looked at it, he couldn't come up with a single idea that might work.

"Ung!" He tried to scream in frustration, but the tape muffled it, turning it into a feeble grunt.

Just then, he heard a clicking sound.

A doorway opened nearby. Thin gray light spilled into the room where he lay on the floor, which now looked to be about the size of a small bedroom. A figure stood in the doorway. It remained motionless for several long moments.

As Charlie's eyes adjusted to the pale light, he began to see more clearly. A pair of hands emerged from the center of the person's body, lit by a small orange glow that was cupped between them. As the light became brighter, he saw the arms, upper body, and chin of a man, then hips, legs, shoes, and finally, a face.

It was Dog Man staring down at him. The same blond hair, the same conceited smirk.

"You awake?" the man asked.

Charlie didn't move. For one thing, he couldn't talk at all. And for another thing, Dog Man could go to hell.

"What's wrong, kid? Cat got your tongue?" he laughed.

What was it with these people, Charlie wondered. *Did they always say such corny stuff?*

Dog Man walked over to him and set the warm orange glow on the floor about two feet from Charlie's face. Then he kicked it, and the ball exploded into tiny fragments of light that surrounded Charlie, covering him in a gentle orange luster. It felt like warm air blowing over his skin.

Charlie's arms relaxed, his shoulders stopped hurting, and the pain in his head simply seeped away like water down a drain.

"That should feel better," Dog Man said.

He bent down and began to pry the tape away from around Charlie's ankles. Charlie watched as the light near his feet changed from orange to pale blue. He found that even though his feet were free from the tape, they wouldn't budge.

Next, Dog Man removed the tape at Charlie's hands, and the light changed from orange to blue again. His hands were freed, but they stayed put, unable to receive the signals from his brain to move.

The orange light must have some sort of pain-relieving property, while the blue light acted as a binding spell. That would mean that if Dog Man were going to remove the tape from Charlie's mouth, there might be a small window of opportunity before the glow surrounding his head changed color and bound him.

Charlie summoned the Words, letting the power build near his face, behind his head, so that when Dog Man yanked the tape off of his lips, Charlie's mouth moved fast.

Two things happened at the same time.

The first was that the force of his Words flung Dog Man through the doorway. Charlie watched with satisfaction as his mouth formed a perfectly shocked "O" shape as he flew backwards. Just before he fell to the ground, however, he extended his arms and righted himself, landing squarely on his feet and shaking his head, making a tsk-tsk sound.

The second was that the orange light surrounding Charlie's head changed to blue. He found his mouth trapped shut, rendered useless.

"Check out the badass new witchling!" Dog Man taunted as he walked to where Charlie lay in the blue pool of light. "A mere month ago you were clinging to your mama's apron strings, crying as I beat on her. Now you're using big-boy Words and being on the offensive. Aren't you the tough guy?"

He stopped a few inches from Charlie's stomach. He bent his knee and drew one of his feet back, preparing to kick. The binding blue light made the steel-toed point of his boot shine like a silver star. Charlie squeezed his eyes shut, preparing to feel the sharp impact of the boot in his gut.

Nothing happened. He opened his eyes and looked up at Dog Man.

"You know," said the man, standing now with both feet planted on the ground. "I oughta just kick the crap outta you, little boy. You deserve it. Making all of our lives hell around here. If you had just come back with me when I found you in your little house in Clarkston, it would not have come to this." He gestured, his arms spread wide.

Charlie didn't know what "this" meant. Was he referring to the fact that Charlie was lying on his side, bound by a blue light? Or that they were in a dark room somewhere, most likely in the bowels of some basement? Or did he mean the attacks that he and Grace and the others had been waging?

It didn't matter. The way Dog Man spoke, Charlie could tell he wasn't expecting an answer. He figured that if the man kept talking, he might learn more about where he was and how to escape.

Dog Man bent over and put a hand on Charlie's shoulder. Electric currents ran from his head to his toes as his entire body rose from the floor, face up, until he was level with the man's hips, stiff as a magician's assistant.

Dog Man turned and walked down the hallway. Charlie floated along beside him.

"We gotta figure out what makes you tick, kid," he said as he looked down at Charlie's face. "I mean, really. It took us three attempts to finally get you. What the hell? Doesn't make sense."

He heard another door opening. Bright overhead light forced him to squeeze his eyes shut.

"Put him over there," a woman's voice said.

Charlie felt hands on his body as he was pushed down onto a chair. Although the blue light kept him from moving, the hands forced his body to mold to the contours of the chair so that he ended up more or less in a sitting position with his arms plastered to his sides and his feet stuck to the floor.

Charlie could make out the shapes of several people walking around the room. His nose was assaulted with the overwhelming stink of unwashed bodies. The blue light still floated around him.

"Dude!" Charlie heard someone say. He could see more clearly now and watched as a slim man did an exaggerated moonwalk over to his chair, spun around, then started break dancing in front of him.

"Welcome to the dollhouse, Chuck!" the man said. He stuck his face right up against Charlie's. Charlie recognized him as the man who broke into his bedroom with Scissors Lady those several weeks ago, the one who fought with Beverly.

Charlie could smell mint gum. The man's teeth were extremely white, and dark stubble covered his cheeks and jawline. He thought he could see madness behind the spark of playfulness in the man's eyes.

"Tony Ambrosio at your service, little fellah!" the man said. "And this is Claudia," he bowed and with a flourish indicated the beautiful black woman who'd held the scissors. "I know we've met, but I thought a more formal introduction would be groovy. You are utterly psychological!" He grabbed Charlie's cheeks and shook his head back and forth. "Ooh, I could just eat you right now!"

While the pain in Charlie's head had lessened from what it had been a few moments ago, the shaking motion nearly crippled him.

He feared he would pass out again. The idea of losing consciousness in the hands of this crazy man terrified him. He bit the insides of his cheeks to remain awake.

"Don't mind him," Scissors Lady/Claudia said as she came into view. "He's just plain nuts."

"I am too," Tony said, spinning in place then dropping to the floor in the splits before popping back to his feet and walking away.

"You, mister," Claudia said, shaking her finger at Charlie. "You sure are a tricky one, aren't you?" Her voice was teasing and soft. Charlie tried not to shake as she bent down and looked into his eyes. She brought her hand closer to him. Her fingernails were painted a bright pink, and there were flowery decals in the corner of each one. She extended her pointer finger. The nail began to grow, sharpening at the point. He felt it poke into the side of his face.

"Meow," she said and then ran her finger down his cheek. The point of the nail caught at his skin and tore into it.

The blue glow held his head in place. He could feel the flow of blood trickle down his cheek. It should have hurt, but either the pain in his head overshadowed the gash she was making or he was too numb to care.

"I cut you," she said, fluttering her eyes, "just like I said I would." Her fingernail shrank back, returning to normal size. She smiled, then stood back and looked at him, arms folded, admiring her work for a few more moments before she walked away.

Charlie looked around the room. It was brightly lit where he sat, but the light didn't cover the rest of the area. He tried to see across the room but couldn't make anything out. The smell of dirty bodies permeated everything. He hadn't noticed any stench coming from Dog Man, Tony, or Scissors Lady, so he assumed there were others in the basement too.

"Okay, people," said a familiar voice. Charlie looked to his right and saw Grace walk through the doorway, followed by Malcolm, who kept his eyes locked on the back of Grace's head. Fear swept over him like a cold wind. Grace stopped to survey the room, nodding her head. "This is good. This is very good. Well done."

CHAPTER 26

Coppertop

GRACE WALKED OVER TO where Charlie sat.

"You knew it was inevitable that we would have some time together, didn't you? And since you wouldn't come here of your own volition, well ..." She looked over her shoulder to where Malcolm stood with his hands behind his back, staring at Grace as if waiting for her to give him instructions.

"Hey, people, come on now. I don't see the need for bondage. Really. I'm sure Charlie will mind his manners." She flicked her fingers in his direction. The blue light surrounding him vanished.

His limbs had fallen asleep, but now he was able to move his mouth. He let the Words gather behind him, let them find his lips and move them.

A wooden chair near Charlie's feet leaped into the air and darted toward Grace's head.

"Oh dear," she said, bending at her knees and holding her hands up to the side of her face in mock fear. The chair stopped inches from her head. "What can I do against a little witch as powerful as you, Charlie?"

She moved her arms and the chair flew against the wall, exploding in a cloud of wood and dust.

Rita and Daniel had taught him that once you decided to attack, you committed yourself. This meant that he had already moved his attention to the next spell, his lips moving fast. Objects began to fly around the room.

Grace looked at Charlie, her smile fading as her eyes narrowed.

Quicker than thought, she stood before him in a blur of peach and ginger. "Really, Charlie? You don't get it, do you? How much trouble you're in?"

She struck him across the face with the back of her hand. His chair tipped backwards and his skull cracked against the wall behind him. His hands flew to his head as more pain seared his face and forehead.

"Malcolm, tell him who's really in charge!"

"Do what she says, kid," Malcolm said, his eyes wide, his voice flat. "If you do, everything will be all right."

"That didn't sound very convincing," Charlie said, hearing his voice as if it were a million miles away. He had never experienced pain like this before, so sharp and all-encompassing, like it was a real person standing over him, punching and kicking his head and gut, his neck, without stop. He didn't know how he had managed to talk.

"What is it with you people?" Grace screamed. "I am helping you all, and yet you try to thwart me at every step. What a bunch of ingrates!"

She backed away from him and with a flick of her fingers his chair righted itself, sweeping him upwards into a sitting position. At the same time, overhead lights came on, illuminating everything.

The room was about the size of a double-car garage. More than twenty chairs lined the walls opposite him and to his right. In each chair sat a kid, ranging in age from about ten years old to eighteen or nineteen. All of them sat perfectly still except for their quick shallow breathing. Their eyes were open and dull, lips parted, skin pallid and yellowish. All had gray circles beneath their eyes, though some were much darker than others. He recognized a girl from the framed photograph during the witches' meeting in the basement on Washington Street. In the picture, her hair had been bright red and frizzy; now it hung in greasy, mud-colored tendrils along the sides of her face. Suzette Nickerson. Charlie thought about Mrs. Nickerson wringing her hands during the meeting, while her husband stood still, looking dazed and lost.

"Oh my god," Charlie moaned, the last word rising nearly an octave in dread. The shock of what he saw seemed to diminish the pain in his head, or at least move it a foot or two away from him. "Those kids. What …? What are they doing here? Why are they here?"

Grace smiled. "Don't you see, Charlie? Your grandfather knew what I was doing. He could see how it would benefit us. These kids. Look at them. So fresh, so ready. So ready."

He glanced at their faces, horrified to stare at any one for more than a second or two. Ready for what? What had she done to make them look so, so … dead? Like they were in comas but with their eyes open.

"What is this?" Charlie heard himself ask out loud.

"What is this?" Grace said. "Well, it's the most courageous thing you've ever seen. Nobody has had the know-how, or the guts, to do this. I'm a pioneer."

Dog Man walked over to where Grace stood and looked at Charlie. "As I'm sure you've discovered, new witches are the most powerful right when they're popped. All of that raw energy, unbridled and untethered! But after a week? Nearly all gone. No one has ever been able to regain that level of power," he finished, shaking his head sadly.

"Forget it! I … I don't want to know!" Charlie said, not quite convincing himself. True, he was disgusted by what the witches seemed to be hinting at. But a part of him wanted to know, to understand why the kids were sitting in their chairs, why Malcolm had betrayed everyone to join Grace's side. Hadn't he been curious about this ever since Grace had promised to tell him the secrets she held? He squirmed in his chair, torn between horror and fascination, forgetting for the moment that he was no longer bound by the blue light.

Grace barked a laugh. "Oh, but you do want to know, Charlie. That's the truth, isn't it? Why else would you have agreed to fly off with me during our little nighttime rendezvous? Hmm?

"When I met Thomas here," Grace said, nodding at Dog Man, "he'd been playing around with certain taboos in the witching world, things we've all been told couldn't be done."

"When someone dies, " Dog Man Thomas continued, his voice faster, more excited, "there is a burst of energy that can be quite strong. I developed the ability to grab it and use it, to consume it. The sheer power I gained from it was incredible.

"I showed Grace what I could do. She practiced and practiced and eventually got the hang of it."

But ... Charlie thought to himself. *But Beverly said this was impossible. That it was all a myth.*

"I knew there could be more," Grace said, her volume rising. "A way to use the same principles and apply them to newly popped witches. Just imagine what a burst of juice that would be!

"It took us years. We tried and failed, tried and failed, until eventually we did it. We found a way to harness all that incredible energy instead of letting it go to waste."

"No, no, you can't, you can't just ..." Charlie moaned.

"Oh, but yes. Yes, we can!" she laughed, practically shouting now. Pride widened her features as she indicated the kids in the chairs with a wave of her hand.

Charlie's head spun. He tried to comprehend what Grace and Thomas were saying. Using unpopped witches the same way they got power from dead people?

Kidnapping, killing, harnessing power. It was the stuff of fairy tales. Or nightmares.

"Things really do go bump in the night," his mother told him when they had fled from Clarkston in the Toyota. Had she known what was going on? Had she any idea what Grace was up to?

Why were they telling him all of this? What was Malcolm's part in it? And how was he going to escape?

"What do you want with me? Why am I here?" Charlie asked.

The man and the woman looked at each other. Grace nodded to Thomas.

"Charlie, I bet Elizabeth failed to mention this to you. I don't mean to get all Jerry Springer on you, but ... I'm your dear old dad. I just wanted to welcome you to the family."

CHAPTER 27

Apple and Tree

CHARLIE'S MOUTH DROPPED OPEN AS HE stared at Thomas.

"What? No, you're not. My father was, was …" he began. Was what? The kind-hearted man who worked the fishing boats in Alaska year-round? Who didn't look anything like Dog Man standing before him? How could he have let his imaginary dad become so real to him that he used it as the standard for measurement?

"Oh my god, this is better than Jerry Springer! He didn't know!" shouted Tony, clapping his hands and wiggling his hips. "Look at him, kid. Don't you see the resemblance?"

Thomas walked over to Charlie and bent down so his face was level with Charlie's.

"Same blond curls," the man said, reaching out to ruffle Charlie's hair, who jerked his head away. "Same chin, though you have your mother's eyes. What do you think, Grace? Does he have my nose?"

She came over and kneeled down beside Thomas. "Oh yes, he has your nose, Thomas. Most definitely."

With both adults so close to him, Charlie's vision blurred. How could this be true? How could any of it be true? He knew they were lying, knew they must be saying this to torture him.

But his mind flooded with the secrets that had been revealed to him since late August: the legacy of witchcraft, how his mother had pretended to be someone she wasn't, his aunt and uncle in Seattle, even the secrets of his very own heart. He had grown used to this feeling of denial followed by a slow reluctant acceptance. He had accepted things because he had to, because he couldn't deny the truth, no matter how hard he tried. Broomsticks, dogs that talked, secret societies.

Maybe this was true. Maybe his mother had dated Thomas. Maybe she had even married him. She had hidden so much else from Charlie, why would she worry about keeping this fact from him? Maybe Thomas really was his father. So what? He had no feelings for him, this awful man who was in cahoots with Grace. Well, that wasn't true. He had several: contempt, disgust, hatred, fear.

"How sweet!" said Scissors Lady. "Father and son reunited. Isn't that darling?" she giggled.

"I don't believe you. I don't care. None of it," Charlie sputtered, his words rasping up out of his dry, dry throat.

"Wait a minute, Charlie, which is it?" Grace said. "You don't believe it, or you don't care? It can't be both."

Charlie couldn't sit still any longer. He lurched into a standing position, nearly stumbling on his wobbly legs. This was all too big, too ridiculous, too …

"Wait, Charlie," said Grace. "You don't seem to understand what this means. What it can mean for you."

She walked over to one of the kids in a chair. He looked to be about twelve years old. He had black hair. Most of it was matted to his head. He had Asian features and light brown skin. He stared straight ahead the way people sometimes stare at the TV: eyes lifeless, mouth hanging open. His chest rose and fell with rapid shallow breaths.

"Thomas and I figured out a way to use the power of these teens, Charlie. The way it boosts our own natural abilities is incredible. Watch."

She placed her hand on top of the boy's head. Immediately his neck stiffened and his breathing froze. His face tightened and shriveled into something that looked like torment.

Grace's head shot back, exposing the creamy softness of her neck.

She held that position until a sigh slid from her lips, a sigh sounding very much like pleasure. She dropped her chin and looked at Charlie. Her eyes sparked is if they were filled with lightning.

"The sheer force of it all, you can't understand, Charlie. What it allows me to do. You have no idea."

She vanished, appearing on the other side of the room. He watched as her body grew larger, then smaller, Alice-in-Wonderland style.

"I can do things that were previously impossible," Grace said. Her body burst into flame, and she rose into the air, spinning with heat and embers. Just as quickly, she stood still, back on the ground, flames extinguished. She disappeared again, then reappeared next to Malcolm, who jumped nearly a foot and then stepped several feet away from Grace before resuming his flat lifeless expression.

Charlie stared, dumbfounded, at Grace's display of power.

"Your grandfather understood that it was time for witches to come out of hiding. That we had lived for far too long under cover, running from angry townspeople, suffering persecution, all because we didn't have the sheer power to control the human population, to take our rightful place as their sovereign leaders.

"This," she said, pointing to the kids in the chairs, "This is the way to do it. To strengthen ourselves."

A vague element from Charlie's dream swam into his mind, where the orderly from the hospital bit random children until they popped like water balloons. He shuddered as he remembered how she kissed Diego, then sank her teeth into his shoulder until he exploded in a burst of water, his skin a wasted elastic shell falling to the schoolroom floor.

Had it been one of those dreams that Beverly had described? What had she called it? A dream of … premonition? Had his dream been trying to tell him that this was what the witches were doing to the kidnapped teenagers?

But what good were his dreams if they didn't help him prevent bad things from happening? Just like the dream he had had with the German shepherds, when he hadn't known what to do with the information or how to prevent Principal Wang from having a heart attack, the dream with the orderly was useless. Too little, too late. He shook his head in frustration.

Forget the dreams, Charlie, he chided himself. He looked up at Grace, narrowing his eyes at her.

"You would use kids as, as batteries, just to lord it over non-witches? And you'd call that good?" he said, shaking his head in disgust. "It's not exactly helping those witches be free, is it?" He asked, pointing to the kids in their chairs.

"Charlie," Grace said, speaking to him the way a teacher does to a dull-witted student, "you're missing the point. It's about freedom! Freedom from hiding. You, of anyone, should understand that. Freedom from the stupid tedious little games people like your Aunt Beverly have to play every single day of their lives. Freedom to dominate the air, the streams and rivers, the oceans. Freedom to arrest the destruction that human beings cause on this planet, to return nature to her true balance, to use her gifts as is our birthright!"

Charlie doubted that Grace was an environmentalist at heart. But he could tell that she believed what she said. Wasn't that what made people crazy? And dangerous? When they had some insane idea that they really believed in?

"You go along with all this, Malcolm?" Charlie asked, staring at the man.

Malcolm opened his mouth, then shut it abruptly. He looked at Grace as if waiting for her to instruct him, a look of confusion on his face. Charlie couldn't understand what was going on with him. First, he betrayed Beverly, making it so Charlie would get kidnapped, even hurting Amos. And now he showed none of the fire or strength that Charlie had come to associate with his mentor. He just stood there, waiting for Grace to tell him what to do.

Thomas spoke. "Malcolm has recently been helping us find the perfect candidates, Charlie. He has more exposure to witching covens and their unpopped youth than anyone we know. With a little persuasion, he agreed to help us out."

Grace smiled and walked over to Malcolm, who winced as if he were about to be struck. She reached up and placed both of her hands on his head. His body began to shudder. When she stepped away from him, he stopped moving. His mouth dropped open, arms slack at his sides. He looked catatonic.

"What did you do to him?"

But Grace ignored his question.

"Here's where you come in," she continued, walking over to where he stood.

"You see, Thomas and I have learned a lot. We've figured out how to use that little burst of life force when someone dies. And we finally understand how to tap the potential of young witches. Combined, the power is incredible. Immense. But we haven't been able to expand it. We've had to stay relatively near these kids to use their gifts. If we don't, whenever we travel farther away from them, the power fades. We needed your help to learn how to …"

"How to go mobile, Charlie," said the man Thomas who might be his own father. "Right now it's like a landline. We want it to be more like a cell phone." He smiled as he finished, as if this explanation were the most obvious thing on the planet.

"That's right. With no roaming fees," Tony added with a giggle from where he stood in the background. Scissors Lady Claudia gave him a warning look, but Grace just ignored him.

Charlie crossed his arms over his chest. "Why do you think I can help you? Why do you think I would? I won't, you know," he said, keeping his eyes locked on Grace.

"Oh, you'll help us all right," the witch said as she walked over to him. "We just aren't sure yet how it's all going to work."

She put her hands on either side of Charlie's shoulders and peered into his eyes. Charlie's skin crawled at her touch. He tried to wriggle away from her but found his feet stuck to the floor.

"You see," said Thomas, walking over and standing next to Grace, "one night a few months ago, I felt you. Just like that. I woke up and I felt you stirring in my gut." The man placed his hand over his stomach.

"I didn't even know you existed. But I could feel you far away, and I knew that somehow you could help. You're my offspring. My blood is in you. My legacy is also in you. I knew you had to be part of what Grace and I have been building.

"It took a while to track you down. I'm just happy to have you here, son, ready to help us with our plans."

"I told you, I won't help you. I'm not your son. I ..."

Thomas spread his arms out to either side of him and turned his hands palms up. Then he raised his arms above his head. Charlie felt himself lift up off the ground. For a brief moment he floated in midair, horizontal, facing the floor, a foot or two above everyone else. Then he was thrown hard against the ceiling.

The wind whooshed out of him as his head exploded in pain. He was struck blind for several moment as white heat seared his eyeballs. He cried out in spite of himself.

"Remember that? I sure do. I thought I'd let you know what it felt like and remind you that you will definitely be helping us. Just so you know this isn't a negotiation."

As his vision returned, Charlie looked down at the room from where he lay pressed flat with his back against the ceiling, at the kids sitting like zombie schoolchildren in their chairs, at Claudia and Tony who were smiling up at him, at Grace and Thomas directly below him, eyeing him the way people look at monkeys behind bars at the zoo, at Malcolm who stood stock still, staring off into space.

Charlie wanted to summon Words, wishing he could wreak havoc on the witches below. But he didn't know how to wreak havoc. He wasn't powerful enough. Plus, if he could, he might inadvertently hurt one of the captured kids. And he had no illusions that he would be any match for even one of the witches standing beneath him, let alone all five.

It was time that he faced reality: he was stuck, helpless, glued to the ceiling, held captive by the scariest witch on the planet, with no idea whatsoever how to get away, save his life, or keep from becoming a human battery pack himself.

CHAPTER 28

The Link

"SHALL WE GET STARTED, THEN?" Grace said, grinning like the hostess of a summer tea party.

No more than five minutes had passed since Thomas had thrown Charlie up against the ceiling. Now he sat on a chair facing one of the catatonic kids, a boy older than himself with big shoulders and an unshaven face. He stared at a spot just beyond Charlie's right ear, his chest moving with that terrible rapid breathing.

Tony and Claudia stood behind Charlie's chair, their hands pressed down on his shoulders. They had been instructed to subdue him if he even so much as tried to summon a single Word.

Grace and Thomas sat in front of him, on either side of the big-shouldered boy.

Charlie looked over to Malcolm, hoping against hope that his teacher had snapped out of his stupor. But the man remained in a daze, eyes half closed and glassy, standing a few feet away.

"We've been waiting a long time for you to be here with us," Grace said.

Charlie shivered.

"Whatever this is, I'm not going to help you!" Charlie said, hoping his voice sounded braver than he felt.

"Now's not the time to talk, okay, son?" Thomas said to him. Then, "Now only take a little, Grace," he continued, jutting his chin at the boy opposite Charlie. "We just need to make contact and get the flow started."

Grace nodded. She placed her hand on the boy's head. He squinted. It didn't look like he was in pain as much as he was concentrating on something. Grace's head didn't fly back like it did the previous time, but her eyes widened and her breathing increased.

"Good, good," said Thomas. Then he placed his hand on the boy's head. Thomas closed his eyes as a shudder ran through him.

He opened them and looked at Grace. "Now," he said.

At the same time, the two witches reached out toward Charlie with their free hands.

"No!" Charlie tried to squirm away.

Tony and Claudia gripped his neck and the back of his head, holding him firmly in place.

Charlie closed his eyes, wishing he could be anywhere other than here, wishing there was something he could do.

He felt pressure on his scalp as the witches' hands pressed down on the top of his hair.

And then everything changed.

There was a momentary dropping sensation in his gut like he had fallen from a short height.

His skin flushed with a pleasant heat as if someone wrapped a warm towel around him after he had stepped out of a cold swimming pool.

And just like that, Charlie felt himself thrust inside the boy's head who sat across from him. He knew all sorts of things. He could see and feel what the boy saw and felt. The boy's name was Todd Laramie. He hoped to go to college on a basketball scholarship. Charlie watched as a pretty young girl walked up to him. He grew aroused as he kissed the young girl on a bed somewhere. He felt himself sweating on a basketball court, dribbling the ball, jumping up and making a three-pointer. He heard a crowd cheering, felt teammates clapping his back.

He saw cats. He felt himself running on all fours, and now he leaped, not like an athlete but an animal. No effort. Pure joy. He was fully feline, chasing rodents at night, stretching in a pool of sunshine during the day.

He could feel the confusion and terror in Todd's mind. The boy didn't understand what was happening to him, even as he enjoyed the thrill and speed of being a cat.

But above all else, above the sensations and the confusion, the memories and the cat dreams, the intrusion into Todd's world, Charlie felt a stockpile of power, of amazing raw strength stretching far out in front of him like a vast reservoir of water.

This seemingly endless supply of raw power made everything that he had learned before about witchcraft look like child's play.

He knew things: about air and trees, about the hair follicles of humans, about whistling up the winds and racing moonbeams across the sands of the great deserts of the world. He knew himself as both human and as something greater, something better.

And ... he wanted it. He wanted this thing that promised to carry his heart and his mind into a single point of utter clarity and confidence, confidence that had previously been unimaginable. He wanted this force that would give him dominance over everything. Over everyone.

Before Charlie could fully grasp what was happening, the flow of power cut off as suddenly as it had washed over him, and he felt himself wrenched from Todd Laramie's head and dumped back into his brain.

He opened his eyes as his entire body shook.

Grace and Thomas were staring at him expectantly, their hands now at their sides.

"Oh yeah, that's it. You felt it, didn't you, my boy?" said Thomas.

Charlie's teeth chattered, and his skin itched as if a thousand sand fleas scampered and burrowed across its surface. For a moment he feared he would shoot up off his chair and through the ceiling, the aftermath of the invasion into Todd's head was so strong.

"Now, how can you say that's a bad thing, huh, Charlie? How can you say that?" Grace asked, true sincerity in her words.

The raw rush of power was diminishing, its fiery edges softening, turning dark, the way the edges of land do as the sun sets behind the horizon.

Yet he could still feel Todd's life force, still knew all the details, as well as sense the boy's latent spark of witchcraft marking him as an echo, his connection to cats, even the inner secrets of his mind and heart. It was all still there, but as if it were in a room, and the door of the room was slowly closing, and Charlie was being pulled away from it, down a hallway, maybe to never go inside the room again.

A moan slipped from his lips, and a small puff of white vapor floated from his mouth and hung in the air in front of his face. Charlie watched it for a moment, fascinated, while a part of him mourned the loss of the rich all-encompassing power.

The vapor slid into his nostrils causing him to sneeze. His head jerked to the side, and he saw Malcolm standing still, not watching anything, just staring at the far wall. He forgot who Malcolm was for a moment. But as the surge a of power continued to wash away from him, and his mind sharpened in focus, he began to remember. He remembered that Grace was using Malcolm somehow to find more children, find them and turn them over to her so that she could drain them dry, leaving them sitting on chairs like corpses.

The way the three of them had just drained a large quantity of energy from Todd Laramie, the basketball player.

Oh my god! Charlie thought in a panic. *I didn't mean to. Did I just …?*

Yes. Yes, he had. The life force that they had just drunk was now gone from Todd, as if they had eaten months off of his life span, or maybe even years. Charlie knew in his gut that the boy could never get that vitality back.

He looked over at the line of children against the wall, sitting zombie-like and captive, waiting to be used by Grace as nothing more than power boosters.

Charlie felt his skin crawl. He had just been forced to drink a portion of Todd Laramie's actual life. What was worse, a part of him had liked the power, had wanted more, had wanted it to go on forever. But now that it had stopped, Charlie knew it for what it was: stealing, siphoning away someone's life, the worst kind of violation.

Even though he still didn't understand how he fit into their plans, he knew that Grace and Thomas wanted to make Charlie help them, to maybe drain all of the children, and mostly likely many more.

He felt his head shake from side to side.

"No," his mouth formed the silent word. He wouldn't do it. He wouldn't steal like that again, and he wouldn't be a part of any plan that would let the witches steal from children.

It's time then, isn't it? he said inside his mind. *It's time to fight.*

As if from far away, he heard Grace's voice, pleasant and matter-of-fact.

"Let's continue, then. Let's see if Thomas's theory about you being a strong conduit is right."

Before Charlie could stop them, hands were one again placed on his head.

"No!" he tried to scream. "I won't let you. I can't …"

A violent lurch. He was no longer in the basement.

He gasped as the dropping sensation came on again, only this time much stronger. This time it felt like he had been tossed from a cliff.

Something shadowy encircled his face as he fell, hissing in his ears. A cold wind stippled his skin in gooseflesh, and dark shapes darted beyond his line of vision.

Pleasure flooded his senses filling him with a longing so sharp that it almost hurt. He reached out to grab at something, anything, for balance, and then his feet landed on what seemed like solid ground. The euphoria increased, but this time a pall of anguish, like dark ink, sullied its surface. At first he couldn't figure out why it was there.

And then as clearly as if someone had flipped on a light switch, Todd Laramie now stood less than two feet from him on a vast expanse of arid land. The sky overhead glowed silver, and the air threatened to suffocate him with its heat. Todd's eyes, alert, were staring at Charlie. He didn't look like a wasted zombie anymore. He stood tall and hale. But something was wrong. Tears began to run down the boy's face. His mouth moved as if trying to speak, but Charlie couldn't make out what he was saying. He looked so incredibly sad right then, so grief-stricken, that Charlie felt his own heart lurch in torment without knowing why. Drops of brown-red blood began to seep from Todd's neck, and he shook his head slowly as if surrendering something. As if giving up.

Charlie reached out and touched the boy's neck, diverting one streamlet of blood onto his index finger. He heard his own sharp intake of breath. It was as if he had been parched with thirst for days at a time only to finally drink from a cool glass of water. He could feel his skin cells, his organs, his nerve endings, being slaked.

Having drunk his fill, he pulled his hand away from Todd's neck. The look of grief dissipated from the boy's face, replaced by a blank stare. Then he shuddered once, closed his eyes, and collapsed in a heap to the dry ground.

Charlie stared at the boy's crumpled form at his feet. What? What happened? Why was he …?

Charlie squatted down on the ground and gave Todd's shoulder a slight shake, already knowing the boy wouldn't, couldn't respond.

"Todd, wake up! Todd, it's okay! Come on, wake up. Wake up!" he managed to squeak out before his throat squeezed closed. Tears stung his eyes as he shook the boy harder.

Charlie groaned, patting at the boy's shoulder, his arm. He looked around for help but only saw sand stretching for miles beneath the silvery sky. He tried to grab for Words, Words which could enter his mouth and reverse what he feared had just happened. But none came. Only the sounds of his own whimpering, his cowardly denial falling from his lips like an August rain too late to save the failed crops.

Todd Laramie was dead. Charlie had sucked at his life force just as it was leaving the boy's body. He had stolen from this young man again, had taken his very essence from him, and the proof of it lay in the lifeless body at Charlie's feet. It didn't matter that the witches forced him into it. The boy was dead and Charlie had participated in his death.

His hands flew to his mouth in horror as a wail began to build in his throat. But before he could make a sound, his eyes snapped open. He found himself once again on the chair in the basement. He couldn't make sense of what he saw in front of him. Todd still sat on the chair opposite him, Grace and Thomas still on either side, eyes closed as they rode their waves of pleasure. At first he thought that the boy was smiling. But his smile was wrong. It was too wet, too red, and the angle was strange.

The boy wasn't smiling. His head rested back against the chair. His throat had been cut wide open. It wasn't a mouth that Charlie saw, but a fatal gash administered by the knife Claudia held in her hand where she now stood behind the boy, morbid glee dancing in her eyes.

Blood had gushed down Todd's front, along Claudia's arm. There were patches of it on Grace's face, more smeared over the front of Thomas's white shirt.

"No! No, no, no, no, no!" Charlie began yelling. He tried to stand up, for he wanted to run away, to be free of these power-hungry murderers, and even more strongly, to acquit himself of any role he had played in Todd's death. But Tony held Charlie to his chair, and Grace and Thomas kept their hands, the ones not grasping onto Todd's body, pressing down on Charlie's head maintaining a buzzing circuitry and forcing Charlie to stay locked within it.

There was no escaping, no fleeing from the horror of Grace's world. He couldn't run away. The witches had forced Charlie into a nightmare of violence and death. He couldn't free himself from it. Nor could he ever again pretend that it didn't exist.

But he had to do something. Hadn't he decided that he was going to fight?

If he couldn't get away from these people, then what could he do?

In that moment, deep inside himself, below the horror of Todd's murder and his own part in it, underneath his own hopelessness at ever escaping from Grace and this hellish basement, even beneath the deep troubling satisfaction of being filled with the dead boy's life force, Charlie glimpsed a small window of opportunity. It seemed too easy, too implausible, but just maybe, if he acted quickly, he could slip through that window while it was still open.

CHAPTER 29

Window of Opportunity

BEFORE HE COULD TALK himself out of it, Charlie gave a sharp shout and lurched forward in his chair, slamming his right hand on the top of Thomas's head, his left hand on Grace's. Their eyes flew open, and he heard Claudia shout, "No!"

But it was too late.

Charlie's hands interrupted the flow of power. With Todd's life force completely gone, the circuitry sputtered and popped, then reversed direction, searching for and finding the only other sources of vitality left in the closed loop: Grace and Thomas. Twin screams erupted as the loop began to suck power from the witches and dump its entirety into Charlie.

The sheer vastness of the power shooting into his body threatened to overwhelm him, to tear him from limb to limb, but he bore down on the rush, sure that he had to take this risk if he wanted to put a stop to things. By keeping his hands on the witches and draining them, they were as helpless to escape as he had been only moments prior.

In the split second before Tony could pull Charlie back and break the circuit he had just created, everything else seemed to come to a standstill, as all the knowledge available to him sped into his veins like an injection from a hypodermic needle.

And just like he knew everything about Todd Laramie, he now knew everything about Thomas and Grace.

Or very nearly everything.

Images, emotions, colors and sensations, plots rife with murder and darkness, flooded through him.

He couldn't comprehend everything at once, for too many things were flashing too quickly through his mind. But with the onslaught of information came an ability to navigate it, so he narrowed his focus as if he were taking quick gulps from a torrent of fetid water.

Grace. He had known she was formidable, had known that she was power-hungry and untrustworthy, but now he saw more clearly into the vast network of her machinations, saw into her heart, empty of even an ounce of benevolence, and knew her rage-filled and cunning ways, surpassed by nothing other than an endless ache of single-minded greed.

Charlie felt himself yanked along the twisted trails of her thoughts, grasping more of her motivations and schemes.

He plunged into a pocket of her memory where she was having a conversation with Thomas about whether or not Charlie would be as useful to her plot as Thomas thought he could be. She had her doubts but was willing to try if the boy could somehow give her the boost of power she so craved.

Another pocket pulled Charlie in. This time he saw Malcolm through Grace's eyes, standing outside the gate to his property on Snoqualmie Pass, bending over his rickety old mailbox and looking for mail. Four shadows emerged from the forest and crept toward Malcolm from four different sides. The crunch of gravel alerted Malcolm, who spun around, just as Claudia threw what looked like a cloud of yellow dust at his head. Grace and the others ran out of the way as Malcolm raised his hands above his head, but he crumpled to the ground before he could protect himself. Charlie watched as Grace ordered Thomas and Tony to pick up Malcolm's unconscious form and carry him into a shiny black car parked nearby.

Charlie dove deeper into Grace's psyche, looking for more of her secrets. This time there were no words, no scenes, just a realization: Grace planned to kill off Thomas, as well as Claudia and Tony, once her system of semi-popped teenagers was complete. They knew too much and were more of a hassle than useful, but until things were set, she needed them.

Charlie bumped up against a small cluster of Grace's thoughts and motivations that would not open to him, as if they were behind a locked door. He tried to break the cluster open, but it wouldn't budge. A voice in his head pressed him to try harder, to gain access to Grace's innermost thoughts. But the dark pocket she had hidden away remained inaccessible. He was mostly relieved because he sensed that, if he did manage to get inside the cluster, it would be like falling into a radioactive cesspool of toxicity and madness.

Charlie released himself from Grace's thoughts and felt himself thrown forward, lost, scrambling for a foothold somewhere, until …

Thomas. Snapshots and thoughts flooded into Charlie's mind, less cogent and more fragmented than Grace's had been.

Thomas believed in Charlie. Or at least he believed in his own sense of superiority, which clouded his judgment. He held tightly to the notion that because Charlie was of his own blood that he was the powerful conduit they needed for their plans.

Charlie waded through the detritus of pride and arrogance until he found what he was looking for: the truth of Thomas's claims of paternity, coming at him in flashes and blurry memories.

A much younger Thomas discovering Charlie's mother as a teenager, hiding in a different basement from the one in which Charlie was being held captive.

"What, how … how could you do that?" his mother stuttering, a look of pleading and abject horror on her young face.

"Get her out of here!" Grace whispering. "Her father's upstairs! We can't let him find her down here!"

Thomas dragging his mother into a side room, her shouts of "Dad! Dad!" muffled by his hand over her mouth.

"You thought you could sneak in here and spy on us?" Thomas sneering at Elizabeth, then striking her upside the head, with Grace's voice carrying down the staircase from the living room above: "Demetrius, how nice to see you again."

The sound of clothes tearing, a bare shoulder, Thomas pressing down on top of the wide-eyed teenaged Elizabeth, her cries further stifled by her own sweater pressed over her lips, her hands slapping at his face.

Muted screams, grunting, more exposed skin, the flashing of teeth.

Thomas, red-cheeked and gloating, resting against the side of a sofa to catch his breath.

Elizabeth's foot connecting with Thomas's groin, icepicks of pain stabbing in his gut.

"Bitch!" Thomas screaming, squeezing his eyes shut and falling to his right side.

Elizabeth's form flickering, fading to a shadow.

A door to the backyard opening, a gray shape slipping outside.

A man's voice calling to Thomas from outside the room. "Let her go! Bigger fish to fry."

"Run!" Someone shouting from far away, throat squeezing with the threat of tears, Charlie recognizing it as his own voice after a short while.

Charlie shook his head, releasing Thomas's thoughts.

For a quick moment, he only felt relief, the relief of being free from the witches' sullied minds and memories.

Then the realization hit him in a flash as the blanks in his mother's story filled in.

She had stumbled upon the witches using deathcraft and learned of their plot to sell it to her own father, Demetrius, in exchange for his access to the Seattle coven.

She had fled, but not before being overpowered by Thomas.

This was why she had left Seattle, why she never wanted to come back, why she never told Charlie about his father.

All of this information, all of Grace's scheming, Thomas' violent act, Charlie's origins, all of it organized itself in Charlie's head in less time than it took to blink his eyes. It surged through Charlie's cells, his mind, as he sucked away at the power and knowledge inside the witches' heads.

In the next second there were three more things that Charlie learned.

One of them was that he wasn't special. Thomas had been wrong. There was nothing unique about him, no talent imbedded in him to be the conduit that Thomas had hoped he would be. Charlie wasn't sure how he knew this, for the truth of it wasn't rooted in his father's heart or Grace's mind, but he knew it to be true just the same.

The second thing was that, even though he was not a conduit, Charlie had inadvertently gained vast knowledge and power just now from the witches. Not because he was special but because he had turned the tables on them and stolen from them the way they had been stealing from their captives. He had taken advantage of the situation and now knew nearly everything that they did.

And the third thing was this: he could use the knowledge that he had just stolen from the witches to defeat them. He didn't know how yet, didn't know if he was capable of doing it, but knew that he had what he needed to try.

Ignoring the agonized grunts of the witches subdued beneath his hands, he saw doorways inside of him opening, watched as new kinds of Words rushed down hallways toward him, finding his lips, his mouth, coalescing inside of him into such a savage buildup of potency that he feared his head would explode.

In the split second it took for him to gain all of this vast knowledge, just before Claudia and Tony could get their hands on Charlie and break the circuit, he opened his mouth and unleashed the Words.

Claudia, hand flashing toward Charlie as she prepared to bury her knife into his heart, flew backwards through the air and crashed into the far corner, her weapon clattering to the floor. Strips of material tore loose from an old couch nearby and sailed toward her, binding her mouth, her arms, her legs.

Tony's hands barely touched the back of Charlie's neck before a funnel of water erupted from the floorboards and engulfed the man, lifting him several feet off the ground and spinning him in a sickening blur. As the funnel began to slow down, several pieces of heavy furniture from different parts of the room arced through the air and descended on Tony, flattening him to the ground as he screamed in gargled agony. Charlie could hear bones breaking.

Without pausing to consider his actions, Charlie turned his head and looked at the back two walls, focusing on the kids sitting in their chairs. He felt parts of him extending, like long tongues, licking at the teens the way a mother cat licks her kittens. Soon their eyes lost their dull stares as they jerked awake. Some of them fell forward, too weak to remain sitting. Some of them shook their heads and rubbed their faces with their hands, trying to understand where they were.

Charlie swept his gaze along the walls, waking them all, freeing them, one at a time. He passed over Todd's body slumped in the chair opposite him, knowing it was too late for the boy. His gaze reached Malcolm, and he watched as the man's body shuddered, watched as his face came alive with awareness.

Then Charlie looked at Grace and Thomas, who squirmed and writhed in their chairs while Charlie continued to drink from them.

"Enough, kid! Enough! You've got to stop," he heard Malcolm's voice from somewhere in back of him, shaky and weak, but clear and earnest enough to be understood.

"Stop, Charlie! You'll blow a fuse!"

Charlie turned his head to see Malcolm standing right behind him.

"Get away from me!" he yelled at the man. "You're one of them!"

He was confused. The stream of power he continued to suck into himself splintered his thoughts. Competing voices yelled in his head.

Malcolm is one of them.

It wasn't his fault. The witches had controlled his mind.

Witches can't control people's minds.

Don't trust him. He betrayed you.

Malcolm is good. He's one of the good guys!

In his heart of hearts he knew Malcolm wasn't one of them, at least not anymore, but his mouth kept shouting accusations.

"You kidnapped me! You betrayed Beverly! You lied to us! After you told me I couldn't lie about things."

Invisible hands yanked Malcolm's body into the air, flipping him upside down. Other than a small grunt, the man made no sound.

The desire to do the right thing was fading in him. He had known he had to stop Grace and Thomas, had to free the teenagers, but now … now his head swam. He couldn't concentrate. Too much power sizzled and spat in every cell of his body. He was losing his ability to distinguish between right and wrong.

He brought Malcolm closer to him, raising his body in the air so that his face floated inches from his own, upside down. The man's cheeks and forehead turned bright red from the pressure.

"It's okay, kid. Really. You did the right thing. That's good."

He nodded at Charlie, but he looked funny upended, like he was trying to do a sit-up. The power flowing from Grace and Thomas into him was thick and sweet, heavy. It felt good. Really good.

"Charlie, listen to me. You're going to have to stop now. You can't keep taking from them. You're going to explode."

"You're trying to trick me! You told me witches couldn't read people's minds. But I can. I know everything about them!" He shouted, gesturing with his chin to Thomas and Grace, who continued to wither beneath his palms.

"Kid, I didn't know about that when I talked to you before. I didn't know they could get to me this way. Honest," he said in a matter-of-fact tone, as if he were explaining the properties of algebra, not hovering, inverted, in Charlie's clutches.

Charlie's arms started to shake. The sheer might flowing through him felt incredible, but his legs were quivering and he thought he might fall to the floor.

"I'll help you. All you have to do is …"

"No! I don't believe you. You'll just …" he said, his voice trembling, his words losing conviction.

"I'm right here, little man. I am not going to trick you."

The words "little man" reached into Charlie and pulled on his heart, softening him. "I c-c-can't! I don't know how to stop!" he choked. His throat was raw and scratchy. "I just … I just want a glass of water!" he finished, surprising himself.

"Yes, you do. You do know how. Just stop. You can do it," Malcolm said. His expression of concern was clown-like and strange.

Charlie's hands started to burn. He looked at them and could see smoke rising from Grace and Thomas's hair.

He was scared. He didn't know if he could trust Malcolm. Or if he should. But he had to do something. He couldn't hold on any longer.

So he did the only thing he could do. He let go.

CHAPTER 30

Exodus

SEVERAL THINGS HAPPENED AT ONCE. Malcolm fell to the ground, landed on his hands, and flipped himself right-side up, nimble as a gymnast. Grace howled and tried to stand from her chair, only to fall flat on the floor. She jerked and spasmed, unable to make her muscles cooperate. Flinging her fingers at Charlie's face, her lips moved, trying to find Words. Nothing happened. Thomas fell off the side of his chair, flopping about like a fish thrown into the bottom of a boat.

Charlie stood bent over with his hands on his knees, frozen as he watched Malcolm kick Grace hard in the face, once, twice, then turn and kick Thomas in the back, the side, the head. The two witches wailed and writhed about, unable to summon the strength to protect themselves. Charlie wondered absently why Malcolm kicked them instead of using the craft to bind them.

With the connection broken and the surge of power dissipating, Charlie's mind began to clear. He was breathing hard and had to blink away the sweat that dripped into his eyes.

"Charlie! Get these kids out of here!" Malcolm yelled. "They need your help!"

The loud words startled him.

He looked at Malcolm, unsure if the man had returned to normal, or if this was just another trick.

Impatience, authority, and a boot-quaking glare emanated from the man's face. Charlie decided his mentor was back.

"But what about them? Her?" he asked, pointing to Grace.

"She's weak for now. I'll hold them off while you get the kids upstairs."

Charlie pitched forward as his legs gave out. He wasn't sure if he righted himself with witchcraft or pure will, but he regained his balance, then wobbled over to one of the walls and tried to open a side door.

"No!" Malcolm shouted. "Over there!"

Charlie stumbled to where the man pointed and yanked open another door, revealing a well-lit staircase leading to the floor above.

When he looked back at the teens, he saw that they all stood or sat stock still, unsure what to do, eyes squinting as if waking from a long sleep.

"Hey, kid," Malcolm whispered to him. "Can you …?" he said, then waved his hand in front of his own face. Immediately his features blurred, looking fuzzy and hard to follow.

"So they don't know …" Malcolm added, tilting his head in the direction of the teenagers.

Charlie nodded, slowly understanding that it would be better if these kids couldn't recognize him in the future. He stepped out of sight into the stairwell. A few simple Words, and he knew that his features became unclear and difficult to remember.

"Hurry!" Charlie gestured to them as he stepped back into the basement. "You've got to get out of here. Come upstairs."

A few of the older-looking kids stood up and began to help the others. They stumbled toward the lit doorway, clutching onto each other, some of them crying.

"Kid! There are people upstairs. Be careful!" Malcolm warned.

His balance and strength coming back to him, Charlie bolted up the stairs in front of the group of teens. He breathed in fresh air, relieved to be away from the funk of stinky bodies and moldy lumber. When he reached the upper floor, he saw several women, holding cleaning supplies, standing in a large white living room, staring at him.

"Get out of here!" Charlie yelled. They fled from the room, buckets and spray bottles dropping from their hands.

Two large armed men, one wearing a sport coat and tie, the other a track suit, entered through a side door and aimed their weapons at Charlie.

"Stop right there!" one of the men yelled at him. "Where's Grace?"

Even though he wasn't tapped into the full force of power that he felt earlier, Charlie still had more than enough of it flowing through him. He held his hands up. Both men shouted as their guns flew from their fingers. Their bodies were thrown through the air, landing on top of lavish white couches.

"Stay," he said, then strengthened his command with the force of his new Words. The men struggled against the invisible pressure that held them in place. One more final Word, and the couch began to blur. It was enough to camouflage it from the children.

Charlie watched to make sure they couldn't get up, then hurried to help the rest of the kids up the staircase.

"What's your name?" Charlie asked an older girl with black hair and tattoos on her bird-thin arms after he had brought the last kid up from the basement. She seemed more alert than the others.

"Laura."

"Okay, Laura, get everybody together and wait here."

The girl nodded and began to corral everyone into a tight-knit circle while Charlie ran back downstairs.

He looked around. Grace lay unmoving on the floor near Todd Laramie's lifeless body. Tony seemed to be unconscious. Claudia, the Scissors Lady, was still bound and gagged in the corner, struggling weakly against the cloth that held her.

Malcolm stood over Thomas, who sat on a chair with a look of dazed defeat on his face. Malcolm held his hands out in front of him, obviously doing what was necessary to keep the man seated and subdued.

Charlie took one look at Thomas and forgot what he was supposed to be doing.

"You! Dog Man!" Charlie yelled, pointing his index finger at the man. Thomas and Malcolm's head jerked in his direction.

"You raped my mother!" he screamed.

"Charlie!" Malcolm's voice was sharp. "I have it under control. You need to get out of here!"

Charlie ignored him.

"You raped her! How could you?" he was yelling and crying, and an upswell of power surged through his feet, rising up through his legs and chest, into his scalp, as his outstretched finger continued to point at Thomas's face.

"Charlie, no! Stop, you can't ..." Malcolm shouted, but Charlie wasn't listening. He couldn't erase from his mind the images of Thomas forcing his mother.

A few simple Words shaped his mouth, and he watched as Thomas' weakened body flew off the chair and rushed toward him, much like Malcolm's had done only a few moments before. He stopped a foot from Charlie, hovering in the air, right-side up.

The man was now fully aware of what Charlie was doing and saying. He began to plead with Charlie, to beg, to whimper.

"I didn't plan to! Sh-sh-she was in the way, I had to ..."

"Shut up!" Charlie screamed. The floor beneath him shuddered, then made a loud cracking sound. He slapped the man once across the face. Hard. Then he backhanded him. Then slapped him again. Each slap elicited a cry from Thomas.

Red rage filled Charlie's head, driving his anguish away. He wanted to tear the man apart, to rip his head from his neck, to unleash the storm of violence coursing through his veins.

"Charlie, don't do this. Don't, son," he heard Malcolm say.

"But he did that to her! And he killed people. I'm gonna destroy him!" he yelled. More cracking, and then a long groaning sound filled the room, as if the joists in the walls and floor were about to snap. The pressure was building in him, and he felt it sparking out of his eyes and ears, spitting off of his fingertips, making hissing sounds.

"You're right. And it would probably feel really good," Malcolm continued, now standing next to him, his voice close and warm in his ear.

"But it's a long-term solution for a short-term problem."

"Malcolm!" he yelled. "Don't give me any of your psychobabble. I am going to kill him!"

Malcolm stepped in front of Charlie, blocking his view of Thomas.

"Get out of the way!"

"No, Charlie. Don't do this. It's a choice you'd have to live with for the rest of your life."

"But …" he grunted, afraid that he couldn't hold the rage inside anymore, afraid that it would hit Malcolm in the process. The air shimmered and crackled around his own head.

"I know you, son. You'd only feel temporary relief. Then you'd feel guilty for the rest of your life. Don't do it."

"But …"

"Don't."

"Malcolm," Charlie cried in agony. "Puh-puh-puh-please leave me alone!"

Charlie felt like he was being torn from the inside, ripped in half by his desire to destroy Thomas. Only a small part of his mind could grasp what Malcolm was saying. The rest of him wanted to unleash everything on Thomas.

But the small part of his mind heeded Malcolm's warning. It knew that Malcolm spoke the truth. Without knowing what else to do, unable to extinguish the rage in him, he turned to the side and released the full force of everything inside of him at the far wall.

A funnel of molten red light, crackling through with silver streaks, shot from his outstretched arms and pounded into the wall, blasting a huge hole in it and sending flames up to the ceiling.

A tormented bellow exploded from Charlie's mouth while a second blast, this time thick, waxy, and yellow-colored, exploded from his fingertips, destroying the rest of the wall.

The noise of the crash and the sight of the flames licking at the ceiling above their heads frightened him. He was out of control and didn't think he could stop if he tried.

"M-m-m-Malcolm! Help! I … I can't stop!" he yelled.

"Let it go, son. It's okay. I've got you," Charlie heard the man say from somewhere through the gray acid-smelling smoke that was now filling the basement.

With a last anguished cry, Charlie slumped to the floor while a brilliant flash of blue snapped off of his body in a wave and shot outward. He heard human grunts and the sounds of furniture and other things crashing into each other.

Climbing to his hands and knees, Charlie looked up to see Malcolm crawling to his feet, pulling a weakened, but alive, Thomas up with him.

"Oh my god, oh my god, oh my god," Charlie whispered, turning his head and taking in the destroyed wall, the floor torn wide open in places, fire racing across the floorboards and the ceiling, the bodies of the witches strewn about like neglected backyard tools.

Malcolm walked toward him, one arm dragging a stumbling Thomas behind him, one arm raised up to the ceiling. His mouth was moving, and Charlie watched as the flames above their heads shrank, diminishing to smoldering red lines. He moved his hand downward, and the flames running havoc across the floorboards dwindled down to nothing but smoke.

"You did the right thing, son."

"But I ... I almost ..." he said, his throat dry and burning.

"You didn't. That's what counts."

"Are the others ... the other witches ...?" he croaked out, looking around the room.

"They're okay. None the worse for wear."

"I, I uh, I don't ... thank you, Malcolm, I ..." he coughed.

"Listen to me!" Malcolm yelled, pulling Charlie to his feet with his free hand. "Those kids upstairs need you. You've got to get them out of here. The police will be here any minute. There will be time to think about this later, okay, kid? Now you have a job to do."

"But ..."

"Look at me, Charlie. Look at me. Get upstairs and help those kids. Get them out of the house. Nod if you understand me."

Eyes locked on his face, Charlie nodded.

Behind Malcolm, Thomas moaned. Malcolm gave the man's shirt

collar a hard shake, then ignored him.

"Good. That's good, kid. Put that face glamour back on so they can't remember what you look like. Take them out the back way, all the way to the lake. Once you hit the lake, go right, and you'll come to a big park. Luther Burbank Park. Get the kids there, and you'll be okay. Follow?"

He nodded again.

Malcolm reached into his pocket and handed Charlie something small and silver.

"Take my phone and call Beverly once you're there. Tell her you're at the park. She'll be able to find you. What's the name of the park?"

"Luther Burbank," he said, trying to keep his focus on Malcolm's instructions.

"Good job. Which way will you turn once you hit the lake?"

"Right."

"Good. You were very brave. You did the right thing, little man," Malcolm said, a grim but true, smile on his face.

Charlie nodded, feeling woozy on his feet. He wasn't sure if he had enough strength to climb the stairs again, let alone walk the kids to the park.

"Now go!" Malcolm said, turning Charlie by the shoulders and pushing him toward the door.

Charlie felt himself once again moving up the staircase. He had to pull on the handrail to make the final few steps. He rubbed at his face and let the glamour hide his features. When he stepped onto the second floor, he saw that the kids stood huddled together, whispering and looking terrified. Some still seemed dazed while others appeared to have recovered from their stupor.

"Who-who-who are you?" one of the boys nearest him stammered. He clearly didn't recognize him from before. "What happened down there? What's all that noise? Wha-wha-what's going on?"

"I'm, uh, I'm a friend," Charlie replied, glad that his glamour was holding up. "We need to get out of here. We'll go out the back. By the lake. Turn right. To Luther Burbank Park," he said in a rush so that he wouldn't forget Malcolm's instructions.

"I know where that is!" a girl yelled from the circle of kids.

"Good. Now stay close together," said Laura, the girl with the dark hair and the arm tattoos, who herded the group toward the back of the house. Charlie followed, relieved to know that she and some of the others were there to help.

They walked through a large kitchen with shiny steel appliances. The first door they tried opened onto a giant pantry filled with dried goods and cleaning supplies. The second door led to a four-car garage.

"We'll never get out of here!" cried a young boy.

"Shh, sweetie, shh," said Laura, wrapping her arms around his shoulders.

Someone turned the knob of the third door and early morning sunlight spilled onto them, blinding their eyes. Charlie was shocked to see that it was daytime already. He wondered how long he had been in the basement.

The kids stumbled out onto a large cedar deck, trying to both hold hands and block the sunlight from their eyes at the same time. They rushed down a wooden staircase, through a well-landscaped back-yard, over a green lawn, and down to the edge of the lake, before turning right.

"There's the park!" someone yelled.

Charlie saw a series of slender docks, like fingers, floating out into the lake, and a cluster of giant pine trees rising up from the shore.

Remembering the rest of Malcolm's instructions, Charlie pulled the cell phone from his back pocket and dialed Beverly's number, as the entire group tottered along the lakeshore toward the safety of the trees.

"Malcolm?" he heard his aunt's voice on the other end. "Where are you? Where's Charlie? What's all that noise?"

"Aunt Bev, it's me. Charlie. And a bunch of kids. Will you come get us?"

CHAPTER 31

Backyard Prayers

"... THE POLICE ARE STILL searching the house for evidence. Once again, if you have just tuned in, nineteen teenagers, all of whom have been missing from different parts of the Greater Seattle area over the past year, were found together today at Luther Burbank Park. Police officials say they escaped from a nearby Lake Washington home, though the details are still being gathered. The body of an unidentified adult male was found in the basement of the home.

"The teens have been taken to nearby hospitals to be treated for severe malnutrition, head injuries, amnesia, and exposure to the elements.

"A religious cult is expected to be behind this bizarre event.

"Once again, if you are just tuning in ..."

The TV screen went blank as Rita pressed the off button on the remote.

Charlie sat between Beverly and Randall on a couch in their living room, having given up trying to remove his aunt's protective arm from around his shoulders. Amos lay at their feet, every so often sighing deep sighs as he slept with his head resting on his forepaws. Jeremy paced back and forth in front of the fireplace, chewing on his thumbnail. Rita perched on the edge of a love seat, while Daniel sat with his arms crossed over his chest in one of the room's reclining chairs. All of the adults, save for Daniel, had red puffy eyes. Rita clutched several tissues in her hand, occasionally dabbing at her face.

A fire burned in the fireplace, its cheerful light at odds with the grief and shock, heavy as morning fog, hanging in the air.

"SPD will have a lot to sort out, calling family members and bringing in different county services," Daniel said, his voice even more somber than usual. "None of the kids remember much of anything until they were away from Grace's house and walking with Charlie. I got there before the crime unit did. I cleaned up all of the leftover traces of witchcraft, though there wasn't enough time to remove Malcolm's body. When I left, the CU had dispatched officers over to the park. The official story will probably be something like a mass kidnapping."

"What about the cult theory?" Randall asked, gesturing toward the TV with his left arm, the one with the blue cast.

Daniel shrugged. "It depends. We'll use it if it keeps the SPD and any other group off our trail. But if it invites a lot more snooping around, we'll quell it."

Daniel's comment made Charlie wonder about all the times he had heard people on the news debating theories and discussing controversies. How often were witches behind these debates, using them to distract the world from their existence? The possibilities were chilling. He set the thought aside. Now wasn't the time to think about witch-based conspiracy theories.

Randall turned to look at his wife and nephew. "But won't the kids be able to identify you guys?"

"Charlie and I used glamours to conceal our features. They won't remember us," Beverly explained. "They think they escaped on their own, and some nice people found them and brought them to the park to wait for the police. Once I knew they were going to be okay, I got Charlie and myself out of there before the officers could spot us and start asking questions.

For a while the only sound was the fire crackling away in the hearth.

"Honey, you could sit down if you wanted," Rita said, after blowing her nose.

"What? Oh, no, I'm fine. It's just … it's all so …" Jeremy stopped mid-sentence, looking around as if the words he wanted to use could be found among the living room's furnishings.

"Let me get this straight," he continued, one hand on his hip, the other stroking his beard. "Grace and her crew had been kidnapping unpopped witches and bringing them to her basement? Keeping them in a perpetual state of semiconsciousness to siphon off their power? And Malcolm supplied some of the kids, although they acquired the others on their own?"

He stopped, then shook his head in disbelief.

"But how could they have controlled Malcolm? Witches can't get inside people's heads!" Rita declared, her cheeks flushing with anger.

"And deathcraft? I thought that crap was just myth."

"We all thought it was myth, Jeremy," said Daniel from his easy chair, the firelight flickering in his eyes. "We all thought it was."

Charlie untangled himself from his aunt's embrace and stood up.

"I, uh, I think …" he said, looking down at the floor, then around the room. All the décor—the warm beige furniture, the soft throws draped over the couches, the photographs of Beverly and Randall's wedding—was familiar to him and yet looked vaguely different, as if everything had been painted over with a slightly duller shade, or as if each object had been moved a few degrees from its original location. It was still the same old living room, but changed somehow.

"I'm gonna, um, just go outside, and …" He stopped, unsure how to explain why he wanted to leave.

"Charlie, we don't have to talk about it anymore if you don't want to. We're just confused, is all," Randall said, patting the couch cushion next to him.

"Nah, it's all right. You guys should. We need, er, you guys need to …"

His voice broke, and he felt his eyes burn and moisten.

He turned and walked through the living room toward the kitchen.

"Buddy. Buddy! Come on, you don't have to do this alone. You don't have to …" continued Randall, his voice starting to plead.

"Let him go, Rand. He needs time to himself," Charlie heard his aunt say.

Charlie stepped outside and felt the cold wind blow on his face. He slid the door closed behind him, walked the short distance to the edge of the deck, and leaned out over the cedar railing.

"You're such a baby," he said aloud, angry that he didn't have the guts to stay with the adults and answer more of their questions. But he had been so hot in there with Beverly's arm around him, and he didn't want to cry in front of everybody anymore. They were all being nice to him, worrying over him, trying to give him things to eat. They had spread an ointment onto his cheek where Claudia had cut him, reassuring him that it would heal without a scar. Rita even asked him if she could rub a poultice into his temples.

"It'll help you forget, Charlie. Not permanently, of course. But it'll put things aside for a bit. So you can have a break."

He declined her offer.

He didn't deserve a break.

He deserved to remember what happened. Everything that happened. Even though he couldn't bear to talk about it with them anymore.

Some vestiges of the terrible power he had ingested in Grace's basement still lingered, keeping his senses sharper than usual. He could hear the adults talking in the living room through the thick glass of the deck door. It reminded him of what it was like right after getting popped, though it was nowhere near as strong nor as haphazard.

"… just let him be for a while. He's not one for talking things out, if you hadn't noticed," he could hear Beverly say in a scolding tone.

"I know that, Bev. Jesus. I just think he needs some help. With all that happened," Randall said.

Charlie hoped they didn't get into an argument over him. They probably would. One more thing to add to his list of things that were his fault.

"He's not going to get over this any time soon, you guys," said Jeremy. "I mean, being held captive in that closet, Grace threatening him, that kid being killed right in front of him …"

An image of Todd's slit throat flashed into his head. He squeezed his eyes shut while his hands slammed down on the wooden railing.

He shook his head, making the voices behind him fade away until he couldn't hear them any longer. He looked out over Puget Sound, searching for something to focus on, anything to get his mind away from Grace's basement.

He spotted a ferryboat bound for Vashon Island far below him, watched as it coasted along the choppy waters. By extending his vision forward and down, he felt transported away from the house with its heavy emotions.

Charlie squinted his eyes until he could see the name *Klahowya* painted in thick green lettering on the starboard wall near the captain's station on the upper deck. He looked below at the car deck and saw two young girls sitting in the back of a large pickup truck playing a game of patty-cake. Their hands clapped, opened, slapped, and closed in dizzying repetition.

Concentrating, he listened closely, attempting to catch what they were saying.

At first, all sound was drowned out by the drone of the ferry's engine and the frothy churn of the boat's wake.

But then the girls' words drifted into his ears as if they were in the yard below him, not nearly a mile out to sea.

See-see oh playmate, they sang, their voices high-pitched.
Come out and play with me,
And bring your dollies three,
Climb up my apple tree,
Slide down my rain barrel,
Into my cellar door, and
We'll be jolly friends,
Forever more more,
More more!

Their hands slapped together two times in quick succession, then the girls collapsed onto each other in giggles.

An old man walked past the pickup truck, eating a granola bar. Charlie heard the foil packaging crinkle, heard the chewing sound coming from the man's mouth.

"Quit hiding, you baby!" Charlie chided himself.

He blinked his eyes and shook his head again. His vision and hearing returned to normal, bringing him back to the deck where he stood.

Well, almost normal.

"… glad that Amos is okay. Malcolm must have used one of those sleeping spells on him," he could hear Randall saying from the living room.

"But you mean that asshole is really his father?" Jeremy asked.

"He raped Lizzy, and that's how Charlie …" Rita stopped, unable to finish the sentence. "God, it's so awful."

"He told me," said Beverly, "that even though he's not the conduit they hoped he was, he jumped into the circuit, learned everything about Thomas and Grace, grabbed at all that boosted craft, subdued them, and freed up the kids."

"Jesus, Mary, and Joseph!" declared Jeremy. "What a brave kid!"

Charlie shook his head again. He couldn't bear to hear it, to hear them complimenting him. Because he hadn't been brave. He had been stupid and chickenshit. Why didn't he do more? Why didn't he go back and get Malcolm out of there?

Without thinking, he leaped over the deck railing, the waning power still coursing through his veins more than strong enough to give him a soft landing on the grass below.

That boost isn't going to last forever, Charlie, he thought to himself.

Ignoring the thought, he walked out to the edge of the backyard.

Not that long ago, when Malcolm wanted privacy, he had surrounded them both with silence. Charlie reached up and plugged his nose, imitating the man's gestures. He felt pressure against his cheeks and forehead as he closed his mouth and tried to blow air out through his nostrils. His ears popped.

And then, nothing.

Silence.

All sound gone: all noise, conversation, compliments, questions, worried sentiment, everything outside of his small, cone-shaped spell of protection, gone.

The only thing left was the noise in his own head. Words and images bumped against each other, yelling for his attention.

Todd. Todd is dead. And Malcolm too. Dead. You sat there while they butchered that boy, and you thought about wanting more of that power. You did. You did.

I didn't know! I couldn't help it, I just ...

Malcolm's dead because of you. You should have gone back downstairs and helped him.

I know.

How could you leave him down there? With her? With the others? Of course they killed him! You knew you shouldn't leave him, but you did anyway.

They slit his throat, they slit his throat, they slit his throat.

Violent images arose in his mind's eye once again: the gaping maw in Todd's neck, the blood spattered everywhere, Claudia's cruel smile as she stood there, holding the knife.

The look of sad acceptance on Todd's face when it had been only the two boys, facing each other. Charlie drinking all that power in huge hungry gulps, Todd knowing that it was too late for him, that he was about to die.

No! he shouted inside his head. *No! I didn't want that! I didn't ask for it. They made me drink. She made me take it all. No!*

Grace's face floated into his brain, with her tricky, soft smile, her bright red hair, her creamy skin, all so oddly gentle, inviting, belying none of the savage cruelty just inches beneath the surface.

I stopped her! I broke that circuit, and I stopped her. I ...

I saw into Grace's deepest thoughts, at the filth and brutality floating around in there. He saw it all again, picturing eel-like shapes swimming beneath black oil.

Malcolm is dead. Malcolm is dead. Malcolm is dead.

You freed up those kids, Charlie. Malcolm's voice talking to him now, disembodied, his firm, gentle words meant to comfort him, meant to give him strength. *You did the right thing. You harnessed all that power and you freed up the kids.*

No! I don't deserve comfort.

Come on, little man, you gotta ease up on yourself, okay? For Pete's sake! The wrinkles above Malcolm's cheeks crinkled as he winked at Charlie.

Grace and Thomas, Claudia and Tony. They all escaped. But how? Malcolm said he had it under control. And why did they leave Malcolm's body but take Todd's? Maybe it was some sort of message?

I know what'll happen next. Grace'll go into hiding. She'll rebuild her strength. Then she'll do it all over again. I know she will. She'll kidnap more kids, kill more teenagers and adults, it won't stop, it won't stop, it won't stop! The phrase continued reaching a deafening volume in his head.

Cha-a-a-a-arlie.

His body jerked hard and he looked around the yard, expecting to see …

Because it wasn't a voice in his head this time, it was …

No. Impossible. Impossible! How could …

Right inside of you, little man.

It was Grace's voice coming from somewhere inside his chest. Vibrating just above his sternum.

No! D-d-don't call me that. You never get to call me that again. Those were his words, don't …

I can call you whatever I want, little man. Because I've burrowed up like a little mousey right inside of you.

No!

And I'm going to burn a hole right through you until you turn to ash.

His hands flew up to his chest as he felt a white-hot searing pain stabbing at the area around his heart.

He stumbled, barely catching himself before falling backwards on the ground.

No! he shouted, though he wasn't sure if it was out loud or in his head. *How can she be inside of me?*

The pain burned brighter, increasing until his eyes watered. This time he did cry out loud. His legs gave way beneath him as he crumpled to the ground.

Looking up at the gray sky, he gritted his teeth, then pushed down hard on the bones in his chest.

The pain froze. It didn't lessen, but somehow by pushing on it, he stopped it from getting worse.

No, you can't stop me, boy, I'll ...

Now he could see it inside of himself, see a small flame flickering in the middle of his chest, surrounded by blackness. As he continued to press, the flame began to shrink.

No, you can't. You can't do that ... he heard her scream.

Oh yeah? He said through gritted teeth. *Watch me!*

He pressed harder, and the flame dwindled to a tiny spark. He knew, without quite understanding how, that he had subdued her, that for the moment she could no longer speak to him. A steely satisfaction replaced the burning sensation.

He pushed and pushed, but no matter how hard he tried, the spark would not extinguish. At least the pain in his chest disappeared. Somehow he had stopped her, even though he couldn't get rid of her.

He sucked in gulps of cold air, then rolled over and pushed himself upright until he was on his hands and knees, the grass cold and wet beneath his fingers.

How did she get inside of me?

Did it happen accidentally, when I jumped into the circuit? If so, why wasn't Thomas inside of me too?

Maybe she made it happen. Maybe she slipped inside of me even while I was controlling her.

Don't worry about it now, Charlie. She's subdued for the time being. You've got bigger fish to fry.

He shuddered. *Bigger fish to fry.* The exact words that someone had told Thomas after Charlie's mother escaped out the basement door.

He stood up and brushed wet grass off the seat of his pants.

Like ... like what? What bigger fish?

And for a moment, everything was quiet. There was calm inside his head. Not because he had found the peace and emptiness himself but because his thoughts had run themselves out.

But only for a moment.

You're a faggot, Charlie. What a joke you are.

For some reason, this thought brought him up short.

Really? Really?! After all you've been through, that's what you're gonna focus on?

An image of Diego emerged, looking at him, at their spot in the woods, with the span of the bridge arching above them.

His look of shock, then wonder, and then delight, after Charlie shouted out loud that he was gay.

Calm settled in his mind again as the loud voices and the bright images softened, faded away, like the spark of Grace in his heart: not disappearing entirely but becoming so small that he could rest a bit, could get a break from the all the clamor.

Well, so be it. You're a faggot witch, you were born because some bad guy raped your mother, you've seen murder, you almost killed your father. So what? Get over it, you've got work to do.

He almost laughed, hearing the sharp pragmatic tone of this voice. Was it the same one he had heard when he was still tied up in Grace's basement, telling him there was nothing he could do if Randall and Amos were dead, that he had to calm down to think things through? This voice was new to him. It sounded like himself, only more grown up, like someone who knew a thing or two about the world. Like somebody he could trust.

Charlie reached up squeezed his nostrils closed, then blew hard. He felt his ears pop, then … wind on his face, a bird chirping overhead. The loud hoooo of a ferry's horn below, signaling that it was about to dock.

He couldn't hear the adults talking about him in the living room above.

He stood still, eyes closed, feeling for a moment the simple softness of the grass beneath his feet.

Then the sound of the deck door sliding open.

"Hey, Charlie," he heard Jeremy shout from above and behind him.

He whirled around, feeling stupid as he realized how he must have looked, standing there in the yard all by himself, maybe even talking out loud like a crazy person.

"Yeah?" he replied, his voice a little too loud.

"Rita and I are gonna leave now."

"Oh. Okay."

"You need anything?" Jeremy said to him, and Charlie could see the worry only half-hidden behind his smile.

Before he could answer, Rita stepped out onto the deck and stood next to her husband.

"Anything, Charlie. You just ask, okay?"

"Oh, yeah. Um, thanks. Thanks for coming over," he said, although he wasn't really sure why he had said it.

"You're welcome, Charlie," Rita said. "Get some rest, okay? You've been through a lot."

"Okay. Uh, you too."

Jeremy's smile widened, and for a moment Charlie could see the worry disappear.

"We slept fine last night, you goofball. You're the one who needs a nap!"

In spite of himself, Charlie laughed.

He watched the bottoms of their feet through the slats in the deck, as they walked into the house and slid the door shut behind them.

Charlie turned back toward the water and looked up at the sky. Fat clouds colored gunmetal gray pushed and jostled against each other. It looked like it could rain any minute. But for now there was only a cold wind and the briny smell of the Sound.

He looked at the large maple tree directly above him. Many of its leaves had turned from green to shocks of rust-red and orange. A few branches, however, were already bare. Their naked twigs pointed like accusing fingers, as if blaming October for robbing them of their clothing, some of which lay scattered near his feet.

He reached into his pocket and pulled out his phone. He entered a familiar number on the dial pad. Then he waited, his thumb hovering over the call button.

Should he call her?

Should he call and tell her that he knew? That he knew what happened?

What would he say? "Hi, Mom, it's me. Charlie. I know what Thomas did to you. I know he's my father. I know why you ran away from home."

No. He wasn't ready to have that conversation with her. Maybe she wasn't ready to have it with him either.

Then what would he say? "Hi, Mom, I can fly around on a broomstick now. It's cool. Wanna go for a ride some time?"

That just sounded stupid. And she probably couldn't even fly anymore. If she could, would he want to?

The truth was he wasn't sure what he wanted. He was confused. On the one hand, he was still mad at her for lying to him, for dumping him off and leaving in the middle of the night. Just because bad stuff happened to her as a teenager, did that give her the right to treat him like that? Wasn't she being a hypocrite?

On the other hand, maybe he wasn't being fair to her. He had learned what happened to her by being inside Thomas's mind, not hers. He didn't know what it had been like for her. Maybe he should show her some compassion.

One thing he was clear about: he didn't want to go back to California. Not yet, anyway. As violent and frightening as the past few days had been, he still really liked his life here, with Beverly and Randall, with his new witch friends. With Diego.

His thumb moved closer to the send button.

Charlie waited.

Then he watched as it moved over to delete. It pressed down on the button and held it until all ten digits disappeared from the screen.

"Abracadabra. Just like magic," he said, laughing a mirthless laugh while putting the phone back in his pocket.

He looked again at the tree above him, running his eyes along the thin lines of its branches. He felt into his chest, where there was the small spark that was Grace, small and hot like a tiny ember. It wasn't burning into him like it had before, but he had no doubt it, or she, would try again. Would try to burn a hole right through him. He had no doubts anymore of what she was capable of.

"I'm going to find you, Grace," Charlie whispered out loud, and he pictured the words coming out of his mouth like wisps of smoke. He imagined the wind grabbing at his words and rushing away with them, twirling them up through the bare branches and the dying leaves of the maple tree, drifting upwards and becoming something solid.

Something like a prayer.

Charlie turned and walked toward the door that led into the basement, then went inside.

The Boy Who Couldn't Fly Straight

BONUS OFFER

Bonus for readers of *The Boy Who Couldn't Fly Home* ...

Download a free short story about Charlie's witching world with new characters and challenges that will affect the entire planet!

www.jeffjacobsonworld.com/bonus

ACKNOWLEDGMENTS

I AM DEEPLY GRATEFUL to the following people for helping me to bring *The Boy Who Couldn't Fly Home* to fruition:

To my writing group the Kimchees (Mary, Kim, Cat, and Lauren), and to their unending source of patience as I shared yet another scene of someone flying on a broomstick, to their collective sharp eye, and for sharing their love of reading and writing with me.

To Chris Kapzynksi, for building a quirky, fun website that delights me.

To Howard VanEs, whose marketing ideas, knowledge of how to promote books on Amazon, and kind persistence have been key in making this book happen.

To Dennis Martin, whose keen eye, attention to detail, and design sense made the book easy to read, both digitally and in paper. Also, his friendship is magical!

To Julia McNeal, whose enthusiasm for Charlie's story carries over into her ability to help me edit, reconstruct, and build the best story-telling possible.

To David Darst, for his inspirational lamb burgers. Count yourself lucky if he ever grills for you.

To Ina Garten, the Barefoot Contessa, for inspiring the gourmet s'mores at Malcolm's cabin, and for all of her food witchcraft.

To my family (Mom, Jen, Jack, Jonathan, and Justin) for keeping me grounded and for loving their loquacious storyteller of a family member.

To Maren and Martin, for their constant encouragement and love and for believing in me when my own self-belief plummeted.

To my early readers, whose clear feedback (both positive and constructive) helped me to see if I was writing what I thought I was writing, which enabled me to craft a more cogent narrative.

To my readers in general, whose words of encouragement and praise on Amazon and Good Reads still thrill and inspire me.

To Jeanine and Leza, who listened to many early drafts and ideas and cared enough about Charlie and his character arc to help me make him as real as possible.

To Fly, my Thai kickboxing trainer in Shanghai, and for the Studio MDR in Los Angeles. All of those hard workouts keep me physically and mentally sharp.

And lastly to Terry, who listens carefully to my writing travails, then gently encourages me to get back to it (he knows how much I enjoy it), and who has taught me a great deal about true love.

ABOUT THE AUTHOR

JEFF JACOBSON WAS BORN in Seattle, Washington, in 1968. When he was still in kindergarten, his maternal grandmother told him that she was a modern witch who flew over his house at night on a vacuum cleaner to keep him safe. While he mostly doubted the veracity of her story, he still liked imagining that it was true. This led to a lifelong romance with the idea of witches, and while growing up he read as many witch stories as possible. It only made sense that he would sit down one day and write his own version.

Jeff has also worked as a personal and professional coach since 1997 and has been a faculty member with the Coaches Training Institute since 1999. He recently moved to Southern California after working in Shanghai, China, for three years. He lives in Los Angeles with his partner and their two cats and is busy writing the next book in the Broom Closet Stories. *The Boy Who Couldn't Fly Home* is his second novel.

Made in the USA
Las Vegas, NV
01 December 2020